In Another Man's Bed

In Another Man's Bed

FRANCIS RAY

ST. MARTIN'S GRIFFIN

NEW YORK

This is a work of fiction. All of the characters, organizations, and events portrayed in this novel are either products of the author's imagination or are used fictitiously.

www.stmartins.com

Design by Maggie Goodman

ISBN-13: 978-0-312-35613-2
ISBN-10: 0-312-35613-7

To health-care workers around the world who tirelessly care for those entrusted to their care. I salute you.

Special Thanks

Angelique Boyd, B.S., R.N., an extraordinary nurse
with a boundless energy, ready smile, and unwavering
passion to always be the best that she can be.
Thanks for the unending support.

Prologue

Justine Crandall had seduction on her mind, and in less than ten minutes she would be in bed with the man she adored.

The racy thought made Justine grin, then she laughed out loud at her uncharacteristic naughtiness. Both she and Andrew, her husband of five years, were as conservative as they came, but since they'd been apart for two weeks she didn't think he'd put up much resistance.

In the cocooned luxury of the Porsche Carrera, she sighed in pleasure and anticipation as the sports car easily took the sharp turns up the Appalachian Mountains. She'd been on the road since five that morning and couldn't have picked a better day for the drive.

Spring was in full force. The air was crisp and clean, the sky a startling blue, the roadside bursting with wildflowers. She smiled and slowed as a deer bounded gracefully across the road and disappeared over the steep incline. She'd seen several this morning. It was a good thing DEER CROSS-

ING signs were posted. As owner and operator of It's a Mystery Bookstore in Charleston, she seldom had a chance to enjoy nature.

Last night, after Andrew had finished his last workshop at the men's retreat in Gatlinburg, he'd called to say he was too tired to make the four-hour drive back to Charleston on Sunday afternoon. Justine suggested he stay at their nearby cabin for a few days before returning. He could work on the book he wanted to write.

As soon as she had hung up, she'd begun planning to surprise him. They were going to have two whole days by themselves, something they hadn't had in a very long time. They'd built the cabin as their retreat two years ago, but it had been almost a year since they'd been there together.

Justine patted the Gucci overnight bag on the seat beside her. Inside was a new blue negligee. Andrew loved blue and he loved her.

She'd be the happiest woman in the world if they could begin planning a baby. Andrew wanted to wait until he wasn't away from home so much, but she was hoping she could change his mind. For the past nine months Andrew had been on a grueling schedule conducting a number of retreats for men across the country. There hadn't been very many occasions for "trying." Justine didn't begrudge the time Andrew spent away from her because she felt his work was important. Perhaps if someone had counseled her father, he might not have left her mother for another woman.

Justine knew she'd never have to go through divorce. She and Andrew were committed to each other for a lifetime. Not just because they loved each other, but also because neither wanted to repeat the mistakes of their parents.

Shortly after nine she pulled up to their cabin, a two-story structure with a gabled roof and a balcony that ran along the back of the house. Disappointment hit her on seeing another car parked beside her husband's Escalade. She'd wanted them to have this time alone. Annoyance crept in. He should be resting instead of counseling someone.

People sometimes took advantage of Andrew's goodness. He didn't know how to say no. Usually she stayed out of his business affairs, but lately he'd been preoccupied and easily distracted. It was time he was a bit selfish and put himself first, she thought.

Getting out of the Porsche, a birthday gift from Andrew, she shoved the keys into the pocket of her white slacks and started toward the hand-carved front door. She and Andrew could unload the car later. Right now, she couldn't wait to see her husband after their two-week separation.

As she went up the stone steps, she inhaled the sweet fragrance of the Peace roses that were in full bloom on either side of the house. She made a mental note to put a bouquet of the lush pink flowers in their bedroom.

Upon entering the spacious interior that she had lovingly decorated in warm earth tones and comfortable easy-to-care-for leather, she turned, expecting to find Andrew and his guest in the kitchen. The big plateglass window in the breakfast nook provided a spectacular view of the heavily wooded mountains, which always beckoned them to begin their day there over a leisurely breakfast.

She started in that direction, then heard a sound from upstairs. She glanced at her watch. 9:10. Andrew was an early riser. Worried, she started up the stairs. He didn't take care of himself when he was away from her. She wished he were home more. He was a wonderful, loving—

Her thoughts abruptly halted as an unmistakable moan of sexual pleasure drifted out to her from their bedroom. Stunned, she stood at the top of the stairs, a tightness in her chest, her throat. She wasn't aware of how long she remained immobile before she moved down the hallway in a daze. Her tennis shoes were soundless on the wool runner on the polished oak floor as she stopped at the open door of the master bedroom.

Justine's heart clenched and her breath snagged as she caught a glimpse of a woman's naked butt and shoulder going into the master bath. Her gaze stayed glued to the closed door as if she were putting off looking at the bed for as long as possible. Her hands clenched, she finally made herself look. Hot rage rolled through her.

Her husband lay naked on the wide bed. His eyes were closed, one long leg was drawn up, and a satisfied smile curved his soft mouth upward. Justine tried to remember if she'd ever seen that look of complete satisfaction after they had made love. She couldn't.

She must have made a sound, because Andrew's eyelids flew up. Stunned, he stared at her with those light brown mesmerizing eyes that had swayed and motivated thousands, then he sprang out of bed to cut her off from the bathroom.

"You lying, cheating bastard!" Justine snarled.

Andrew looked as taken aback by the harsh words spewing from his wife as by her appearance. "Justine, please let me explain—"

The open-palmed slap across his face echoed through the silent room. He stared at her as if she'd gone mad.

There were so many hot emotions running through her

that she thought she might just have done so. She'd always been quiet, had never raised a hand to another person, had never given her mother or her teachers one moment of trouble, but right then she wanted to scratch Andrew's handsome face to shreds.

She'd given him everything and he'd left her with nothing. The only reason she didn't slap him again was fear of not being able to stop. He would defend himself and that meant he'd have to touch her. She never wanted his hands on her again.

"I trusted you. I loved you," she said, her voice trembling with rage and pain.

"It only happened once," Andrew told her, his hand on his cheek, his eyes wide and uncertain.

She fought the urge to hit him again. "Do you think that makes the betrayal any less?"

"Hon—"

"Don't." Justine stepped away from the hands reaching for her. "Who is she?"

"It doesn't matter. She means nothing to me."

Justine raised her hand to hit him again, then clenched it into a fist instead. "That takes you even lower." She swallowed the painful lump in her throat. "Don't come home. I'm filing for divorce as soon as I get back."

Fear leaped into his eyes. "You can't throw away all that we mean to each other, all that we've shared."

"I didn't. You did. Now, get out of my way."

"No!" Andrew said, spreading his arms wide so she couldn't go around him. "Let's go downstairs and talk."

Hysterical laughter burst forth. "You're naked and your lover just left the bed I picked out for us. Nothing you can say will change anything. Good-bye."

"Jus—" His hands lifted purposefully toward her.

"Try to touch me and you'll regret it," Justine promised. She looked over his shoulder at the closed door. There was no sound coming from the bathroom. Whoever was behind that door could hear them.

Justine had a few words for her. "There's a word for women like you, but I don't want to foul my mouth saying it!" With that parting shot, she turned and walked from the room. What she really wanted to do was scream and kick and howl.

Her world had just been torn apart, her heart yanked out of her chest. With one arm wrapped around her heaving stomach, she stopped on the stairs for just a second, then continued downward. She had to get away.

Her pace increased. She didn't want to give Andrew or his lover the pleasure of seeing how much their betrayal had hurt her. She ran faster, stumbling on the way out of the door, picking herself up to stumble forward again.

By the time she reached her car, her hands were shaking so badly that it took several tries to get the key into the ignition. As she pulled off, Andrew, always well groomed and fashionable, ran out of the house with his shirt open, his slacks unfastened. He was carrying his shoes. She gunned the Carrera and spun out of the driveway, fighting the upheaval in her stomach, the gut-wrenching loss of her dream, as Andrew leaped into his own vehicle and began to chase her.

Justine was an excellent driver and she used that skill to pull farther and farther away from Andrew. She tried to keep the image of her husband's deceit at bay, but it kept returning.

Her hands gripping the steering wheel of her sports car,

Justine threw a quick glance in her rearview mirror. Andrew was at least a quarter mile behind her. On the winding mountain road his Escalade was no match for her Porsche on the sharp turns of the narrow descent. With each rotation of her wheels, he lagged farther and farther behind. It would be laughable, if it weren't so tragic, that he had given her the means to evade him.

"This car will be carrying the most important and precious person in my life."

Justine's hands flexed on the steering wheel as she fought to keep the tears from falling. Lies. A man didn't love one woman and have sex with another.

Her mind shied away from the scene she had just witnessed. She wouldn't let herself think about it, or she'd never be able to get down the mountain and make good her escape. She had surprised her husband, all right, but not in a way either of them had expected.

Her eyes shut tightly in an attempt to keep the sickening picture of Andrew's betrayal at bay. It was useless. She heard the moans, saw the backside of the woman and her husband's naked body and satisfied expression.

The blast of a car horn jerked her eyes open in time to see an oncoming truck directly in front of her. She yanked the Porsche back into her own lane and out of the truck's path with only seconds to spare. Her heart pumping with fear and anger, she glanced in the rearview mirror again. There were so many questions running through her head that she couldn't sort them all out. She'd worry about them later. Now, she needed to get away.

"Let me explain."

There was no way in hell he could explain away what she'd just witnessed. If it hadn't taken her those several moments on the stairs to stop shaking and compose herself enough to drive, he wouldn't have gotten this close to catching her.

Out of the corner of her eye, she caught a flicker of movement in the thick brush on the side of the road. Three adult deer and one fawn emerged as she passed by. Instinctively she glanced in the rearview mirror.

She eased off the gas and onto the brakes. Her heart pounded even more as she glimpsed the deer crossing the road. She hit the horn just as Andrew's car rounded the curve.

The fawn froze. The others scampered away. Andrew didn't brake; he swerved around the animal, putting his vehicle perilously close to the edge of the ravine.

Justine didn't realize she'd stopped and gotten out of her car until she felt the imprint of the door handle biting into her clenched hand.

She could see Andrew desperately wrestling with the steering wheel, his eyes wide with terror. Then the back wheels began to lose traction. For a moment their eyes locked, then the Escalade slid down the cliff.

Justine screamed, then she was running. She stared in horror as the vehicle flipped over and over before coming to a halt. Through the dense trees and shrubbery she barely distinguished the gleam of the gray exterior of Andrew's SUV. A plume of thick black smoke spiraled upward.

Justine hesitated for a moment, then began to scramble down the hundred-foot embankment toward her lying, adulterous husband.

One

Three months had passed since Andrew's accident, and the flowers, cards, and telegrams continued to arrive daily. The massive outpouring of prayers and well-wishers showed no signs of abating; in fact, it was increasing. A staff member from Having It All, Andrew's firm, had been assigned to keep track of all the mail and send thank-you notes.

"He looks so peaceful. Don't you think he looks peaceful, Justine?"

"Yes, Beverly." Justine answered the way she always did. Andrew's mother had asked the same question daily for the past month since he'd been care-flighted from the hospital in Gatlinburg to a hospital in Charleston. Justine really couldn't tell if he did or not. She'd never been able to look Andrew in the face, not after . . .

"The brain wave patterns are growing fainter each day." Dr. Lane's somber voice intruded on Justine's chaotic thoughts. "Mrs. Crandall, you need to make the decision as to whether you wish us to disconnect life support if brain activity ceases."

Andrew's mother edged closer to Justine, showing her distress, but also her support of Justine's decision. A decision she'd wrestled with since the day after Andrew had arrived in ICCU almost a month ago and his condition had begun to deteriorate.

"There's nothing more we can do. We need to know what you'd like for us to do. Your husband didn't have a living will."

No, Justine thought. They were going to live happily ever after.

"Mrs. Crandall?"

Justine looked at the doctor, a tall man with a long face and bushy eyebrows over tired eyes that looked out from behind wire-rimmed gold glasses. The white lab coat hung on his lanky frame as if he'd lost weight. He was the top neurosurgeon in the state. He was the reason they'd transferred Andrew.

However, Andrew's heart had stopped en route to Charleston. It had been his second cardiac arrest since the accident. This time his heart had refused to beat longer than during the first arrest two months earlier.

"It would be the humane thing to do," the doctor said, sounding as tired and as weary as she felt.

Humane perhaps, but did she want them to disconnect the respirator if he coded and was determined brain-dead because he had betrayed her or because it was the right thing to do? She'd risked her life to save his because it wasn't in her to do anything less. The scratches, cuts, and bruises on her body from dragging him to safety were healed; those on her heart and soul remained open and painful.

"Are you sure there's no hope of him waking up?" Beverly asked, her slim hand stroking the pale, gaunt cheek of her son as the respirator pumped air in and out of his lungs. Always perfect, there wasn't a hair out of place in Beverly's short, stylish black hair. The Albert Nippon pink suit fit her slim frame perfectly. "I've heard that a lot of people wake up from comas."

"The broken bones have healed, but the head injury was more severe. Each time he arrested, the possibility of brain damage became more and more likely. It would be a miracle if he woke up, and if he did wake without brain damage, it would be truly miraculous," the doctor answered, clearly tired of repeating himself over and over.

"Miracles happen." Beverly smiled up at Justine. "Andrew said it was a miracle that he found you. You were there to save him at the accident. Another miracle. He loves you so much. You're the reason he keeps fighting so hard to come back to us, to you."

Not me, the other woman.

Justine clamped her lips together and wrapped her slim arms around herself to keep the angry words from spilling out. Beverly loved her son, almost worshipped him. Justine wouldn't steal her illusions as hers had been stolen. Andrew's mother had welcomed Justine with open arms when Andrew had taken her to meet his mother after their second date.

"I knew from the first time I saw you that you were the one."

Justine's arms tightened. Andrew had told her that lie numerous times since the night he'd proposed—six weeks after they'd met. She'd never doubted him and had counted her blessings that she had such a wonderful, loving husband.

"Mrs. Crandall, the papers are ready for you to sign at the nurses' station."

Justine worked to get her anger under control, but at the same time she wondered if her decision would have been any easier before the day she'd tried to surprise her husband. She didn't know; she just knew she had to find the answer.

If she made the decision for the wrong reasons, she didn't want to live with the guilt for the rest of her life. Andrew had taken so much from her; he wouldn't take her peace of mind.

"Perhaps tomorrow," she finally whispered softly.

The doctor grunted. "Prolonging signing the papers will only make it more difficult."

"My daughter-in-law said perhaps tomorrow," Beverly said pleasantly, but there was a hint of steel in her voice. Charleston-born and bred, she was a true Southern lady, soft, gracious, and charming on the surface, but underneath strong and determined.

Dr. Lane glanced at the diamond-encrusted Rolex on his wrist. "It's almost eight. Visiting hours are over soon. What time do you plan to come in tomorrow?"

Justine hesitated. She'd like to have just one day that she didn't have to come here and pretend. "I'm not sure."

"Her best friend is moving back to Charleston from Dallas tomorrow," Beverly told him. "But once Brianna's settled, Justine will be here. Just as she has been every day that Andrew has been in the hospital. She's devoted to my son. Aren't you, dear?"

Justine wanted to scream "no." She was so tired of the vigilance, the charade. "Yes."

Beverly smiled as if she'd just been given a precious gift.

"Perhaps we'll get a chance to talk in the morning. Think about what I've told you. Good night." The door of the ICCU room swung shut behind the doctor.

"You go on home, Justine, and get some rest." Beverly turned back to her son, a tender smile on her unlined face. "I'll visit with Andrew a while longer. I wanted to tell him the azaleas he had the gardener plant for me are still in full bloom. My neighbor's have withered. Mine are waiting for Andrew to see them."

Justine's hand clenched and unclenched on the strap of her shoulder bag. She was desperate to leave, yet she hesitated. She felt so sorry that Beverly had to go through this. No matter how unscrupulous Andrew was, Beverly loved him. Justine loved her mother-in-law, but if she had to pretend for another minute she might start screaming. "I think I will."

Beverly glanced up at Justine. "When he wakes up he'll be so proud that you're seeing that his company is running smoothly along with all of the other plans you made together. He couldn't have chosen a better wife." Turning her attention back to her son, she brushed her hand across her son's pale forehead. "I wouldn't be surprised if you two begin making plans to start a family afterward."

Unable to take any more, Justine gave Beverly a quick hug, then left. She nodded to the nurses at the nurses' station on passing. She was almost running by the time she hit the heavy double doors of ICCU. She halted abruptly as Marcus Hayes and his wife, Nina, came to their feet in the small waiting room crammed with people and uncomfortable chairs.

Marcus had dark hair, narrow shoulders, and sad brown eyes. He was Andrew's best friend and vice president of operations of Having It All. After Andrew's accident, Marcus had quickly stepped in to take control. Dealing with Andrew's deceit and his critical condition, Justine had been in no shape to make any decisions and had welcomed Marcus's intervention. She still did.

Marcus, his dark-skinned face anxious, quickly came to her. His calloused hands settled on her shoulders. Unlike Andrew's athletic build that topped six feet, Marcus was thin and of average height. "Has there been a change?"

She shook her head, the knot in her throat too large to get the words past.

His hands tightened for a fraction. Marcus and Andrew had gone to college together, but it had always been Andrew who had the charisma, the eloquence in speaking, the stylish appearance. Andrew had been the driving force behind the creation and success of Having It All.

Shamefully, on first meeting Marcus, Justine had thought how fortunate she was that she had a man who always looked perfect, was charismatic and at ease in any social gathering rather than one who was quiet, unassuming, and never appeared to care what he wore. Tonight, Marcus had on a dull brown off-the-rack suit with a white shirt and brown tie. All of Andrew's clothes were tailor-made.

Foolish, foolish woman.

"We came by to make sure you were all right," Marcus said. "We missed you at church today."

Marcus was too down-to-earth and caring to censure her. He had come out of concern and love. Staring up into his troubled face, Justine wanted to ask if he'd known about Andrew's affair. Had he been a part of Andrew's deceit?

"Justine, would you like to go get something to eat?" Nina asked. "Or if you want to go on home, we could pick something up and drop it by your house."

Justine switched her attention to his attractive wife, Nina, who wore a magenta-colored Carolina Herrera linen suit. The fitted skirt stopped at mid-thigh. Nina worked for Andrew's company as well, in public relations. She and Marcus were opposites in dress and personalities. Like Andrew, she had an acknowledged affinity for life's finer amenities. Had she become restless, and sought excitement and a wealthier man? Was she the one?

Justine caught herself and glanced away. She detested that she was so suspicious of all the women who came to visit Andrew, but she couldn't help it. The other woman was usually someone the wife knew or who worked with the cheating husband. Nina fit both profiles. Or had it been a woman Andrew had picked up?

Nina was slender and attractive with the right height and same amber coloring of the woman at the cabin. Her short hairstyle was curly instead of in a flip, but it was the right length and color.

"Justine?" Nina frowned, her smile slipping. "What's the matter?"

Was that guilt in her eyes? Justine thought, then quickly chastised herself. Putting her friends and herself through this continual scrutiny had to stop. She swallowed. "I'm sorry."

"You're probably worn out," Marcus said gently. "How long have you been here?"

Too long. Justine ran her hand through the limp strands

of auburn shoulder-length hair. She'd missed her last two beauty appointments and had washed her hair herself. It was too taxing to repeat Andrew's condition over and over. Often she thought of just making a sign and wearing it around her neck.

"Justine?" Marcus prompted

"Pretty much since around nine this morning," she finally answered. Posted visiting hours were from 10:00 A.M. to 8:00 P.M., but Beverly knew the chief of staff, Dr. Thomas. At Beverly's insistence, and against Dr. Lane's wishes, Dr. Thomas had relaxed the visiting hours for them. They could pretty much come and go as they pleased. Justine felt guilty if she wasn't there. Not about Andrew, but about his mother, who seldom left his side.

"You have to take care of yourself," Nina said, sliding an arm around Justine's waist. "Andrew would want you to."

"He loves you so much," Marcus said.

Justine wanted to laugh at the absurdity of such a statement, but felt tears clog her throat instead. "I . . . I need to go."

Thankfully, Nina released her. "I'll walk you to your car, then come back and see Andrew. Marcus, you go on in."

Justine shook her head and took an unsteady step away. "I'm fine. Thanks for coming. Good night." Turning, she increased her pace, not giving them a chance to stop her. Swallowing convulsively, she hurried to the elevator and jabbed the down button, once, twice. *Please*, her mind screamed.

The door opened and she stepped on the empty elevator and punched G. As the door slid shut, she closed her eyes and prayed to keep it together long enough to reach her van. The moment the elevator stopped, her eyes snapped open.

Stepping off, she easily located the blue van parked next to a white pillar in the underground parking garage. Deactivating the lock, she climbed inside.

Her hand shook as she stuck the key in the ignition. With a flick of her wrist the motor roared to life. Justine reached for the gear shift, but couldn't see it through the sheen of tears in her eyes. Trembling hands clenched the steering wheel. "Damn you, Andrew! Damn you to hell."

The retro music of "Hungry Like the Wolf" had her jerking her head around and down. She dove for her handbag, then searched frantically through the jumbled assortment for the ringing phone among the paraphernalia she carried in her large handbag.

"Please don't go to voice mail," she desperately whispered, finally dumping the contents on the beige leather seat beside her. If Justine didn't pick up, Brianna might think she was busy and turn her phone off.

Two rings later Justine located the phone beneath her checkbook and a notepad with her store's logo. Snatching it up, she flipped it open. "Brianna, thank goodness!"

"Whatever it is, you can get through it," came the calm, reassuring voice.

Eyes closed, Justine leaned her head back against the headrest and fought tears and misery. Brianna Ireland had been her best friend since they'd been in kindergarten. Brianna had been the outspoken one, Justine the shy one. Together they had gone through puberty, first date, first kiss, first breakup. They'd always been there to support each other.

"Did he . . ."

"No," Justine answered Brianna's unfinished question. "But his condition continues to deteriorate. The doctor wants me to sign the papers to disconnect life support if brain activity ceases. I . . . I can't."

"Then don't until you're ready. My plane gets in at eight tomorrow morning. If the doctor continues to hassle you, I'll handle him."

Justine almost laughed, something she seldom did anymore. No one messed with Brianna. She might look soft with her knockout figure, beautiful face, and elegant Southern manner, but she was the epitome of the steel magnolia. "You'll scare him."

"It's what I do best," Brianna said, a smile in her voice. Even when she cut a person off at the knees that smile remained as smooth as glass and as sweet as sugar. Southern women had it like that.

"That you do." Laughter drifted through the receiver to Justine. "Your going-away party. You should be socializing with your friends instead of calling a hysterical woman."

"Who calmed me when Daddy had his heart attack?" she asked quietly.

The unflappable, self-assured Brianna had almost lost it when her father was transferred to a hospital room after being in ICCU for five days and the staff nurse was lax about monitoring his vital signs, and then became flippant when Brianna's mother asked about them. Brianna went off on the nurse, who'd hurriedly left the room. Justine had had to physically restrain Brianna from going after the woman. Eventually Justine got Brianna to see that there was a better way to handle the nurse.

Brianna had opened her BlackBerry and begun making

calls. In less than fifteen minutes, the hospital administrator and the director of nursing service were in Brianna's father's hospital room, apologetic and nervous. Malpractice suits were nasty business. Brianna might be five foot four, but she had a presence about her that told you to tread carefully, and the intelligence and the connections to back up her threats. She walked softly and carried a very big stick.

"I'm so glad Mr. Ireland is doing better."

"He's raring to get back on the golf course." Brianna chuckled. "Mama insists on going with him if he does. I bought her a cute outfit to wear, and a golf cart for them. After drilling me on how much it cost, they'll get a kick out of it."

Brianna and her parents had always been close. Justine and her mother had never shared that closeness. If was as if her mother were afraid Justine would make the same mistake of loving the wrong man, just as she had. Her mother had been right. "I'll pick you up at the airport."

"No need. Daddy and Mama are coming. They'll both feel better if they help. But I'll expect you for dinner tomorrow night. No excuses. We'll stuff ourselves on fresh baked bread and seafood gumbo. Mama can throw down with the best of them."

Tomorrow might be the day Andrew—Justine pushed the thought away. She couldn't keep scheduling her life around Andrew. "I'll be there."

"Brianna, excuse me. Jackson wants you."

Justine frowned. There'd been impatience and censure in the female voice that was loud enough for Justine to hear clearly. Obviously the woman had cared more about Brianna returning to the party than courtesy. "I didn't mean to keep you so long."

"I'm the one who called you, remember? We can talk as long as you like."

Justine's frown didn't clear. "You're sure?"

"Jackson sent one of his lackeys for me," Brianna explained, annoyance creeping into her voice. "I don't heel for anyone. He should know that by now."

Jackson Hewitt was Brianna's former lover and a fellow lawyer at her firm. Brianna had told Justine that he hadn't taken the breakup well and wanted her back. Of course, he was trying to spend every moment with her before she left for Charleston. He cared about her.

Perhaps all of Andrew's out-of-town seminars without Justine should have been her first clue that their marriage was in trouble. People in love wanted to be together. "I should be going."

"You sure?"

"I'm sure." Just because her life was a mess was no reason to impose on Brianna's. "Good night and safe travel. I'll see you tomorrow night."

"Count on it."

Two

Justine hung up the phone, her hand no longer trembling, the tears gone. Brianna might be returning to take over her father's law practice, but she was also saving Justine's sanity. She was the only person Justine could confide in, the only one who wouldn't see Andrew's infidelity as her fault. Her mother certainly wouldn't understand and she could hardly tell Beverly. Starting the van, she backed up and drove away.

Justine pulled out of the parking garage and turned left, away from the direction of her house, which was in an exclusive gated community. She wasn't ready to face the mocking house that was supposed to represent unity and instead was nothing more than a reminder that her husband preferred another woman.

On their third wedding anniversary, Andrew had surprised her by giving her the keys in an elongated white jewelry box while they were out celebrating. She had squealed, jumped up from the candlelit table in the posh restaurant, and kissed Andrew. People around them had applauded.

Too excited to stay, she'd asked him to take her to their new home. Seeing the house with lights blazing in welcome, the dancing fountain in front, she couldn't believe it was theirs, that he could be so generous and loving. She'd considered a home the first step toward eventually starting a family. She'd stepped onto the Italian marble tile inside and felt as if she were the luckiest woman in the world.

"All I have is yours, just as my heart is," Andrew had said softly.

Hand in hand, they'd toured the house. In the master bedroom they'd made love on the thick white carpeting. Afterward, she'd gone to sleep, secure in the arms of the man she loved, a man she thought would love her forever.

Her hands flexed on the steering wheel. Had he been cheating even then, or had it begun later? Was it a lack in her or a flaw in him that caused him to stray? So many questions to which she might never have the answers.

Minutes later Justine pulled up in the driveway of her mother's house, a traditional single-level house in an established neighborhood. It couldn't have been easy for a single woman to keep things going or hold her head up after her husband deserted her for another woman, leaving her with a ten-year-old daughter, but her mother had never complained. But neither had she given her confused, lonely daughter the hugs or touches she'd craved.

Letting down the windows, Justine killed the engine. Quietness settled around her except for the occasional passing car, crickets, and children trying to get in those last precious minutes of play before they were called inside for the night. Justine had been just like them, but she had another reason for wanting to remain outside. Her eyes closed.

Just as she had all those years ago, she prolonged the inevitable and leaned her head back. For some unknown reason she and her mother had never been close. As a teenager she had thought she was adopted, but her late grandmother, a no-nonsense woman, had disputed that story and called her silly. All Justine knew was that she had never been able to please Helen . . . except when it came to her marriage. To her mother, Andrew was the perfect son-in-law.

"Justine?"

Justine jerked her head around to see her mother standing beside the van. She sat upright. "Hi, Mama."

"Did—did something happen?"

From the dim light of the porch lantern, Justine saw the fear in her mother's beautiful caramel-colored face. She looked years younger than her fifty-one years. She still wore the size eight she had as a young bride. On those rare occasions when they were out together, people thought they were sisters.

"No, I just didn't feel like going home."

Her mother nodded once, an almost agitated movement. "You want to come in for a while?"

Justine hadn't expected warmth. The problem was that she didn't know what she had expected. It certainly wasn't the bland tone her mother used as if they were strangers. Her mother was warm to everyone except her daughter. Brianna's mother would have had her in her arms and in the house in seconds, then made her a cup of tea and probably tempted her with her favorite cake, comforting her, loving her.

"No, thanks." It had been a mistake to come here. Justine started the motor. "I better get going."

"I'll be by the hospital tomorrow before I go in to work." Her mother stuck her hands into the pockets of her long robe instead of reaching out to comfort her only child. "If you need anything, call."

"I won't need anything." She thought she saw her mother flinch. She hadn't meant the words to come out so harshly. "Good night, Mama. You better get back inside."

"Good night, Justine." Helen walked back up the winding path to the front door and went inside. She didn't look back.

Justine pulled off. What was wrong with her that her mother couldn't love her or her husband remain faithful to her? More questions to which she'd probably never find the answers. Sometimes she wasn't sure if she really wanted to know.

Brianna Ireland disconnected her BlackBerry and slipped it back into her clutch, then picked up her flute from the balustrade and sipped the vintage white wine. Jackson should know by now that she didn't respond well to orders or pressure. He'd tried the latter after she broke off their relationship a few weeks ago. She'd remained firm. She wasn't sure of her feelings for him, and since she was moving to Charleston for an indefinite period of time, calling it quits seemed the wise thing to do.

Jackson, although brilliant, at times annoyed her with

his high-handed manner, as he had just done. She did as she pleased. Always had and always would.

She'd made that fact clear when the law firm she now worked for had sent a headhunter after her. She'd taken two months to make a decision and upped the initial offer by forty grand a year plus perks that added up to an additional thirty thousand before she accepted the corner office. One thing she knew and knew well was her worth as a lawyer. She was damn good at what she did.

Checking the slim gold Cartier watch on her wrist, she decided to wait another minute or so. Jackson hated to wait. He could have the office staff under him scurrying to please him with merely a look. Her lips curved.

Brianna's five-foot-two mother could have given him lessons. Those piercing eyes of hers could nail you to the wall at twenty feet, but she was also the best mother in the world. She'd jerk a knot in your neck if you got out of line, but she'd stand toe-to-toe with the devil to protect those she loved. That's why Brianna knew how scared she was when she didn't take the nurse to task that day in the hospital room. Brianna had no difficulty taking the unprofessional woman down a peg or two.

Deciding that her prolonged absence had hammered home the point to Jackson that their past personal relationship wouldn't bend her to his will, she went back inside. The tri-level house, decorated in pewter and black, was perched on the rocky cliffs overlooking Lake Ray Hubbard, twenty minutes away from the Dallas city limits.

Brianna placed her barely touched glass of wine on the tray of a passing waiter and joined the jovial group. The gathering of the twenty-seven firm lawyers at the lake home of their boss, Elton Tipton, was part going-away party for her and part celebration of the firm's big win in a lawsuit in which she'd been lead counsel.

As his due as senior partner of Tipton and Todd, one of the largest and most prestigious law firms in the country, Elton held court in front of the massive limestone fireplace on the second floor of the great room, which had a twenty-foot-high wooden-beamed vaulted ceiling. An immense chandelier of brushed nickel and cut glass bathed them in warm light.

People standing around Elton laughed. Brianna surmised it was probably one of Elton's lame lawyer jokes. At sixty-two, widowed, a multimillionaire, and shrewd beyond belief, he was self-assured enough to be able to poke fun at himself. Her lips tilted upward. It had been a good decision to leave her previous firm. Her reputation and stature had grown in the year she'd been with Tipton and Todd. She had the plaques from the Texas Bar Foundation and the stack of won cases to prove it.

Recently she had been awarded the Lola Wright Foundation Award for exemplifying the highest standards of professional ethics. The year before she'd walked away with the Dan Rugely Price Memorial Award, given to the outstanding Texas lawyer. In November *Law & Politics Magazine* named her a Texas Super Lawyer. She'd worked hard in a job she loved to gain those recognitions. She was on a fast track to the top, or would have been if her father hadn't suffered a heart attack two months ago. But he was one of the lucky ones.

Thankfully, he'd survived with very little damage to his heart. He'd recovered while Andrew lingered and made Justine's life hell. If there was any justice, that would be his final destination.

"Brianna, Elton asked you a question."

Hearing the annoyed tone of Jackson's voice, Brianna snapped her head around. Tall, imposing, and handsome in a dark gray pin-striped Brooks Brothers suit, he was easily the best-looking man there and possibly the smartest. Unfortunately, he knew that as well as anyone.

"I'm sorry. I was thinking about my father." Brianna didn't see her answer as lying. She *had* been thinking about her father. Lawyers learned early to shade and embellish, within reason, of course, and only when necessary. This was definitely one of the latter. Andrew was too well known for her to give even a hint of the ass she thought he was.

"Understandable," Elton said magnanimously. "I hate to see you leave the firm, but I understand."

"I'm trying to talk her into staying," Jackson said, his smile as polished as the hardwood floor beneath their feet.

Brianna didn't even try to keep her displeasure from showing. The man she'd known for a year and had had a brief affair with should understand and support her. Instead he kept selfishly trying to talk her into remaining to continue their affair and their climb to junior partners in the law firm.

At the moment her father's health wouldn't allow him to return to the thirty-five-year private practice he'd cultivated in Charleston. The only way she, her mother, and the doctor could get him to stay at home and therefore cut down on the stress was for Brianna to take over his practice. Her father didn't trust anyone else to handle his clients, some of whom had been with him since he began his practice. Luckily, she was certified to practice in South Carolina as well as in Texas.

"My father needs me, and that's that," she finally told him, her voice more clipped than she had intended.

People around them shifted uneasily. The amusement in Jackson's brown eyes turned to censure.

"Whenever you return, you have a position with Tipton and Todd," Elton slipped in smoothly. His expertise as a negotiation lawyer came in handy with a staff of over sixty. "I was delighted I was able to woo you away from Thompson and Thompson to join us. Your expertise has proven invaluable. You and Jackson are a dynamic duo."

Jackson curved his long arm around Brianna, forgiving her. "She's smart and has nerves of steel in the courtroom. I couldn't have asked for a better associate to work the Gipson case last month."

Brianna relaxed. She didn't want them to part as enemies. "You aren't so bad yourself."

Everyone laughed, and the earlier tension was gone. "Wish I could say the same about Mitch Drummond. We had to do most of the research ourselves on the Gipson case," Jackson commented.

"It wasn't that bad," Brianna said. "He's young."

"That's no excuse for incomplete or sloppy work," Jackson said. "We put the case together with very little help from him."

"Hmmm. Everyone has to carry their weight. I'll look into it Monday." Elton said, a frown puckering his smooth brow. Elton remained trim and fit. The smattering of gray in his black hair made him look even more distinguished. "Now, let's go onto the patio and eat." He extended his arm to Brianna and Jackson. "The special guests should go first."

Brianna looped her arm through Elton's and forced a smile. She disliked Jackson's irksome trait of tattling. She couldn't say anything now, but later she'd have a thing or two to say to him.

Two hours later she had her chance when she entered her high-rise apartment in downtown Dallas. She had barely closed the door before Jackson pulled her into his arms, his lips seeking hers, his hands sliding up her sides. Before his mouth and hands reached her lips or the soft swell of her breasts, she pushed out of his arms.

Typical Jackson—he hadn't believed that they weren't getting back together when he'd insisted on taking her to the party. She'd shipped her car to Charleston earlier that week.

"Be reasonable, Brianna. You can't throw what we had away," he said, twin lines running across his forehead.

Brianna tossed her clutch on one of the several closed packing boxes in her living room. Except for her four-poster, all of her furniture had already been shipped. The movers were coming back in the morning for the bed. She loved her pillow top mattress and had no intention of sleeping on a rental. "Why did you have to take a swipe at Mitch?"

The frown cleared, he smiled the smile that made women sigh, and slid his arms around her waist. "You're leaving in the morning. Surely we can find something better to talk about."

She pushed against his chest until he released her. "Jackson, I don't like it when you do that."

Anger stole across his handsome face. "I can't believe we're having this conversation. Mitch was less than worthless, and you know it."

"No, I don't. This is his first year as a paralegal. He's still learning, just like we had to learn." She folded her arms. "With your comment, he might not have a chance. Elton doesn't carry dead weight."

"Rightly so. Whatever happens to the kid is no skin off my nose." He went to the kitchen and poured himself a scotch, then tossed it back. "I don't understand you sometimes. We were on the fast track to be junior partners. Then you toss it and me away to run home like some baby. You're throwing our future away."

"Whoa." Brianna held up her hand. "My father means more to me than any partnership."

The crystal tumbler hit the counter. Eyes narrowed, chin jutted, Jackson stalked back into the room. "What about our plans? Let someone else run your father's practice."

"He wants me, and that's what he's going to get. I won't build a future at the expense of my father or anyone else, as you seem to want to do."

His well-groomed head snapped back; his expression hardened. "What are you talking about?"

"Tonight isn't the first time you've tried to make yourself look good at the expense of someone else. It's not an endearing quality," she said flatly. "Before Mitch, it was Sally—you just happened to mention to Elton that she had the allocations for a will incorrect."

"She was going to let Clayton sign the will without specifically leaving his wife the majority of his estate as he'd wanted."

He was always ready with an excuse. Nothing was ever

Jackson's fault. "She asked you to check it over. She was unfamiliar with all the antiquated laws in Texas that have been on the books too long."

Jackson was unforgiving. "Then she should have stayed in California," he snapped. "I'm not going to baby-sit anyone."

Brianna was seeing a side of Jackson she didn't like. "Whatever it takes to get ahead. Right?"

He smiled and reached for her. "Right."

She let the lower half of her body sink heavily against his. Her fingertips grazed the curve of his mouth, which was descending toward hers. "And if it meant throwing me to the wolves, you'd do it, wouldn't you?"

A full second passed before Jackson's body tensed against hers. "No, of course not. Don't be silly."

Brianna had cross-examined too many witnesses not to be able to tell when one was caught off guard and lying. Straightening, she stepped out of his loose hold. "Good night and good-bye, Jackson."

"Brianna, you're overreacting and jumping to conclusions."

"If I were overreacting, I'd be on the phone calling Elton's private line."

Something leaped into Jackson's dark eyes that she had never seen before. Fear. "Don't be crazy."

"Call me that again and you'll regret it." She stalked to the door and opened it. "If I hear Mitch lost his job, I'm calling Elton."

"I don't have control over what he does," Jackson told her.

"Your problem, and if you aren't through this door in five seconds I'll make the call anyway." Scowling at her, he made it in three. Angrier than she could ever remember, Brianna slammed the door. She prided herself on being a keen judge of human nature. It irritated her that she hadn't seen through Jackson's polished veneer to the selfish, underhanded person that he was.

She didn't accept excuses from others and she wouldn't accept them for herself. She'd gone into the affair shortly after her father's heart attack. Jackson had been there to lend a broad shoulder and unending reassurance. He and Elton had even flown down on the company's jet on two occasions to visit while her father was in the hospital, and offer their support.

It really peeved her that she had been so gullible and needy and slept with him. Damn. If Andrew needed company when he reached his final destination, she knew just the person.

Three

Shortly after midnight, Dalton Ramsey sat behind his desk in his spacious home office in Buckhead, outside of Atlanta, and stared at the blinking cursor on the nineteen-inch flat computer screen. A third of the way down the page "Chapter Twenty-six" was written in bold black letters, and regrettably nothing else. He'd stared at the annoying cursor for the past five days, hoping for some spurt of inspiration, some nugget of an idea, but nothing had come.

Dalton blew out a pent-up breath of frustration, palmed his bearded face, then continued to run his hands over his thick, black hair, which brushed the collar of his open cotton shirt. In less than two weeks his agent, his editor, and his publishing house expected *Sudden Prey*, the eighth book of his Edgar Gunn series, to be finished and on their desks.

Sudden Prey was a lead title for January, six short months away. The hardcover was already listed in the publisher's catalog. The sales force was already vigorously selling the book. Orders were up by eighteen percent and expected to go higher. Marketing, publicity, and tour dates were being finalized. There was no wiggle room.

Dalton had four chapters, roughly eighty pages or so, to go before Brock Jernigan, the lead character, tracked down the serial killer terrorizing Willington, the fictional small Texas town where he was helping an old football buddy, the local sheriff. Dalton, an ex-cop with the Detroit Police Department for thirteen years with four of those as a detective, knew the solid police work and occasional blind luck needed to apprehend a criminal.

Usually by this time, Dalton's long fingers would be flying across the keyboard, trying to keep pace with his characters in a breakneck race to what he always hoped for and always feared it wouldn't be, a nail-biting, satisfying conclusion.

Not this time, and he knew the reason.

Getting up from his cluttered desk in his office lined with birch shelves overflowing with research books and the books he'd purchased for pleasure, but never seemed to have the time to read, Dalton made his way to the ultramodern kitchen in the four-thousand-square-foot home he'd recently purchased and poured his umpteenth cup of decaf coffee.

After a couple of sips of the strong black brew, the restlessness intensified. Taking the mug with him, he walked beneath the vaulted ceiling of the great room to the lighted terrace.

Stretched out before him was a rectangular pool with a waterfall, lush flowers, and manicured shrubs. The Mediter-

IN ANOTHER MAN'S BED

ranean blue waters reflected the full moon. Crickets chirped. The July night was a pleasant seventy-three degrees and peaceful. Peace, for far too many years, had been something he had longed for, but never hoped to find. But by some miracle he had . . . until now.

Just as he turned to go back to his office, the doorbell chimed. He didn't need two guesses to know who was at the door. Placing the coffee on the black granite counter, he went to the front door and opened it. On the curved stone steps were his two older sisters in their uniform smocks. Slim and trim, their shoulder-length braids sprinkled with premature gray, they were attractive, take-charge women. Both were registered nurses and worked the three-to-eleven shift at Mercy General in Atlanta.

"Go home."

Essie, the oldest, studied him closely, clearly seeing the tiredness in his face. She'd had lots of practice. "Story still giving you trouble?"

"You'll get it. You always do," Martha, the middle child and perpetual optimistic, added.

He hadn't expected anything less from either of them. There wasn't a thing in the world they didn't think he could do. From his earliest memories they had been there to protect, to guide, to praise. Was it any wonder that when his life had crashed he'd come to them?

"You gonna keep us standing here all night?" Martha asked.

Dalton stepped aside. He might be thirty-five to their forty-five and forty-three respectively, but to them he would always be their little brother to boss and take care of. "Why don't you go home and worry Sam and Bill?" he asked, referring to the husbands who worshipped the ground their wives walked on, men who would bend over backwards to please them.

"Because we'd rather worry our little brother." Martha affectionately patted him on the cheek. He caught her arm as she passed. "I'm already packed."

"Then it won't hurt for me to check." With that, she was gone.

He looked around for Essie and didn't see her. She was either in the kitchen or his office. He found her pouring coffee down the kitchen sink. "I just made that."

"I can tell. Thick as motor oil and probably tastes as bad." Turning on the faucet, she washed the carafe, then prepared more coffee. "If you have to drink the stuff, at least learn how to make it."

Dalton stuck his hands in the pockets of his jeans. "I'm used to the taste."

Essie cut him a look over her shoulder. "Yeah, right."

The corners of Dalton's mouth kicked up as he dumped the contents of his cup down the drain. He'd never been able to get by with a lie, even when he tried. The smile died on remembering three years prior when he'd desperately wished that wasn't the case.

"You forgot the extra shave kit," Martha announced, opening the refrigerator for a can of the diet cola she'd started drinking to help her lose a few pounds.

"I don't suppose you'd believe that I planned to put that in there in the morning," he said. This time the smile was full and teasing.

Martha turned the can up and took a huge swallow. "Sure, just like I believed you the time Dad caught you sneaking in and you said you were sleepwalking."

Dalton grimaced as his two sisters laughed. "I was grounded two weeks."

Essie grinned, showing the gap in her front teeth. "Mama added on the extra week for lying."

They grew quiet for a moment. Elvira Dalton had been a five-five dynamo who didn't take mess from anyone. She had taught her three children to be the same way. She'd died six months after their father had made the transition four years ago. "She was tough."

"But not as tough as Daddy." Essie shook her dark head. "That man had eyes in the back of his head."

Martha chuckled. "Caught you kissing Freddie Haynes down by the creek."

Essie rubbed her butt. "Don't remind me."

"We had some good times growing up in Charleston." Dalton reached for a mug as soon as the coffee began to fill the carafe.

"Which brings us to the question of what are we going to do about the home place down there?" Essie asked. "We all live here. My and Martha's kids are in college. I hate to let the place run down, but I don't want to sell it either."

Both women looked at him. In some things they deferred to their baby brother. "I don't want to sell the place either. I'll look it over when I'm down there."

"Maybe you can use it like a writer's retreat?" Essie suggested.

"Maybe," Dalton said. He didn't know what his plans were where Charleston was concerned. Perhaps he was crazy for even thinking of going back.

"Does that coffee mean you're going to write instead of sleep?" Martha said, her mouth pinched with disapproval.

"Deadline," he said. "Besides, I plan to leave around seven, so why go to sleep?"

Both women frowned at him. "You shouldn't drive without sleep."

"It's only a couple of hours. I'll be fine."

Their frowns didn't clear. "You don't usually do signings this close to deadlines."

The unspoken question of "why" hung in the air. "I don't usually get stuck either," he answered evasively.

Essie nodded her graying head. "You're probably working too hard. Maybe this trip is good . . . if you weren't driving there without any sleep."

Dalton threw an arm around each sister and headed them toward the front door. They were too good at making him reveal things he didn't want to reveal. "Don't worry. I've pulled all-nighters before."

"Call the minute you check into the hotel."

"Don't I always?" Dalton answered.

"Safe travel." Essie gave him a hug, then stepped back as Martha did the same.

"Safe travel."

"Thanks." Dalton stood in the doorway until they climbed into Essie's big Lincoln Continental and pulled off. They'd helped him through some hard times. He had thought those were all behind him.

Sighing, he returned to his office, determined to work. Instead, he paused at the corner of the cluttered desk and picked up *The Post and Courier*, the main newspaper of Charleston, his hometown. The story was three months old, but the headline still had the power to chill him: *Wife Risks Life to Rescue Husband.*

The fingers of his other hand lightly touched the picture of the woman, her blue silk blouse and white pants torn, her beautiful face scratched, her hands bleeding from pulling her husband from the SUV, then dragging him to safety before others arrived to help her. Her courage and her love were undeniable. Once he'd thought . . .

"Don't go there, Ramsey." The mug hit the desk. Digging up memories would likely bury him.

She had her life and he was just beginning to have his. She had probably forgotten him. Just as he should have forgotten her.

But did one ever forget their first love? He wasn't sure. He just knew he'd never been able to completely forget Justine and, as life became hell on earth, he'd thought of her more and more, thought of when they'd first met.

He'd been cocky and wild, riding home from work at his father's service station on his motorcycle. She'd been walking home from band practice. He'd noticed her around campus. Every time he'd try to catch her attention, she'd smile and duck her head. If she'd been another girl he would have thought she was being coy.

But it was a well-known fact that Justine was shy. After talking to her, he'd discovered she had the prettiest smile he'd ever seen. Against all odds, they'd clicked. They'd gone out a few times . . . until her mother had gotten into the picture.

What might have happened if her mother hadn't stepped in?

Dalton shook his head and took his seat behind the computer screen. Questions like that wouldn't help. Scooting his chair closer to the monitor, his hands hovered over the keys as he waited for Brock to say something, anything, to the woman he'd loved once and never forgotten, the woman who happened to be the wife of the man lying dead at their feet.

Nothing came.

Dalton had been exorcising his own demons when he'd come up with the plot. Now he couldn't stop thinking of Justine and what she must be going through. Because, if there was one certainty in this world, it was that Justine loved her husband. Something he had never been certain of with his ex-wife.

The thought only brought sadness now; three years ago the pain had sent him into a tailspin. He'd survived by going into seclusion and burying himself in his work. Oddly, being reclusive had helped with book sales. He'd made very few personal appearances, until now.

He glanced at the newspaper photo again. He was going home and, just like Brock, no matter how hard he tried to deny it, no matter how it made him feel like slime, he wanted another man's wife.

Patrick Dunlap was dying.

He knew it with every ragged, pain-filled breath he drew. Faintly he heard the piercing wail of the ambulance's siren competing with that of a squad car, but he knew they wouldn't reach him in time.

He'd been a policeman for eighteen years, had reached the rank of second lieutenant, had pulled his gun less than ten times and fired three of those times, but he'd never thought about his death. He wasn't callous or cocky, he had just chosen to live with optimism instead of fear . . . until now.

Fear lay like a heavy blanket over him. He had so much

to do, so many plans. The surprise birthday party for his sister-in-law at her favorite restaurant, the fishing trip to Alaska with his brothers, the fishing boat he'd been thinking of finally buying. He tried to concentrate, to pray, but the fear and the pain were too great. His thoughts kept slipping away, just as his life's blood was slipping through his clenched fingers. He wanted to live, hadn't realized how much until he faced death.

Then he heard the running footsteps, the frantic voices. Too late. They were coming too late.

"Dunlap, hang in there! Hang in there."

He was trying, but something was dragging him under. It was almost easier to stop fighting, anything to escape the pain, the stench of his own blood. His last thoughts were of his large family. His parents were gone, but the five sons they'd raised with love and a firm hand were as tight as it got. They'd take it hard. He'd miss them, but he was so tired.

He was lifted. Excruciating pain stabbed him. All he wanted to do was escape. He felt himself being dragged down. He couldn't fight any longer.

I'm sorry, he thought. Tears formed in the corners of his eyes as they fluttered closed. *Good-bye. . . .*

Patrick woke up in a cold sweat with the acrid smell of blood in his nostrils, his body tightly curled in a fetal position. His shaking hands frantically clutched his abdomen in a futile attempt to stop the sticky wetness of his own blood seeping through his fingers.

His labored breath shuddered out as he jerked upright in bed and tried to separate reality from his dream. Reaching over, he snapped on the light on the bedside chest, his other hand lifting his damp T-shirt from his stomach.

There was no blood, but his breathing grew more labored. The ten-inch jagged scar was a horrific reminder that there had been blood and pain. The fight to recover had been long and difficult, but he'd made it. His partner hadn't.

Standing, Patrick stripped off the white cotton T-shirt and tossed it on the foot of the king-sized four-poster as he went to the balcony and opened the French doors. Cool air bathed his perspiration-drenched body instead of the putrid stench of the filthy alley.

His hands gripped the iron rail as he stared down at the marina on the Ashley River in Charleston. By the light of the full moon he could see the *Proud Mary*, his boat, riding at anchor on the pier. He wasn't in a rat-infested alley, praying to live, and then praying that his family mourn him and then go on if he didn't.

He was alive. He was safe.

Slowly his breathing returned to normal and he went back inside the condo. The clock radio's red dial on the nightstand blinked 5:15 A.M. He could try to go back to sleep or pull on clothes and take the boat out to meet the sun.

In the next instant, Patrick grabbed the discarded T-shirt on the way to the bathroom. One thing that dark alley six months ago in Myrtle Beach had taught him was to grab life, never wait for a tomorrow that might not come. He was going to live each day to the fullest.

Less than fifteen minutes later, Patrick was on the pier, waving to a few friends with charter boats getting ready for the day. On occasion and when he felt like it, Patrick hired out his craft. The counsel of his thrifty mother more so than the pension from the police department had given him the financial freedom to do as he pleased and to buy the town house from his unpredictable and lovable niece, Brooke, after she had married last year.

Untying the rope, Patrick smiled as he continued to think of Brooke. She was the only child of his oldest brother, and the other single brothers had enjoyed spoiling their niece. She'd grown up with expensive taste and had a job that could afford her the best. They all expected her to marry some high-powered, driven executive. True to form, she'd done the unexpected and married a great guy who owned a garage and had two adorable children and made him and his other three brothers very happy uncles and her parents instant adoring grandparents.

On board, Patrick stood at the wheel of his craft, the running lights on as he aimed for the mouth of the marina, heading for the open sea. Life's little unexpected turns were often the best. His hands went to the scar on his stomach beneath his shirt and windbreaker.

Then there were times you just had to hold on and pray. Opening the throttle, he pointed the boat toward the pinkish sky.

Patrick arrived back at the marina shortly after nine. The nightmare that had driven him from a peaceful sleep was a distant memory. Securing the boat, he started up the pier, waving to friends and acquaintances as he passed. Most of the residents in the condo were friendly and easygoing. Many of the berths of his charter and pleasure boat friends were empty.

He waved to diners sitting on the deck eating breakfast from the restaurant inside the pavilion. Occasionally he dined there, but another thing his mother had taught him was to be self-sufficient.

"Morning, Patrick. Want to join us for breakfast?"

"Good morning, Pasha," he greeted, never slowing his long strides. Pasha was a five-foot-eight beauty with long legs and a sleek body. She wore a bikini top that strained to cup her full breasts and a smile that said he could have more than breakfast if he wanted. "Maybe another time."

Disappointment etched fine lines across her brows. "Sure."

Another thing that night had taught him was not to play games. He wasn't wasting his time or a woman's. He had turned forty last month. There were a couple of gray hairs in his jet black hair. He was old enough to want something from a woman besides a hot body. He was patient enough to wait until he found what he was looking for.

Hands stuffed in the pockets of his white shorts, Patrick followed the curving walkway that led to the four-story condo, glistening like a diamond in the morning sun. Situated on the Ashley River, the upscale Millennium let the residents have the best of living near the water and the convenience of quick access to the city.

He entered the spacious lobby, and cool air greeted him. Summers in Charleston were hot and muggy, but so was Myrtle Beach. The open area was filled with lavender-colored leather furniture, ten-foot-tall palms, and seascape paintings by Carolina artists. He headed for the elevator, planning to take a shower and then drive to his niece's house for breakfast. His mouth quirked. He pushed the elevator button.

It was still difficult to think of Brooke ecstatically, happily balancing marriage, her two stepchildren, and a growing business. Fifteen months ago Brooke was more interested in the newest fashion must-have and rising in the corporate world in marketing. Marriage certainly changed people. He had yet to know the feeling.

He had seen too many of his friends' marriages fail. He wasn't anxious to follow suit. His older brother's happy marriage was the exception rather than the rule. There were five brothers and Sam, Brooke's father, was the only one who had taken the plunge. But that was understandable because his wife was an exceptional woman. Patrick didn't want to play games, but he wasn't ready to get married, either.

The heavy wooden doors with an ironwork grille dating back to the early nineteenth century opened. He saw several pieces of designer luggage. The corner of his mouth tilted upward. He easily recalled the amount of luggage and trips it had taken them to move Brooke, who had enough clothes for three women. His gaze went beyond the luggage. He saw a good-looking, well-dressed older couple.

"Morning," the man greeted. He wore a long-sleeved white shirt, open at the collar, and a beige lightweight sports coat. "I think you can squeeze on. We've already taken one load up."

"Daddy." The sultry voice was filled with affection and good humor, but he had little difficulty imagining it whispering in his ear on moon-draped sheets.

"Thanks." Intrigued, Patrick stepped into the domed elevator just as the doors began to close. He saw the owner of the midnight-and-lace voice immediately. She was stunning in an off-the-shoulder white knit top, lime green linen pants, and a sterling silver chain belt loosely draped around her narrow waist. Her long black hair was in some kind of coil atop her head. He'd like nothing better than to take it down and run his fingers through the thick, lustrous strands.

"Which floor?" the man asked.

Patrick whipped his head around. From the knowing smile of the man this wasn't the first time a man had been totally captivated by his daughter. "Four."

The older man punched in the number. "Do you live here?"

"Yes." Patrick smiled at the daughter. She gave an almost imperceptible nod. "Welcome. I'm Patrick Dunlap."

The older man extended his hand. "I'm—"

"Daddy."

Patrick glanced around, but the woman's attention was centered on her father. Neither said a word, but some type of communication must have passed between them, because the older man clasped his hand lightly and said, "Charles. Pleased to meet you."

"Nice weather we're having," the older attractive woman said, filling what could have been an awkward moment.

"Yes, it is." Patrick's attention went back to the daughter again. Smart and beautiful. They didn't know him, and introducing themselves to a total stranger wasn't a good idea, but Patrick wanted to know her name, know more about her.

The grilled elevator door slid open on the third floor. The daughter picked up the larger of the five suitcases. The father saw the direction of Patrick's gaze and his mouth firmed.

"Let me have that."

"Got it, Daddy. Hurry before the door closes."

Reluctantly, the older man picked up the overnight Gucci case and a train case and stepped off. His wife followed with two smaller pieces.

"Can I help?" Patrick asked, holding the door.

"No, thank you," the daughter said, stepping past him. He caught a whiff of some exotic scent that made his body tingle and recall that he hadn't been intimate since his accident. The door started to close and he punched the open button. She turned. And simply looked at him.

Tipping his head, he pushed the close button. His time was coming. He'd been good at his job and had a knack for uncovering information. Before the week was over he was going to find out who the mysterious and beautiful woman on the third floor was, and if she was worth knowing better.

Instincts told him she was. Life had just gotten more interesting.

Four

Justine woke up slowly and stared at the bedside clock. 7:19 A.M. Her bookstore didn't open until ten, but Beverly liked to be at the hospital by 8:30, a full ninety minutes before the regular visiting hours.

"Andrew was always an early riser and he expects me."

Justine curled tighter as if she could hear her mother-in-law's voice. She didn't want to go, but she had little choice. Beverly expected her, needed her. Justine had finally figured out that as long as they kept vigil over Andrew, Beverly was able to convince herself that he'd improve.

Justine knew that he wouldn't. As much as he had hurt her, she didn't want him to die. She just wanted out of the lie that was their marriage, wanted to be able to stop the charade.

Throwing back the covers, she went into the bathroom. The soft blue guest room and bath was half the size of the master suite, but she hadn't been inside the master bedroom since the day she'd come home a week after the accident.

Once home, she hadn't stopped until she'd moved all of her things to the guest bedroom. The maid thought Justine had moved because sleeping in their bed would have been too painful.

The housekeeper was partially right. The rice-style bed was a reminder of his betrayal and of what a gullible fool Justine had been.

Dressed, she grabbed her keys and purse off the dresser and went to the kitchen. The automatic coffeepot had the coffee ready. She poured herself a cup, added sugar and cream, then stared out the window as she sipped. The kitchen looked out onto the side of the house, where pink crepe myrtles grew surrounded by St. Augustine grass an inch thick and so green it looked artificial.

Andrew had hired a lawn service along with a maid even before they moved into their house. With both of their busy schedules neither one of them had time to maintain the huge, landscaped yard or the forty-five hundred square feet of living space. Their dream home.

Her prison.

Justine's slim fingers clenched on the handle of the delicate cup, a wedding gift. Many of their three hundred wedding guests had commented that they'd never seen a happier couple or one more in love. They'd been wrong, or had they? When had the lies started? How long had Andrew cheated, or was it his first time as he'd said? No matter. Once or a thousand, the betrayal couldn't cut any deeper than it already had.

Rinsing out the cup, she put it in the dishwasher. She'd go to the hospital to be with Beverly, and hope she'd be able to leave soon thereafter. She wasn't sure how much longer she could keep pretending to be the dutiful loving wife. But she had to. Other people depended on the illusion.

"Andrew, you have a lot to answer for."

"Mrs. Crandall, your mother is wonderful," Carolyn, the dark-haired head nurse for the seven-to-three shift, commented the moment Justine entered the ICCU patient area.

"She sure is," Sadie, the ward clerk, agreed, then grinned and patted her protruding abdomen. "She brought brownies. I'll have to start my diet tomorrow."

Carolyn rolled her eyes. "You're always saying that."

"And I always plan to," Sadie said, her grin growing.

Amid the laughter and good-natured ribbing, Justine hoped no one noticed that her steps had slowed. The few times her mother had visited, the nursing staff had relaxed the rules to allow all three women to be in the room instead of the required two.

Not for the first time Justine wished the chief of staff, an old friend of Beverly's from high school, and the nursing staff weren't so accommodating. Taking a deep breath, Justine pushed open the door and paused. Beverly and her mother stood on either side at the head of the bed, staring down at Andrew as if they expected him to wake up and start talking. Both looked up as she entered.

"Good morning, Justine. Look who's here, Andrew." In a lime green suit Beverly looked as crisp and as well turned out as she always did. Justine didn't know how she managed. It was an effort at times for her to drag herself out of bed. Her mother looked equally well dressed in a black gabardine pants suit and white silk blouse.

"Good morning, Justine." Her mother greeted her as if the stilted conversation between them last night hadn't happened. In public her mother was the epitome of a loving, supportive mother. When it was just the two of them they were awkward with each other, and the conversation always dragged.

"Good morning, Mother, Beverly." Justine let the door swing shut behind her. "Thank you for bringing the nursing staff the brownies." She'd long since gotten over being hurt when her mother did for others and not her.

Her mother had been room mother for each grade from pre-kindergarten through high school graduation. There had been very few years in which she hadn't been a PTA officer. If there was a committee, her mother's hand was usually the first to go up. Perhaps that was why she and Andrew hit it off. Both presented the perfect picture outwardly, but in actuality were frauds.

"They deserve it for taking such good care of Andrew," her mother said, visibly swallowing.

Justine wondered, not for the first time, if, were she in that bed instead of Andrew, her mother would keep a vigil over her the way Beverly did. "Yes, they do."

"I was telling your mother that Andrew had a good night." Beverly beamed down at her son lying lifeless on the white sheets.

"That's good to hear," Helen said. "It will be so good to have him back with us."

Beverly smiled and patted Andrew's still hand. "It's just a matter of time. I feel it."

Justine glanced from one woman to the other. They

continued to watch Andrew as if they expected him to open his eyes and sit up. "Did the doctor say anything different this morning?"

Beverly rolled her eyes. "I don't need him to tell me anything. I feel it. Mothers are instinctive, aren't they, Helen?"

"Yes," her mother answered.

If Beverly heard the hesitancy in Helen's stilted voice, she didn't comment.

"Justine, you can take my place and keep Andrew company while Helen and I go for a cup of coffee." Beverly picked up her black Louis Vuitton purse. "You can tell him all the wonderful things you're going to do together when he comes home."

"Beverly, the doctor doesn't—"

"No." Lips tight, Beverly held up her small hand to cut Justine off. "There'll be no more negative talk in this room. Dr. Thomas will have a talk with the neurologist today. If he can't keep an open mind, we'll find one who will."

Justine didn't want to point out that Dr. Lane didn't appear to be the type to take orders from anyone. Not even the chief of staff.

"Justine agrees wholeheartedly with you, don't you?" her mother said, her lips pinched.

Both women stared at Justine, almost daring her to challenge them. She was still a coward in so many ways, but only to a point. "I'll do whatever it takes."

Beverly smiled. Helen studied her, as if recalling that her daughter didn't like confrontation and might appear to be agreeing while in actuality planning to go her own way, just as she had with the opening of the bookstore.

Helen had thought Justine was crazy to leave her job as an elementary school librarian in Charleston to open a bookstore. Her mother had predicted she'd go broke in six months. Justine had gone ahead with her plans and hadn't consulted her mother again. The success of the store hadn't changed her mother's opinion. She'd been to the store exactly three times since it had opened.

"Go get your coffee," Justine finally said.

"Thank you." Beverly went to the door. "We won't be long."

Helen shoved the strap of her bag over her shoulder. "Good-bye, Justine. We'll talk later. I'm leaving from the coffee shop for work."

Justine hadn't expected her mother to come back up. She was there for Andrew, for Beverly, to play the part of the good mother, but not for her daughter. "Good-bye, Mother."

The door closed behind them. Justine wrapped her arms around herself and looked anywhere except at the bed. The day couldn't get any worse.

Two hours later she discovered she was wrong. Her cell phone rang just as she stepped on the elevator. Since it wasn't Brianna's dial tone, she ignored the call. If it was the bookstore, she'd be there in twenty minutes.

With Andrew's condition so unstable since he was transferred to Charleston, she hadn't been to work for longer than a couple of hours at a time. She had a good manager in Iris, but it was past time for her to take care of things herself.

By the time she pulled out onto the street from the parking garage, there had been three more calls. Deciding the caller wasn't going to give up, she fished the cell phone out of her oversize drawstring bag at a signal light and answered. "Hello."

"Justine, good morning," Marcus greeted. "I hate to bother you so early, but could you come over here?"

"Here?" she said, but she already had a good idea.

"The foundation."

No! her mind shouted. She didn't want to look at all those sympathetic faces and hear all those platitudes. "Why?" If it didn't mean people would lose their jobs or all the projects be scuttled, she wouldn't care what happened to Andrew's growing empire.

"Please, it's important." Marcus paused, then continued. "You haven't been here since Andrew's accident. People need to know they have to keep hope alive, they need to know that things will be all right. Your presence will reassure them."

A horn blast startled Justine into looking up. She pulled through the green light.

"I know it's a lot to ask, and I understand why you haven't been by. I know how much you love Andrew, how painful it would be if you came here," he went on to say.

She glanced out the window at the passing scenery. Everyone thought they knew what she was feeling. She'd never known until Andrew's accident that so much sympathy could be draining.

"Justine, it's important."

Marcus wasn't the type to complain. The firm was more important than Andrew or her hurt feelings. Regardless of Andrew's deceit, he had touched people's lives and helped them to be better, happier. Too bad he hadn't listened to himself when he discussed honesty and fidelity. "I can be there in fifteen minutes."

"Thank you, Justine." The relief was clearly heard in his deep voice. "I'll be waiting in the front of the building for you. I'll okay it with the security guard to leave your car in front."

Justine disconnected the phone and prepared to be inundated by well-wishers with questions. *Lord, give me strength.*

The Having It All foundation occupied the entire top floor of an office building near downtown Charleston. The white façade gleamed in the morning sun. As promised, Marcus was waiting on the sidewalk for her. Andrew would have sent someone unless the person arriving had very deep pockets.

Marcus was at the door of the van by the time it stopped. "Thank you, Justine."

"The foundation is important." She got out of the van, her hands gripping the strap of her shoulder bag.

"I knew you'd understand." Taking her arm, he went inside the building. The sympathetic gazes of people followed them to the elevators on the first floor. "They mean well."

She glanced up at him. She hadn't thought he was so perceptive. She'd been so wrong about so many people.

They stepped on the elevator and Marcus punched 10. Justine concentrated on trying to relax. Thankfully, they went straight to their floor. The shiny metal panel doors slid open.

The first thing she saw, as every visitor did, was the life-size oil portrait of her and Andrew. The artist had captured what he thought he saw, a young couple very much in love and extremely happy. Dressed in a light blue sleeveless dress, she leaned back against Andrew, who wore a blue shirt and tan slacks, his back braced against the trunk of a big oak tree, his arms circling Justine, his hands clasped at her waist.

"Andrew loved that picture and what it represented. Total love, total commitment for a lifetime."

She couldn't say anything. Apparently Marcus understood. Taking her arm, they continued down the hall. People going about their normal business in the office saw her and immediately came to take her hand or give her a hug or both.

More employees came out of offices as news spread that she was there. The foundation had a staff of over fifty. All she could think of was to hold on, that she could get through this.

Just when she didn't think she could stand another sympathetic, often tearful face, Marcus intervened. "Justine appreciates your concern and prayers. But why don't we let her have a chance to catch her breath?"

"Thank you for caring," Justine mumbled as people tipped their heads and moved away.

"Let's go in here, where we can talk," Marcus said.

Justine readily followed him, only to stop short when they entered Andrew's outer office where his secretary had her desk.

"I hope you don't mind," Marcus said, for the first time sounding nervous. "Andrew's office is bigger than mine. I needed the space for meetings and think sessions. Except for moving my files in here, nothing has changed."

"It's all right," Justine said. She passed through the outer office, briefly wondering where Andrew's secretary, Teresa, was, then pushed open the door to Andrew's office herself.

She didn't expect the stab of remorse on seeing the executive desk and Andrew not sitting behind it. They'd picked the oversize mahogany piece out together. He had joked about one day coming back when everyone was gone and making love on top of it. They never had, but had he made love to someone else there?

The thought made her remember her trip to the cabin to seduce him. She cringed inside. Perhaps that was why Andrew had strayed, perhaps she wasn't daring or spontaneous enough.

"If you'd rather, we can go into my office," Marcus said.

"No." Crossing the carpeted floor on trembling legs, Justine took a seat in one of the twin blue leather chairs in front of the desk. Trying to find the reason behind Andrew's unfaithfulness would drive her insane.

Closing the door, Marcus went to her. "Can I get you anything to drink?"

She shook her head. What she wanted was to get out of this office as soon as possible.

Marcus nodded, then pulled the matching chair around so he could face her as he sat down. "I can see this is difficult for you, so I'll be quick. Andrew was a dynamic force and following in his footsteps is a big job, perhaps impossible. He drew people to him."

Especially women. Justine glanced away as if Marcus could read her mind.

"He was booked a year out. Programs had to be canceled, money refunded."

Her gaze slowly came back to Marcus. She'd never thought about money. Kent Taylor, Andrew's business manager, the business manager for the foundation, had come to her the first day at the hospital and told her not to worry about finances. She hadn't. Money had been the last thing on her mind. "Is the foundation broke?"

"No, no," Marcus hastened to assure her. "Andrew was a smart man, and Kent watches the bottom line like a hawk."

"I don't understand."

Marcus rubbed his hand over his head. "Nina says I always take the long road. But this is hard."

"Say it."

"We're fine financially, will be for a while, but with the cancellation of the retreats and seminars, we won't be if things continue in this way."

"Andrew . . ." Justine began.

"We'll come through this," Marcus said, his voice as determined as Beverly's. "Long ago I promised him I'd take care of you, his mother, and the foundation in that order if anything happened to him. I don't break promises."

With so many loyal people who loved Andrew, why hadn't he been worthy of their trust and respect? "I know you will."

There was a knock on the door. Marcus stood. "That's Kent. Come in."

In walked a rotund man with wire-rimmed glasses, dressed as fashionably as Marcus was out of fashion. The pocket square matched the silk tie, the wingtips were Italian, and so was the fine gray wool pin-striped suit.

"Justine, it's good of you to come. I know this isn't easy."

She realized something as he gently squeezed her hands and stared down into her face. "It hasn't been easy on any of us."

Kent pulled a chair from the small conference table that seated six. "How much has Marcus told you?"

She repeated what Marcus had said. "What can be done?" she asked.

The two men exchanged nervous glances. "One thought was for you to lead a benefit recept—"

"No." The word was out before he finished.

"Told you," Marcus said. "I'm for restarting the retreats."

"But how?" Justine asked, her brow furrowed.

"Me," Marcus said, holding her gaze. "With your permission, of course. I've studied under Andrew. I can offer the same solid foundation. We wanted to see how you felt first."

She honestly couldn't see Marcus taking Andrew's place. "I don't know."

He smiled wryly. "I know Andrew dressed better, looked better, and charmed better." His expression turned serious. "But I want to do this; I feel I can help people. Nina promised to pick out the clothes." He chuckled softly. "She's been wanting to do that for a long time anyway."

"We'd start small," Kent said as if he sensed her reservations. "A retreat in Summerville with about fifty men."

Andrew's goal to help marriages stay strong was a good one. Both of them had grown up without their fathers in the home. "If you're asking my permission, you have it."

Both men blew out breaths. "Thank you, Justine," Marcus said. "Nina will be with me for the first couple of meetings, just as you were with Andrew. Seeing a happy couple helps people believe."

Justine said nothing. Luckily Marcus continued. "I don't mind saying that I'm proud of her and blessed to have her in my life. Sometimes I can't believe she chose me."

Justine had often thought the same thing. Now she understood why. "Anyone who knows you can answer that. You're a man of strength and character."

"Thank you. Andrew always said you were incredible," Marcus said.

Justine concentrated on keeping the smile on her face. "Thank you."

"There's one more favor we have to ask," Kent said, watching her closely.

Unconsciously, Justine pressed her back against the leather back of the chair. "What?"

Kent leaned forward. "There is a ministerial luncheon in about an hour at the Doubletree hotel. Many of those attending have pledged their support both financially and personally to the senior citizen complex that the foundation is spearheading. Ground breaking is scheduled in two months."

She knew what was coming next. "You want me to attend the luncheon."

"Please," Marcus said. "Nina is going with us. We have to show them that nothing has changed. We're still committed to building this senior citizen complex. It will have everything the occupants need to live with dignity and purpose. Andrew's vision will continue."

There would be too many people asking the same question, hugging her, offering her comfort when there was none to be had. "Many of them have visited the hospital and assured me of their support. I don't think my attending is necessary," Justine pointed out, hoping, praying it was enough.

"People change their minds and so do ministers." Kent edged closer. "Until I have the check in the bank, I prefer to cover all bases."

Her gaze went to Marcus. He was proving to be more perceptive than she'd thought. He answered her unanswered question, saying, "Kent's right."

Her lashes fluttered down briefly, then lifted. The senior citizen complex had been her dream as well. Too many elderly people didn't have a safe, caring place to live where they were treated with dignity in their declining years. Having children didn't guarantee that they would be cared for.

Seniors shouldn't have to eat cat food to save enough money to buy meds or live alone with no one to care if they lived or died. People needed to know someone cared. She couldn't have made it these last months without Brianna. "I'll need to go home and change first."

Kent and Marcus stood immediately. "We'll pick you up in forty minutes."

Justine came to her feet as well. "I'll be ready."

"Excellent. I have some calls to make. Thanks again for coming." Kent left and they slowly followed him.

In the outer office, Nina, in a cropped red jacket and matching slim skirt, was behind the desk instead of Andrew's old secretary. She immediately stood and joined them. "Hello, Justine."

"You've changed positions?"

Marcus curved his long arm around his pretty wife's slim shoulders. "She's been invaluable to me."

Andrew's secretary had been young, energetic, and efficient. "What happened to Teresa?"

"She resigned shortly after Andrew's accident," Nina said when her husband didn't offer any information.

Suspicion sprouted in Justine's mind. "Why? Was there a problem?"

"No problem. She just decided to move back to Mississippi with her parents." Once again it was Nina who answered.

"I see," Justine said when she didn't see at all. If she recalled, Teresa came from a tiny town in Mississippi and had always proclaimed she'd rather eat dirt than go back.

"It's worked out great." Marcus's dark face split into a wide grin. "I like having Nina near, since I can keep an eye on her to make sure she takes care of herself."

Nina cut her gaze at Marcus, who suddenly looked stricken. "Why is that?" Justine asked, although she was sure she already knew the answer.

Nina gave one last annoyed look at Marcus before answering. "I'm pregnant. With all that's been happening in your life, we wanted to wait and tell you."

"I told her you'd be happy for us," Marcus said, obviously trying to defend his slip.

Justine wasn't sure how she felt. "How far along are you?"

"Not that far. Probably a couple of months," Nina said.

Women were usually more definite about the length of their pregnancy, especially with their first one. Justine wondered if there was a reason for her being vague, then berated herself for doing so. She was driving herself crazy with her suspicions. She hugged Nina. "Marcus was right. Congratulations."

"Thank you," Nina said. Was there relief in her voice?

Justine straightened. She had to get a grip. "I better get home so I can change."

Leaving them standing there, she once again walked the gauntlet of concerned employees, who offered more hugs, prayers, and well wishes.

At the elevator she turned. Through the glass door she saw Marcus and Nina. Neither seemed happy. Although Justine had once thought of them as the odd couple, they had always appeared happy in the past. But she'd learned the hard way that looks could be deceiving.

The elevator doors opened. Before stepping on, she saw Marcus take Nina's arm and enter Andrew's office, closing the door behind them. Interesting.

Five

Shortly after seven that night, a bone-weary Justine arrived at Brianna's condo and rang the doorbell. Lies wore a person down.

They had barely gotten out of Marcus's Lexus at the downtown hotel before others arriving for the luncheon recognized her and hurried over. As at the foundation offices earlier, they were joined by others. By the time she entered the ballroom of over five hundred people, she had an entourage.

She'd hoped they would be seated in the back and tried to keep smiling when they were led to a reserved table near the raised speaker's dais. She had thought the ordeal was surely over when the program began. She wasn't that fortunate.

The guest speaker, a nationally known minister and a friend of Andrew's, recognized her and asked her to stand. The standing ovation that followed made her head pound and made her feel like a fraud. But this time she put the blame where it belonged, on Andrew.

When they left the luncheon almost two hours later, the foundation had numerous promises to have checks ready by the next day, and several ministers had asked Kent or Marcus to stop by their office that afternoon. The senior complex remained on schedule, and Justine was drained.

Brianna opened her door. For reasons that Justine couldn't phantom her throat clogged, tears filled her eyes. Seconds later she was encircled in a hug filled with love and understanding. She'd called Brianna from the bookstore after returning from the luncheon and told her everything. Justine just held on and swallowed to keep the tears from falling.

"It will get better," Brianna murmured.

Justine's eyes closed. No, it won't, she thought, then realized she didn't have to hide her true feeling or watch every word anymore. "When?" she pleaded.

"I don't know, but it will," came Brianna's fierce reply.

Justine straightened before either of them gave into more tears. "I'm glad you're here."

"So am I."

"I want the grand tour," Justine said, glancing around the beautiful apartment in calm, neutral colors of beige and cream. "It's beautiful."

Brianna laughed, a rich, full sound. "Thanks to you. I detest shopping."

"You have exquisite taste. You're just impatient at times." Justine glanced at the hand-tufted rug beneath her feet in ecru and pale blue, the exact colors in the drawn draperies framing the bank of windows and the French doors on the other side of the room. A chair in front of a narrow window was a stripe of the two colors. "Elegant and understated."

"Hopefully, the maid coming next week will help me keep it that way." Brianna wrinkled her nose. "Unlike you, I'd rather chew nails than keep house."

A shadow crossed Justine's face. "I haven't done much cleaning lately."

"You're entitled. Besides, a little dust won't hurt," Brianna said, looping her arm casually through Justine's. "I am an expert on the matter. The bathroom is spectacular, with a crystal chandelier and Italian marble. I might not want to leave to go to work each morning."

Justine smiled as Brianna had obviously planned and went into the bedroom, where a queen-size brass bed with cream and blue bedding dominated the room.

"I thought you wanted a balcony in the bedroom," Justine said.

Brianna made a face. "Only the corner units have balconies in the bedrooms. I thought I had one, but the tenant decided to sell to a relative."

A frown knitted Justine's brow. "They backed out of the sale?"

"If she had, I would have hauled her butt into court. When I was looking at this one to buy, the concierge mentioned the owner of a corner unit was thinking of selling instead of leasing. But when I contacted him about it a week later I was told she had decided to sell to a relative."

"Well, this place is beautiful, and you must have a wonderful view from the balcony in the living area," Justine consoled.

"I do, but I told the concierge to keep an eye and ear out for anyone in those corner units who might want to sell." Determination narrowed Brianna's tawny-colored eyes. "I'm not sure how long Daddy is going to need me to run his practice. If one of those units comes up for sale I intend to grab it, then lease or sell this place."

"You'll get it," Justine said. "There isn't much you've wanted and haven't gotten."

"There's always a first time, but hopefully it's in the far distant future. Let's leave the rest of the tour for later and get a drink." In the great room, Brianna released Justine and poured them each a glass of red wine.

Tossing her shoulder bag on the striped sofa as she passed, Justine accepted the glass. "I'm not sure this is a good idea on an empty stomach."

"Not for long." Brianna glanced at the diamond dial Cartier watch on her slim wrist. "Garlic bread will be ready in five minutes, or we can empty the bottle and you can stay here for the night like old times."

Justine sipped her drink and remembered. "Your mother always said she couldn't imagine what we had left to talk about so much since we stayed on the phone all the time."

Brianna grinned. "She probably had a pretty good idea it was about boys."

Justine's fingers flexed on the delicate stem. "You always handled the many boys in high school so well, and the men afterward. You wouldn't have been duped."

"Don't compare yourself to me or anyone," Brianna said fiercely. "You loved him, trusted him. You didn't expect him to be unfaithful."

"No. Unlike our parents, we were going to be happy

and together forever." Justine walked through the open French doors leading outside to the wrought-iron-rimmed balcony. A gentle breeze touched her face, tossed her hair. The sun was setting behind the boats riding at anchor in the harbor below. "I looked through his papers and e-mails, but didn't find anything that might tell me who the woman was. Not knowing makes me suspicious of every woman who visited Andrew. I hate that."

"But statistically speaking, she's probably someone you know." Brianna leaned against the rail. "I've seen it too many times to count."

"Nina said Andrew's secretary went back to Mississippi to be with her parents. I can't help thinking there might have been another reason," Justine said.

"I can hire someone to check her out if you'd like," Brianna told her.

"No. I won't do that." Justine sipped her wine. "I might have suspected even you if I hadn't known you were a thousand miles away," she said, turning to face her best friend, waiting for the hurt to appear in her face. "Forgive me."

Brianna hugged her. "He put you through a lot. You're still going through it, but you'll survive."

"I'm going to try. Your parents are one of the lucky couples," Justine said, feeling miserable because she couldn't shake feeling jealous and angry that she and Andrew hadn't been able to keep their marriage together.

"They still hold hands and snuggle," Brianna said, a smile touching her lips.

"I don't remember my parents ever doing either." Sighing, Justine walked back into the room. "Mama was always so afraid I'd fall for a ladies' man like Daddy. She was right. At least we didn't have a child."

"Children often get caught in the crossfire, but you wouldn't have let that happen."

Justine's eyes briefly shut. "No, I would have loved any children we might have had even more. On the drive up there I was hoping I could change his mind about starting a family. I had even purchased a new nightgown in his favorite color."

"Was that the blue one you tore to shreds at the hotel in Gaithersburg?"

Justine nodded. She'd used her manicure scissors to cut the gossamer silk, then finished ripping the material by hand. "Childish and unsatisfying."

"Since you couldn't vent your anger on Andrew, you used a substitute," Brianna said. "Andrew is a bastard."

Shock widened Justine's eyes. "He's in a coma!"

Brianna's hard gaze didn't waver. "That doesn't excuse him for what he did or is."

"I've thought and called him worse." Justine glanced down at the fading scars on her hands. "But I couldn't just leave him."

"Honey, no." Brianna arms circled Justine's shoulders. "You did a brave, stupid thing, and I couldn't be prouder of you."

"At times I can still smell the gas fumes, feel the jar of the earth beneath my feet as the Escalade exploded, feel the heat of the flames on my face."

"Don't think about it," Brianna ordered.

"I try to forget, but it keeps sneaking up on me," Justine said, misery in her voice and face. "I feel trapped and angry. And so tired of this limbo I'm in. But I don't want him dead."

"You just want to be able to move on."

She should have known Brianna would understand. "Yes. Sometimes I just want to scream or tell people the truth, but it would hurt more than it would help." She ran a shaky hand through her hair. "Can you imagine the scandal if I tried to divorce the renowned and beloved Andrew while he was in a coma?"

"The people and press would eat you alive. Especially since you have no proof of his affair."

"And it would hurt his mother, the foundation, and jeopardize plans for the senior citizen facility that a large number of churches are backing financially. Even my mother. She thinks he's the perfect son-in-law."

"We both know differently." Looping her arm through Justine's, Brianna started for the kitchen. "The timer just went off."

"I'm not hungry," Justine said, dragging her feet.

Brianna ignored the resistance. Tonight she was putting a stop to Justine not taking care of herself. "You'll change your mind when you smell the gumbo."

In the spotless ultramodern kitchen in blue and stainless steel Brianna seated Justine at the dining table for four, then picked up a large blue bowl with a crawfish on the side. "There's fresh homemade bread."

"Your mom makes the best. How is she and your father?"

"Great." Brianna placed bowls of gumbo on the table and sat in a black leather chair across from Justine. "I'm going into Dad's office in the morning. Mama and I have a bet as to how long it will be before he shows up."

Justine's lips curved as she picked up her spoon, stirred. "Probably an hour."

"That was my guess." Brianna tore a chunk off the loaf of bread and handed it to Justine. "Food is for eating."

Justine accepted the bread, then glanced at the thick gumbo filled with shrimp, sausages, chicken, and vegetables, and then back to Brianna. "Your mother is a great cook, but I don't have much of an appetite."

Frowning, Brianna eyed her best friend critically. "You've lost enough weight. Eat. Don't let him take any more from you."

Justine's sad brown eyes lifted. "I don't seem to be able to help myself, and I'm ashamed for that."

"Don't be. Give yourself time to go through the grief process." Brianna placed her arms on the table. "Soon you'll be able to move on with your life."

"But I can't." Justine bit her lower lip. "You said yourself, a divorce would be disastrous."

"It would cause fallout, and that's what angers me," Brianna said. "Andrew is the one who cheated and caused this. Not you."

Sighing, Justine leaned back in the chair. "I wish I knew what to do."

"Take your time. I'm here now."

"At least for the time being," Justine said. "Did Jackson persuade you to take him back?"

Brianna's expression hardened. "Jackson and I are through for good. He thought I should care more about a junior law partnership with my firm than helping Daddy."

"I'm sorry."

"Don't be." Brianna tore off a chunk of bread for herself and placed it on her bread plate. "If I hadn't found out how selfish he was, I might have wasted even more of my time on him."

Justine propped her elbow on the table and rested her chin in the palm of her cupped hand. "Where are the good men?"

"I don't know, but I'm not going to be looking." Brianna stirred her gumbo. "I've sworn off men."

Justine straightened abruptly. "You can't be serious. You were the most popular girl in high school, and in college you could have had a date every night if you'd wanted. I can't imagine letting myself be that vulnerable again, but just because things with Jackson didn't work out is no reason for you to forgo men altogether."

Brianna turned introspective. "I completely misread Jackson. That's never happened before. I won't allow it to happen again. I don't want another man in my life or my bed for a long, long time."

Justine sighed. "Me either."

"I'll eat to that." Brianna picked up the spoon and began eating.

Justine followed suit. "This is good."

"Stick with me and you'll gain back the weight you lost in no time."

Justine lifted her head. "I'm glad you're home."

"Me too," Justine said just as the doorbell rang. "You're expecting someone else?" Justine asked, taking another bite.

Brianna frowned. "No. I haven't given anyone except you my address."

"Perhaps it's your parents or the concierge?" Justine offered.

"Or a nosy neighbor," Brianna said, her mouth tight.

The doorbell rang again.

"A new admirer?" Justine guessed, then smiled as Brianna's eyes narrowed.

"A man, a tenant he said, tried to get chummy with me when Mama, Daddy, and I were bringing up the luggage. We got off on the third floor. Since this was the only new listing on this floor, it wouldn't be difficult for him to find me," she explained.

The teasing smile disappeared from Justine's face. "Do you think you should be concerned?"

Brianna shook her head. "He didn't look the type, although, after Jackson, my judgment might be off."

"The point is you did find out about Jackson, and I bet you gave him a send-off he won't soon forget."

Brianna's grin was pure devilish satisfaction. "Guaranteed."

Justine dipped her spoon in her gumbo. "Then handling this guy should be easy."

"It won't take longer than three seconds." Rising, a glint in her eyes, Brianna headed for the front door.

Justine leaned back in the seat, envying Brianna her strength. Jackson might have fooled her for a little while, but she'd seen through him on her own. How long had Andrew cheated on her? Or had it really been his first time? Occasionally, to her shame, she wanted to believe it had been.

A scream jerked her out of her thoughts. She was out of her chair before the sound died, the spoon clenched in her hand. She stumbled to a halt a few feet inside the living room when she saw the broad-shouldered man with his arms around Brianna's tiny waist.

Six

"Dalton." She wasn't aware of saying his name, but she must have because he glanced up. Time tumbled backward. He'd filled out since he was a senior in high school. Broad shoulders tapered to a narrow waist. His long, muscled legs were lovingly encased in faded denim. Her gaze lanced back up to his face. The full beard was new, but it gave him a rakish, dangerous look that he'd begun to perfect in high school. He still had the most beautiful black eyes she'd ever seen.

"Justine."

She was running to him before the word completely left his mouth. He let go of Brianna and caught Justine to him, his arms going around her, holding her against the hard strength and warmth of his muscled body. Unexpected tears clogged her throat and misted her eyes.

"I'm so sorry," he murmured.

Her hands flexed. For one glorious moment she'd forgotten.

Setting her away from him, Dalton stared down into her pale face with an intensity that made her tremble. "Ask and, if it's in my power, it's yours."

He'd said the same thing on the night over seventeen years ago when they'd parted. Perhaps if she'd told him what was in her heart then, she would have been spared the pain she was going through now.

Too full to speak, she simply shook her head.

The calloused base of his thumb brushed the tears away she had been unaware were falling. "Cry if you want, but I wish you wouldn't."

She trembled. Tears made men feel uneasy. After Andrew's accident, they'd always turned away or tried to get her to stop crying. But then Dalton, despite his bad boy image and reputation, had always had an uncanny perception of what she needed. "No tears."

He smiled, a flash of strong white teeth in a darkly handsome face that still did unexpected things to her stomach. She tried to step back and found his arms still tightly clasped around her waist.

He frowned, as if realizing that he still held her. Slowly, he released her. "Does the spoon in your hand mean you were going to protect Brianna or am I interrupting dinner?"

Justine took a shaky step back and glanced at the spoon clutched in her hand. "Both."

"Sorry, I—"

"Don't you dare apologize. Come into the kitchen and join us." Brianna led the way to the kitchen and pointed to a chair while she prepared another place setting and bowl of gumbo. "There's more than enough. I guess Mama and Daddy told you how to find me."

"Yes, they did." Dalton said, pulling out Justine's chair

for her. "I hope neither of you mind my dropping by without calling first."

"You're always welcome, and you know it." Brianna placed the food on the poppy-colored place mat. "I'll get you a glass of wine."

"Thanks," Dalton said, but his questioning gaze remained on Justine.

"It's good to see you. Brianna told me you'd called several times. Thank you," she finally managed.

He nodded, his hands lightly fisted on the table. "I thought about coming, but . . ."

Her hand briefly touched his shoulder. "There was nothing you could have done." A bit startled that she had reached out to him, she placed her hands in her lap.

"Here you are, Dalton." Brianna placed the wine on the table, then reclaimed her seat.

"What brings such a famous author back to Charleston?" Justine asked, unconsciously smoothing her hair behind her ears.

"Hardly famous," Dalton said easily. "I'm signing at your bookstore tomorrow night."

Justine's eyes widened. Embarrassment flushed her cheeks. Another thing she'd let go was being on top of things at her bookstore, but it was easier to hide from people in her office during those infrequent times she was there. "Dalton, I'm so sorry."

"Don't be. You have a lot on your mind." He took a bite of the gumbo. "This is good."

"My mother is a great cook. Too bad I didn't inherit her skills," Brianna said.

"You took after your father." Dalton grinned, deepening

the laugh lines around his eyes. "He told me you were pretty famous yourself."

Brianna rolled her eyes. "He'd tell anyone who stood still longer than two seconds."

"Brianna is just being modest," Justine said, well aware that Dalton had gracefully let her off the hook. "She's the youngest Texas Super Lawyer that *Law and Politics Magazine* has ever selected."

"And now you're coming back to Charleston to shake things up," Dalton said, his black eyes twinkling.

"To borrow a word from you, hardly." Brianna sipped her wine. "Taking over Daddy's general practice is going to be easy compared to the workload I left behind in Dallas at the corporate law firm."

"Will you miss it?" Dalton asked

"Yes, but Daddy comes first."

Dalton nodded as if he'd expected the answer. "This hits the spot. I haven't eaten since I left the house this morning."

"You still live in Buckhead?" Justine asked, recalling that he was divorced.

"Yes." He finished off his food and reached for his wine. "I drove straight through and checked into Charleston Place downtown."

"Well, I hope you plan to stay for a few days." Brianna propped her elbows on the table.

"As a matter of fact, I do." Dalton glanced at Justine. "I want to look at the home place and try to decide if we want to sell it or take my sister's advice and make it a writer's retreat for myself."

"My vote is the retreat," Brianna remarked.

Justine was aware of the lengthening silence and that some remark was expected of her. How could she advise someone else when her own life was such a wreck?

"I'll take that under consideration," Dalton said. "Justine, members of the South Carolina African-American Police Association are supposed to be at the signing, so it should be a good one."

The tension seeped out of her. He had let her off the hook again, but presented her with another problem. "Women might go for punch and cookies, but men want something more substantial at signings," she commented.

"I didn't tell you that for you to be concerned or go to any trouble. I've been to plenty of signings where the audience was lucky to have a chair or I was lucky to have one person there," he told them with a hint of a smile.

"Signings can be humbling," Justine agreed, but she still planned to call Iris, the store manager, first thing in the morning.

A little after nine that night, hands stuffed in the pockets of his jeans, Dalton walked beside Justine to her van in the underground parking lot of Brianna's condo. Seeing Justine again had affected him as profoundly as he had expected. "You sure you don't want me to follow you home?"

She smiled, finding it easier each time. "Despite the bad boy image you cultivated in high school, you were always a softie."

"It was easy around you."

Justine flushed. She shouldn't feel the warmth spreading through her. "Good night. Your books sell well, so you'll have a crowd."

He chuckled. "Like I said, I remember when I was the only one to show up at my signings."

The sound was rich, deep, and inviting. It was nice knowing Dalton hadn't changed and could still laugh at himself. "That definitely won't happen tomorrow." She got in and closed the door. "Night."

"Night, Justine. It was nice seeing you again."

"Welcome back, Dalton." Starting the motor, she backed out of the space and pulled away, glancing in the rearview mirror for one last look. Catching herself, she jerked her head around. Dalton was a friend, nothing more, and it was going to remain that way.

Dalton watched the van pull off, then went to his Cherokee and got in. In the three-car garage in Buckhead was a vintage Corvette and a custom-made Harley. He'd gone through a wild spending period before he realized that he was attempting to compensate with things for the mess his life was in, and, as his two sisters pointed out, if he didn't stop he'd be broke in a year. Thankfully, he'd listened.

He'd closed accounts, cut up credit cards, stopped hanging out with his buddy, Jim Beam, and worked hard to keep his life on an even keel after three years of constant upheaval. Six months later he'd read the headline in *The Post and Courier* and his calm world shifted once again.

Dalton watched Justine pull through the iron security gates of the condo and followed her onto the quiet street, his thoughts troubled. He still remembered how slight she'd felt in his arms when he held her, the dark smudges beneath her sad eyes, the lingering anguish in her beautiful face that never went completely away even during those infrequent times when she smiled.

His hand flexed on the steering wheel. She still made his gut clench, his body want.

Not good, and it wasn't likely to get any better. Blowing out a breath, he stopped behind her at a signal light. He should do the signing tomorrow night, then stay the hell as far away from Justine as possible. But he knew he wouldn't. She was hurting.

She looked lost and miserable. He'd been both. If there was the slightest chance that he could ease her pain, even if it was just to remind her that others cared, he was staying.

The light changed to green and Justine pulled off. After a moment's hesitation, Dalton followed instead of turning left toward his hotel. He told himself he'd just worry about her reaching home safely if he didn't follow to make sure. He'd lied to himself before and, although he'd promised himself never again, he had a strong suspicion that Justine was going to make him break more than one promise.

The phone was ringing when Justine entered the house through the four-car garage. Her hand on the doorknob stilled, her heart raced. An image of Dalton's darkly handsome bearded face popped into her mind before she could draw another breath. With the second ring, she chastised herself, then continued to the phone on the kitchen counter.

"Hello."

"Justine."

Guilt punched her in the gut as she heard Beverly's anxious voice. "Is Andrew all right?"

"A bit restless, but I think it's because you weren't here tonight," came the response.

Justine's hand clutched her stomach. Andrew hadn't made any type of voluntary response since the accident, but for the past three weeks Beverly kept insisting he had. The reactions always came when they were alone. "Do you want me to come?"

"No, it's late. I'm sure if you'll just say good night to Andrew and tell him how much you love and miss him, he'll rest more comfortably. Just a moment and I'll hold the phone to his ear."

Justine's grip on the receiver tightened. The phone would be positioned where Beverly could hear as well. Justine had no choice. She lied. "We all love you and want you to come back to us. Sleep well, Andrew."

"You're such a good wife and daughter-in-law. He's calming already," Beverly reported. "We'll look for you in the morning."

I don't want to go. "Do you want me to bring you anything?"

"I'm fine. I'm going in a bit since Andrew is resting better," she said, a smile in her voice. "I knew he would once he heard your voice. He loves you so much. Did you and Brianna have a good time?"

Guilt hit Justine again. "Yes, an old friend stopped by," she said, telling Beverly about Dalton as if that would make her momentary lapse of lusting after another man all right. "He has a book signing at the store tomorrow night."

"I seem to remember reading about how popular he is, but I'd rather read my Bible or a biography. There's too much evil and dishonesty in the world for me to waste my time reading about it."

And your son is at the top of the list. "In Dalton's books evil is always punished." *Unlike in real life.*

"But not before some innocent dies," was Beverly's quick comeback.

"Innocence dies in a lot of ways," Justine said, thinking of her own situation when she'd seen another woman leave a sexually sated Andrew on the bed they'd shared, a bed and bedding Justine had bought.

"I suppose that's why Andrew is such a godsend to men and women having problems," Beverly said.

Justine couldn't think of an appropriate lie, so she didn't say anything.

"He's touched so many lives," Beverly continued.

I know of one up close and too personal.

"Good night, dear. Andrew is asleep."

If Beverly wanted to believe that she could tell if Andrew was asleep or anything else, then Justine would not try to change her mind. Justine had ceased trying to figure it out or worrying if her mother-in-law was going over the edge. Beverly was a mother who was in danger of losing her son; she was dealing with it in her own way. Justine had read on the Internet and heard from the ICCU nurses about similar situations. "Good night, Beverly."

Hanging up the phone, Justine picked up her purse and continued to the bedroom. She had just taken off her dress when the phone on the nightstand rang. Her gaze went to the caller ID. Relief hit her. Picking up the phone, she plopped on the bed.

"How do you always know when to call?"

"You know my maternal great-great-grandmother was a voodoo priestess. What's up?" Brianna asked.

Justine had to chuckle. "That would surprise your mother, since she's very proud of the fact that your ancestors were free people of color and educators in Charleston."

"So she was an educated voodoo priestess. Stop stalling and give."

"I just hung up from talking with Beverly," Justine said and repeated the conversation with her mother-in-law.

"If Andrew does wake up, I'd like to be there to slap him silly," Brianna said.

Justine scooted up in the bed and leaned back against the padded headboard. "I just want to be free." She didn't want to talk about Andrew any longer. "Thanks for dinner, and please thank your mother for cooking."

"Anytime. We both love you. And speaking of . . . did you see the way Dalton was looking at you? I couldn't decide if I wanted to fan myself or leave the room. Girl, that man still has a thing for you."

Justine straightened. Heat flushed her face. "He's . . . he's—"

"Still a sexy hunk with black eyes that could melt a woman at ten feet. Admit it and shame the devil."

Justine twisted uneasily on the bed before saying, "All right. I admit he still has it."

"What if he decided to stick around?"

"Despite a lapse or two on my part tonight, I won't break my vows the way Andrew did," Justine said.

Brianna snorted. "Too bad you can't be like some cultures in the Middle East and just say the words and be divorced."

"You wouldn't have had a successful career if that were the case," Justine said.

"True." There was a slight pause. "Justine, don't turn your back on possible happiness."

Standing, Justine went to the closet and hung up her dress. "I think we're getting way ahead of ourselves. Looking doesn't mean anything."

"If it does?" Brianna asked.

Justine blew out a breath and went into the bathroom and turned on the faucet over the Jacuzzi. "Having a friend who is a lawyer can have its drawbacks at times."

"You love me anyway. You're stalling again. Answer the question."

Wedging the phone between her shoulder and her ear, Justine picked up the crystal bottle of 24 Faubourg perfumed bath cream and poured a liberal amount beneath the running water. "I'd be flattered and leave it at that."

"You're sure you want to leave it at that?"

She sat on the wide lip of the tub and momentarily placed her head in her palm. "Men are off our list, remember? I can't take any more complications, Brianna. Not now. I just can't," Justine said, her voice quaking.

"I understand and I'm with you in whatever decision you make, you know that."

Justine's head lifted. "That helps. I wonder if you know how much."

"I do. What time is Dalton's signing?"

Justine watched the fragrant bubbles fill the tub. "Probably seven. I'll call you on your cell and let you know the definite time."

"I'll be there early."

Justine shut off the water and stood. "It will be your

first day at your father's office. You'll probably be swamped."

"I'll be there," Brianna repeated.

Unlike Justine's mother, Brianna had never made a promise to her that she didn't keep. "To run interference, no doubt." Justine sat on the top of the toilet. "Despite his bad boy image in high school and the fact that you've always gone for the preppy type, you've always liked Dalton."

"I like Dalton, but I love you. Get some rest. Good night."

"Thanks. Welcome home again and good night." Justine disconnected the call and began stripping off her undergarments. She might be flattered that Dalton still found her attractive after all this time, but she had to remember that he had left her as well.

There had been few romances after her sophomore crush on the popular senior who had lettered in every sport and whose name was whispered amid girlish giggles and wistful sighs. She could count on one hand the number of serious relationships she'd had before meeting Andrew.

Perhaps she didn't inspire loyalty in a man. She didn't have the lush body that lured and kept men. What she knew about lovemaking, Andrew had taught her.

Stepping into the tub, Justine sank deep into the scented water until it closed around her neck. Leaning her head back against a plastic pillow, she closed her eyes. If she kept thinking about her shortcomings she'd start crying again. If she wasn't woman enough for Andrew, then that was his problem, not hers.

Nicely put.

Justine just wished she could convince herself that she believed it.

Seven

Dalton pulled up in front of It's a Mystery Bookstore at a quarter to seven Tuesday night. Getting out, he removed the orange cone one of the store personnel had said in an e-mail last week was to designate his parking spot. Good thing, Dalton thought as he climbed back in the Jeep. There wasn't a parking spot to be seen on either side of the bookstore in the strip shopping mall.

Parked, he climbed out again and headed for the double glass front doors. In the old days before he'd made best-selling lists, he'd carried a small briefcase filled with bookmarks, booklets, and a signature book. Now, the marketing department of the publishing house took care of all that.

Through the glass window he thought he caught a glimpse of Justine among the people in the store, and paused. He was adept as any other brother in keeping his feelings under wraps, but he'd found out last night that with Justine that was next to impossible. He'd wanted to keep holding her, give her whatever it took to make the smile reach her dark eyes. The only way to do that was to put her back in the arms of the man she loved, her husband.

He'd didn't want to delve too deeply into how he felt about that. He wasn't the type of man to step on another man to get a woman, but he was woefully human and at times selfish. He just hoped he could also be noble as well.

He'd seen her embarrassed blushes last night when he'd come close to stepping over the line. Justine had been surprised and he hoped a bit flattered. But she wasn't the type of woman to cheat. He knew that as surely as he knew his name. The blushes were a dead giveaway.

She remained the sweet unassuming girl he'd fallen hard for in his senior year in high school. And she belonged to a man fighting for his life. Only the scum of the earth would make a play for a woman at a time like this. He'd done some things he prayed to forget, but he hadn't stooped that low.

Opening one of the doors, he stepped into the spacious and comfortably crowded bookstore. The area was light and airy with white shelves and blue molding around the recessed ceiling. The expected cardboard dumps of bestselling novels were positioned on either side by the door. He was pleased to see one with his books among them. Three books remained out of the thirty-six the dump usually held.

Several people with *Hidden Prey*, his latest, or with one or a couple of his earlier books milled around the store or were seated in gray padded folding chairs in front of a wooden podium. There was a group of men in police uniforms in a line of about fifteen people in front of the cash register on a raised platform directly ahead of him.

To his left was a three-by-five-foot table with greeting cards and stationery. A few feet farther was a rack of African-American greeting cards. A bit farther was the children's book section. Several animated mobiles hung from the ceiling. Two small children, a boy and a girl who looked to be about six or seven, sat at the small white table, reading.

Something tugged at his heart. He had yet to figure out if it had been a blessing or a curse that Gloria hadn't had any children.

"Mr. Gunn, er . . . Ramsey?"

Dalton turned to see a slim fair-skinned woman in her early thirties with waist-length braids. People were often confused as to which name they should call him. He smiled and extended his hand. "Right both times. Please call me Dalton."

Her hand trembled in his. "I'm Iris Palmer, the store manager. It's such a pleasure to meet you. I've read all of your books."

"Hello, Ms. Palmer. It's always great to meet a fan and a bookseller," he said, meaning every word.

Her eyelashes fluttered. "Iris, please. I feel old enough when the children say ma'am."

They laughed together. "Believe me, I understand."

"We'll be ready to start in a moment. I'll take you to the podium." She turned and headed in that direction. "You can see people are already waiting."

Dalton nodded to people as he followed the bookseller. Several men in uniform were already seated. "Thank you, Iris," he said, ordering himself not to ask if Justine was there.

"Do you want water or anything?" Iris motioned to a table with an African print covering, two trays, and a punch bowl on the other side of the room. "We plan to have refreshments afterward, but we have a café if you'd like anything now."

"I'm fine."

She sighed. "I'll just go tell Justine you're here."

His heart shouldn't have thumped. It did, and there was nothing he could do about it. "Thank you." As the manager walked away, Dalton turned to greet the people already sitting and waiting. He needed to get his mind off Justine. "Thanks for coming."

"He's here, Justine, and as yummy as the picture in his press kit," Iris said, her eyes dreamy. "It's great when you can hand-sell a book that you enjoy. A few women might have picked up the book for a male friend, but they came back because they'd read the book themselves."

Justine slowly rose from her heavy oak desk and brushed her hand over her navy linen slacks. She was one of those addicted to Dalton's lead character, Brock Jernigan, a man committed to righting the wrongs of the world. "Thank you, Iris."

"This is going to be great. I'll just pop back out."

"Looks like Dalton struck again." Brianna stood as well as the manager left. The raspberry-colored business suit with the fitted short skirt suited her almond complexion.

"Yes."

Brianna eyed her critically. "You can go home, you know."

Justine was already shaking her head. "I've put my life on hold and hidden enough."

"But still it's not enough," Brianna guessed.

"No." Justine glanced at the phone. "Beverly asked me to come back by before I go home. She's called twice. She said he's agitated since I left."

"Bull crap. You just arrived from the hospital, and why the hell should you care?" Brianna hissed.

"Because I'm his loving wife," Justine said simply. "Let's not talk about it, or I'll never get through this."

"My lips are sealed."

Justine looked over her shoulder at her best friend. "Your eyes and face are shouting."

"Then I'll put on my lawyer face." She hooked her arm through Justine's. "Come on, let's get this show on the road. And despite what you say, I'm introducing Dalton. No arguing, and afterward you're eating some of that food you had catered."

Justine didn't argue. Brianna wasn't the type of woman you could push, especially when she had right on her side. In the store, Justine passed people she knew and, as always, they wanted to know about Andrew.

"He's holding his own," Brianna said. "Please excuse us. We have to get the signing started."

In the wake of people saying, "Give his mother my best" or "I'm praying for you" they made their way to the podium. She could feel the eyes on her. She gave the idea of wearing a sign around her neck more thought, felt laughter tickle her throat, and realized if it erupted it would be high-pitched and hysterical.

Besides last night, she hadn't eaten a decent meal in weeks, wasn't sleeping. She couldn't go on like this.

A sort of hushed silence slowly permeated the store as Justine and Brianna reached the podium. They were showing respect for the wife. Those who didn't know were quickly told in hushed whispers. The half-smile Justine tried to keep on her face kept slipping. She was about to give up pretending when she saw Dalton.

The hot intensity of his stare stopped her in her tracks. She didn't move until she felt a slight tug from Brianna. *Don't do this to me*, she wanted to shout, but wasn't sure to whom she'd shout the words.

Brianna's eyes narrowed. Dalton's laserlike gaze was pinned on Justine and, as any red-blooded woman would have reacted, she trembled. Except that Justine's reaction was part fascination, part shame. If Andrew did wake up, Brianna was going to make him wish he'd kept his zipper in place.

Dalton started toward them. Brianna gave a short, negative shake of her head. He stopped and moved to the other side of the podium. Brianna reluctantly released Justine's arm and stepped to the microphone. Then she was the one who hesitated.

In the third row, a half-smile on his sexy mouth, was the man from her condo. He couldn't have followed her because she'd come from her father's office. She didn't like coincidences. He winked and she wanted to throw a book at him. Instead she ignored him and the sudden rapid beat of her heart.

"Welcome to It's a Mystery Bookstore. I'm Brianna Ireland. It's been my pleasure to know Dalton Ramsey before he set the literary scene on its ears with his nail-biting suspense novels," she said, comfortable with crowds. "A former police officer with the Detroit Police Department, he knows of what he writes. I see we have Charleston's finest and other members of various law enforcement agencies with us tonight. Welcome. Without further ado, I give you our native son, Dalton Ramsey."

Applause erupted. Brianna stepped back to let Dalton take her place, then went to stand by Justine, who resisted her urging to return to the back. Brianna looked around for a chair and almost jumped when the stranger from the elevator offered his.

"Thanks."

"My pleasure."

The voice was deep and as sexy as the man. She turned her back on him and pushed Justine into the chair before she fell down. Luckily, when she stepped to her friend's side, the man was gone.

Dalton's hands gripped the side of the wooden podium as he waited for the applause to stop. He resisted the urge to look at Justine. From the annoyance in Brianna's face earlier, he'd flubbed it again. It was bad enough they knew how he felt without anyone else catching on.

Justine didn't deserve ugly whispers. Leaving town as soon as the signing was over was looking better and better. Later he'd come back to look at the house, when Andrew was well. Maybe he'd hire someone to handle it.

"Thank you for coming," he said, then went into the rehearsed spiel about his reasons for writing—an extension of his childhood dream after watching dozens of episodes of Peter Gunn, and his fascination with mystery writer Edgar Allan Poe. Thus his pseudonym, Edgar Gunn. The audience would have been shocked and probably a bit titillated if he had told them the truth—that writing had been an escape from the hell he'd lived in daily. And at times he'd felt as if he were the main character in one of Poe's macabre novels.

Fifteen minutes later, when he finished and asked if there were questions, a woman in the front row raised her hand. "Why did you decide to reveal your identity?"

A few of the police officers shifted uncomfortably. Dalton pretended not to notice. Even thousands of miles away, they had probably heard about the scandal. They certainly could have checked him out.

"It was time." Since he'd practiced that lie as well, it rolled easily off his tongue. Not for the first time, it occurred to Dalton that for a man who valued truth and honesty, he certainly told a lot of lies. But at the moment it was the only way for him to survive.

Another hand. This was from a uniformed police officer. "Sergeant Haskell, with the Charleston Police Department."

Dalton applauded and was joined by others. "Thanks, Sergeant Haskell, for coming and keeping the city safe."

The gray-haired officer nodded. "The guys at the station had a bet that you were a policeman even before you did those interviews in *People* and *Black Enterprise*. We wondered about Jernigan, the homicide detective. He's tough and often curt even to his commander. Is that a bit of a payback?"

Dalton's mouth curved upward. "All I'll say is that in my first book a police captain was captured by a serial killer. Jernigan saved him, but the captain went mad."

Several officers whistled through their teeth. A man, the same broad-shouldered one who had given Justine his chair, raised his hand. "If you need any names for police officers who meet an unpleasant end, I'll give you my e-mail address."

Laughter erupted. Dalton's lips twitched. People often talked about going postal, but there was probably twice as much pressure and crap going on in the police station. "I'll remember that."

A woman in the front row raised her hand. She clutched Hidden Prey to her chest. The friend beside her had been nudging her for the past few minutes. "Yes, thank you for coming."

"Please read the opening. I bought it for a friend, but started reading it after I was caught in a traffic jam."

"He never got the book," the nudger said with a laugh.

The woman who had spoken frowned as if the friend had admitted too much. "I don't see him anymore in any case." She moistened her red lips. "Could you please read the opening? It is so riveting."

"And grisly." The woman on the opposite side gave a delicate shudder. "I had to keep the lights on that night to go to sleep."

"Bloody, too." This from a uniformed policeman with an unblinking stare. "Like Haskell said, you know the writer has stepped in blood."

The women shuddered, but their eyes remained bright with gory fascination. It wasn't uncommon to be asked to read, and normally Dalton enjoyed it. Tonight he knew he wouldn't. The passage was pretty gruesome. The night he'd written the opening he'd awakened from a sound sleep, sweat pouring off him, adrenaline pumping.

He'd gone to the computer and typed. The officer was right. He had stepped in blood. "There were children in the store earlier."

"They're gone," Iris said from the raised platform. "Please read."

Applause erupted again. He cut a quick glance at Justine. He didn't want her to remember the hell she must have gone through in rescuing her husband. Her long legs were crossed, ladylike, at the ankles, her slim hands were resting in her lap, and her face was composed. Her eyes looked haunted.

His gaze lifted to Brianna, and she gave a slight shrug. Justine wasn't budging.

"Please read," said the woman in the front again.

Dalton opened the hardback, flipped to the first page, and began to read. "Blood was everywhere. Death hadn't been neat or quick. Brock Jernigan crouched over what remained of Bill Tatum and ignored the urge to retch."

Eight

In the audience, Patrick Dunlap leaned against the corner of the raised platform circling the two cash registers and fought the churning of his stomach. The opening Dalton was reading brought back too many horrific memories. That was one of Gunn's books that he had no intention of reading. Ever.

He probably never would have read any of them if Brooke hadn't given him *Deadly Prey* to read while he was recuperating in the hospital. He'd accepted the book and then promptly forgot about it. After all, it had been a selection of the book club she and her two business partners belonged to, which automatically meant it wasn't for a macho man like himself.

That it was a murder mystery didn't bother him. He'd been a police officer in the toughest part of Myrtle Beach for too long for him to be squeamish or flinch just because he'd ended up on the wrong side of a bullet. He'd thought it was probably full of procedural and factual errors.

But Brooke was not a woman to let anything rest. He'd finally gotten tired of her asking him about the book and decided to read it one night when he couldn't sleep, and had been hooked. Thankfully it had been a cat-and-mouse game with chilling accuracy between the killer and Jernigan, who was taking his first vacation in ten years on a cruise ship.

Like the woman in the audience, Patrick hadn't been able to stop reading. He would have had no trouble turning off the lights to go to sleep... if he hadn't read through the night. He still recalled the first lines. *Murder doesn't take a holiday, so why should you?* Patrick had stayed up to finish the book and asked for another. Now he was glad he had for another reason. He'd met the stunning woman from the elevator again, and now he knew her name.

"Jernigan came slowly to his feet, snapping off his gloves as he did. 'Bag and tag. We have a serious nut in our midst, and I have a bad feeling this is only the beginning.'"

Dalton closed the book. The audience stood and applauded. "Thank you."

The woman behind the counter rushed to the podium, her hand over her heart. "Wonderful. If you'll please line up, your books will be signed. There's also refreshments. Thank you for coming."

She looked up at Dalton and even across the room Patrick thought he heard her sigh.

"Thank you so much."

"Always a pleasure," Dalton said.

The clerk sighed again. Patrick shook his head. If the

woman wanted a chance with Dalton she should lose the worship attitude. Most men still enjoyed a challenge.

As people lined up, he positioned himself near the counter so he could see Brianna Ireland, his cautious neighbor. The corners of his mouth kicked upward. She was certainly prickly. Now there was a challenge that heated a man's blood.

He had no difficulty imagining the delectable body beneath the stylish raspberry-colored suit. His hands fairly itched to peel it away, then slowly kiss every inch of her creamy skin as it was exposed.

Brianna jerked her head toward him, her pretty lips pressed together in annoyance, her light-colored eyes narrowed in anger. He tipped his head. Her expression remained unchanged. Well, he knew it wasn't going to be easy.

Now that a woman had finally piqued his interest, he had no intention of letting her get away. Especially since he'd just found out that she wasn't just a stunning face and a heart-stopping body. On his way back from giving up his chair he'd learned that her friend was the owner of the bookstore, and that her friend's husband was in a coma.

He'd asked the talkative stranger about Brianna and was told she and Justine, the owner, had been best friends since childhood. The informative customer went on to say that Brianna had recently moved back to her hometown to take over her father's law practice and was single.

Deciding introductions were in order, Patrick began working his way through the crowd toward Brianna and Justine. However, he soon discovered it wasn't going to be as easy as he'd thought. Every time he started to introduce himself, another person would come up to them. Apparently the store owner and her husband were well known and liked.

"How is Andrew?"

"As well as can be expected," Brianna said. "Did you enjoy the signing?"

The person would usually blink as if unable to follow the switch in conversation, answer in the affirmative, and then move on—usually followed by another unthinking individual who asked almost the identical question. Like most of the people in the community, he'd heard about Andrew Crandall's accident and felt empathy for his young wife.

He thanked God his family had been spared that. The ten-hour surgery he'd gone through had been bad enough. He couldn't imagine what she must be feeling. The well-meaning people who kept asking her how her husband was doing didn't realize how tiring repeating the same answer must be. No wonder Brianna had taken over. If those asking would have taken the time to look at the woman standing protectively by Justine's side, they would have spoken and moved on.

The crowd finally thinned and Patrick quickly moved in. Like everyone else he ignored the barely veiled annoyance in Brianna's beautiful tawny eyes, but not the lost look in Justine Crandall's face. "Hello, I'm Patrick Dunlap."

Like a true Southern lady who is always cordial regardless of her own pain and suffering, Justine extended her hand. "Justine Crandall."

Patrick took the slight hand in his and gently shook it, then he turned to Brianna. "Ms. Ireland."

"Mr. Dunlap," she said with as much warmth as an iceberg.

He gave his attention back to Justine. "I recently

moved to your beautiful city. It's nice to find a knowledge-able bookstore."

He thought he saw Justine's shoulders relax. "Thank you. Is this your first time here?"

"Yes. I came to see Gunn," he explained. "My niece got me hooked on his books."

Justine smiled. "That's easily done."

"There're refreshments on the table if you want any," Brianna said.

It was Brianna's none-too-subtle hint to take himself off. "Speaking of refreshments, perhaps you'd like to go out la—"

"I'm busy," Brianna interrupted.

Patrick lifted a brow. Out of the corner of his eye, he saw Justine turn in her chair to look up. He had a feeling Brianna would have walked off if it hadn't meant leaving her friend. He admired loyalty and was even more deter-mined to take her out. "What is it about me that you don't like?" he asked.

"I don't know you well enough to form an opinion and I plan to keep it that way," she said with studied disinterest.

"Then it appears I have my work cut out for me." He glanced down at Justine, who was watching them closely. "It was nice meeting you. Good night," he said. Then to Brianna, "I'll be seeing you."

"I wouldn't count on it," she said and turned her atten-tion to Justine, dismissing him again.

Patrick briefly wondered what she would do if he pulled her into his arms and kissed her. Not a good idea. The lady looked as if she could take care of herself. Since Patrick didn't want to find himself on his back in front of a room full of people, especially fellow police officers that he had met since he'd moved to Charleston, he nodded his head and walked away.

By the time the last reluctant customer left, it was close to eleven, and there wasn't a copy of any of Dalton's books in the store. Good news/bad news for a bookseller. At the moment, Justine was just glad to lock the door. She wasn't sure how much longer she could have kept up the farce of being the concerned wife.

Thankfully, Beverly had called to say that since it was so late, Justine should go home rather than coming by the hospital. For the first time, her mother-in-law had sounded a bit put out with her. At the moment Justine could care less. All she wanted to do was go home and try to sleep. First, she had to get rid of Brianna and Dalton, her two new protectors who were standing just a few feet inside the store.

"Thank you, Dalton, and you too, Brianna, for helping make this signing so successful."

"All I did was show up," Dalton said.

"Same here," Brianna remarked.

Justine tried to smile and found her facial muscles stiff. "It was more than that and you both know it. Now, scoot."

"Night, Dalton." Brianna crossed to stand beside Justine.

He glanced around the store. "Is there something else you need done?"

Occasionally stubborn friends were a trial. "No. You already helped put up the chairs and Brianna helped clean up the refreshments table. I'm just going to lock up and go home."

"I'll wait," Brianna said.

"No," Dalton said. "It's getting later by the minute. You go on home. I'll follow Justine since I'm the reason she's out so late. Let me help the little that I can while I'm here."

Brianna leaned her head to one side and studied him. "When did you learn diplomacy?"

He chuckled and pulled Brianna to him in a brief, friendly hug. "Two older sisters. Now, scoot. I'll call before I leave town."

Brianna's gaze flickered to Justine and back to Dalton. "I'll miss you."

"Same here. I know you'll take care of Justine."

"Always."

"Please don't talk as if I'm not here, and for your information I don't need anyone to take care of me," Justine told them.

Both ignored her as Dalton walked Brianna to the door, unlocked it, then locked it again. "Do we need to go out the back or front after you set the alarm?"

She could have become angry, but that would take too much energy. "The front."

He slipped his hands in his pockets, tightening the jeans. At another time she might have been caught by the sheer male beauty of the man. "I'll just be a moment." She escaped to the back.

"Brianna."

Brianna whirled, crouched, her hands raised defensively. Patrick was a few feet away, a half-smile on his sensual mouth, his long-fingered hands upraised. "Sorry."

She straightened, annoyed because her heart beat crazily in her chest. She wasn't sure if it was because of the scare she'd experienced or the sexy man in front of her. He wore a white shirt with the cuffs rolled back and a pair of creased jeans that molded to his muscular thighs. "You'd be a lot sorrier if you had been closer."

"Why do you think I was so far away?" He swept her purse up from the sidewalk and handed it to her.

She took the bag and shoved the chain and leather strap over her shoulder. "What are you doing here?"

He glanced around the shadowy shopping mall. The parking spaces were deserted, as were the stores. "I wanted to make sure you and Justine got to your cars safely." He nodded toward a black Cherokee. "Dalton seeing Justine to her car?"

It was a statement more than a question. "Yes."

He looked down the street. "I can't imagine you in a van, so it must be the baby Benz."

A few spaces farther along was a black late-model truck. "Yours?"

"Mine."

Something about the way he said that one word made her skin tingle, her body heat. "Thanks, and good night."

He fell into step beside her. "I thought you might change your mind about—"

"Nope."

"Thought not."

She came to a halt. "Then why ask?"

"With a woman, a man can never be sure," he said, a smile on his lips.

From the light in the shoe store they were standing in

front of, Brianna could easily see the muscled build, the handsome face, the teasing smile. There weren't many men who could laugh at themselves. He'd also shown sensitivity when he hadn't drilled Justine about Andrew. If she hadn't sworn off men, she might take him up on his offer.

"Change your mind?" he asked.

Without answering, she went to her car, deactivated the lock. He opened the door before she could. "I don't suppose you'd consider giving me your cell or condo number?"

"Right the first time." Getting in, she closed the door. Starting the car, she drove away without looking back.

Dalton and Justine emerged from the bookstore in time to see Brianna driving off and Patrick walking to his truck. "Does she know him?"

"No, but he wants to change that," Justine answered.

"You think she'll be all right?" he asked, staring as Patrick pulled out and headed in the same direction Brianna had taken.

"If ever there was a woman who could take care of herself, it is Brianna," Justine said, unaware of the wistfulness in her voice.

Dalton's sharp, assessing gaze snapped back to her. Quickly she went to her van. "There really is no need to follow me."

He opened the door. "I think we already had this discussion."

"Well, then." She held out her hand. There would be no hugs, coming inside at her house, or lingering goodbyes. "Thanks and good night."

His wide-palmed hand closed gently over hers. She felt

the slight roughness of the calluses on the palms of his hands, the strength he kept in check. A strength she wished she could lean on. She swallowed. "Good-bye, Dalton."

"For now."

Her hand jerked in his. Too much of a coward to ask what he meant, she got into the van and started the engine.

"Drive carefully." Thumping the top of the van, he headed for his Jeep. Justine waited until he was inside with the lights on, then she pulled off, telling herself that Dalton's leaving was for the best. Perhaps if she repeated it enough she'd believe it.

As he had the night before, Dalton followed Justine home. He stopped in front of her house as she pulled into the driveway that circled to the back of the house. Lights came on in the front room, then went out. Although he didn't expect her to come to the door and wave good-bye, he was disappointed when she didn't.

It was pure selfishness on his part to want her to want a last glimpse of him half as much as he wanted one of her. Putting the Jeep into gear, Dalton pulled away, unable to resist stopping for one last look. The light shone from a room in the back of the house. He didn't want to imagine her undressing for bed, but his mind wasn't that easy to control.

Teeth gritted, he pulled off again. He wasn't some out-of-control high school kid. He knew how to have power over his body. Only a fool would let himself be led by his zipper. His interest in Justine wasn't just sex. Even when they had gone together for those few short weeks, he'd kept his hands above her waist and made sure not to scare her.

Odd, but she looked scared tonight. Or perhaps haunted was a better word.

In his thirteen years on the police force, he'd developed a sixth sense when something was wrong. He wondered if she and Andrew had been having problems in their marriage. Had she been happy or trapped and miserable like he'd been?

Not your problem, Dalton told himself as he hit the freeway that led back to his hotel. In the morning he was heading home. He had a book to write. What had been first an escape was now his livelihood. He wished Justine what peace she could find and prayed it didn't take as long for her to find hers as it had for him.

Nine

"Mrs. Crandall, your husband's condition has taken a turn for the worse. His blood pressure is erratic, his pulse is weak, the vitals signs are unstable," Dr. Lane told Justine as soon as she entered Andrew's room that morning.

"It's just because Justine hasn't been here lately," Beverly said, dividing the displeasure of her gaze between the doctor and Justine. "He'll be fine once she gets back to her routine."

Dr. Lane ignored Beverly. "Are you prepared to sign the papers now?"

"She is not," Beverly snapped.

Justine jerked her gaze toward Beverly. She couldn't remember a time when her mother-in-law had raised her voice.

"Andrew is trying to wake up." Beverly kept her hand on Andrew's arm, as if daring either one of them to deny it or do anything that might harm him.

"Beverly—"

"Give him a chance, Justine." Tears sparkled in Bev-erly's eyes. "Give my son and the man you love a chance."

Justine bit her lip and looked away. Andrew had killed her love when he'd ripped her heart from her body.

"Just look at him. He missed you," Beverly said.

The pleading in Beverly's voice, the plea of a mother for her child, reached through Justine's pain and anger when nothing else might have. For the first time in months she looked at Andrew.

She flinched at the pale, still figure on the bed. A bar-ber came in every morning to shave him and once a week to cut his hair. Three IVs fed antibiotics and nutrients. The respirator wheezed, pumping air in and out of his lungs.

In and out. In and out. Soon Justine's breathing matched that of the respirator. What if it stopped? *She'd be*—Refusing to let herself complete the thought, she quickly turned away and wrapped her arms around her waist.

"Mrs. Crandall, are you all right?"

She shook her head.

"You've upset her. With all this negative talk," Beverly accused the doctor.

Justine jumped when she felt her mother-in-law's soft hand touch her shoulder. Beverly didn't have to say a word. She had gone from allowing Justine to make the decision to making it for her. Andrew would be allowed to linger by any means necessary and as long as necessary. "I have to go."

"Mrs. Crandall—"

"Run along, Justine." Beverly cut the doctor off, dismissed Justine, then moved back to Andrew's side. "We'll be waiting for you tonight."

Justine stared at her mother-in-law. One part of her mind screamed, "Tell her the truth!" but she knew she wouldn't. Telling his mother of Andrew's affair would change nothing. She would still be trapped in the ongoing farce.

Grabbing her purse off the chair, she hurried away. In the van, she put her head on the steering wheel and let the tears flow.

Less than forty minutes later Justine got out of the van and started down the almost deserted sidewalk to her bookstore. At half past nine the shopping center was just beginning to come alive with the first customers of the day. Thankfully she'd have some time to herself before she had to face anyone.

After pulling herself together in the parking garage at the hospital, she'd started to dial Brianna on her cell, then changed her mind. Brianna would be busy getting her father's law practice in shape after his two-month absence with only a secretary to help.

Instead she'd gone home, put cold compresses on her eyes, and gotten ready for work. Brianna was right about one thing. She couldn't allow Andrew to take any more from her.

Opening the door, she went inside. Iris looked up from the counter, her eyes widening in surprise. If Justine did drop by the store, it usually wasn't this early. "Good morning, Justine."

"Good morning, Iris. Let me congratulate you again on the successful signing last night." Justine stopped at the counter.

A pleased smile on her face, Iris finished putting money in the cash register and then joined Justine on the floor. "Thank you, but a popular talented author like Dalton makes my job easy."

"We both know booksellers never have it easy."

Iris's lips quirked. "Now that you mention it, we don't."

Justine adjusted the wide strap of her shoulder bag. "I'll be in the back."

The front door opened. Dalton entered, balancing a white pastry box and three hot containers on top. Iris rushed to help.

"Thanks. Morning." His gaze skipped past Iris to Justine.

"Morning," Justine greeted. Her voice sounded dry, unused.

"Good morning," Iris said, holding the containers. "I hope this is for us."

"It is," Dalton answered. "I wanted to thank you for one of the most successful signings I've had in a long time."

Iris glanced at Dalton, then at Justine. "We were just talking about that. You made it easy."

"Thanks, but I happen to know how hard booksellers work." He crossed to Justine, who hadn't moved. "Hot chocolate with a layer of whipped cream. Just the way you like it."

Touched and surprised, she felt tears sting her throat. She swallowed, blinked.

"I really wish you wouldn't this time," he said softly. "But if you do, I'll understand."

"Oh, Dalton," she said, blinking rapidly. He touched her in ways that made her want to lay her head on his shoulder or curl up in his lap.

"Where do I put this? Then I'll get out of your hair."

Justine extended her free hand. "I'll take it, and thanks. You're about to get on the road?"

"Yes."

"Safe travel." She wanted to add "I'll miss you," but Iris was listening to every word.

He nodded. "I'll keep in touch this time."

"I'll understand if you don't."

His black eyes narrowed seconds before he touched her lightly on the arm and leaned forward. For a panicky second she thought he was going to kiss her on the cheek. He straightened. "Take care." Whirling on his heel, he started from the store. "Thanks again, Iris."

" 'Bye, Dalton." Iris went to the door and watched Dalton get in his Jeep and pull away.

Justine caught herself staring after him as well. It was just as well that he was leaving. She was just needy and angry enough to do something foolish. Holding the pastries, she went to the break room to put them away, just as she was going to put Dalton out of her mind.

Brianna knew her way around a police station. Unfortunately, she'd gained that knowledge in ways that still angered her. More women than she cared to remember had been physically abused by their no-good husbands. The abusers crossed financial, race, and religious lines. A few of the women had turned the tables and ended up in jail.

However, this morning she was there to post bail for one of her father's longtime friends, a client who had been arrested for disorderly conduct.

Brianna stood on the sidewalk in front of the police station shortly before ten and glanced up at the tall, lanky man in the rumpled, out-of-date suit beside her. A purple tie dangled from the pocket of his coat. The garish colors hurt her eyes. He clenched his tan straw hat between his calloused hands.

It was difficult to imagine him drunk, trying to strip while dancing on the bar at a local club. It seemed he'd pulled the same stunt for the past three years on the anniversary of the day his wife of fifteen years ran off with the part-time help he'd hired for his plumbing business. The man had helped all right, helped himself to his boss's wife.

Harold Hinson was free, and her job, until his trial, was done. More cases were waiting in a five-inch stack on her father's old maple desk. She needed to review briefs, see clients, prepare for other court cases. Yet for some reason she was reluctant to leave the downcast man with his balding pate and slumped shoulders.

He looked pitiful and lost. She was a fighter by nature and couldn't imagine giving up or letting anyone get the best of her. It just wasn't in her to let the other guy win. Especially someone of the opposite sex.

Jackson wasn't the first man to whom she'd given walking papers. She didn't regret their breakup then or now. It wasn't necessary to have a man in her life for her to be happy. But she was aware that many people didn't feel the same way. They wanted, needed to be with someone.

"Come on, I'll buy you a coffee," she told the man.

He didn't say anything, just kept his head bowed and followed her across the street to the almost deserted coffee shop. They'd blatantly jaywalked, a time-honored tradition in Charleston.

Inside the coffee shop the air was cool, the atmosphere reminiscent of the early fifties. There were red-and-white checkered oilcloths on the tables and red imitation leather upholstery for the booths. A Wurlitzer jukebox squatted in the far corner. Except for two men in worn jeans and steel-toed boots hunched over their food at the counter, the place was empty. The breakfast rush was over and it was too early for the lunch crowd.

Sensing that Mr. Hinson was probably feeling a bit embarrassed, she bypassed the tables in front and chose a booth in the back. It was one thing for your card-playing fishing buddy of over twenty years to know you'd made a fool out of yourself, quite another for his daughter to know.

Brianna waited until the eager young waitress had taken their orders before saying, "Do you know that single men outnumber women? You, Mr. Hinson, are a hot and sought-after commodity."

Not by word or action did he respond. She wondered if he'd heard her. Leaning forward, she tried as unobtrusively as possible to see if he wore a hearing aid. There wasn't one that she could see, nor had there been one with the personal effects he'd shoved carelessly into his pockets. But then, he could have lost it doing the hoochie coochie on the bar. "Mr. Hinson?"

"Then why did Cheryl leave me for him?"

Brianna folded her hands on the Formica table. Tricky

question, but she was used to answering them. "Some women don't know when they have a good thing." *Men either, for that matter*, she thought. That slime Andrew was a perfect example.

Slowly, his head came up. Lines radiated from the corners of his sad brown hound dog eyes. "I loved her."

Misery stared back at her. She realized why she was taking time with him. She'd seen the same desolation in Justine's eyes when she'd rushed to Gaithersburg to be with her. It had been there last night as well.

With Justine, Brianna treaded lightly because Andrew's coma had left her in limbo. In Mr. Hinson's case, it was past time for a reality check. Her father had handled the divorce, and the ex–Mrs. Hinson was now living in the next county in a duplex with the hired help.

"She didn't appreciate you. You can keep wallowing in it, making yourself miserable, or put a steel spike in your spine and find a woman who will."

His head snapped up, his narrow shoulders went back. "Charles never said anything like that to me."

"Your coffee," the waitress said. "Can I get you anything else?"

"No, thank you." Brianna shoved the sugar bowl and little container of cream across the table. "That's because Daddy is more of a diplomat than I am. Besides, he hasn't been on the dating scene to know that some lucky woman is just waiting for you."

She could see the idea slowly take root in his furrowed brow. She drove the nail home. "That will show your ex a thing or two."

"I haven't heard from her since—since then." His trembling hands closed around the white mug of steaming coffee. Brianna wondered if it was due to the hangover or to emotions. "I gave her everything. She never had to lift a finger. I hear she's working at a bank to support them while he drifts from job to job."

Brianna didn't point out that for some women boredom was the eighth deadliest sin. Or was it the lure of hot sex? The hired help had been fifteen years younger, thirty pounds lighter in weight, not to mention in the pockets. Apparently the ex-Mrs. hadn't minded the exchange.

Brianna emptied a package of the blue stuff in coffee that she had no intention of drinking. She'd also been in enough coffee shops around police stations to know the food was generally bad, the coffee worse. "What do you think she feels when she hears about your little escapades each year?"

"Sorry that she hurt me?" Mr. Hinson asked hopefully.

"Possibly, but what message would you rather send?" she asked thoughtfully, hoping he wouldn't say that he wanted her to come home. If she hadn't come back by now, it wasn't likely that she would.

"A man with steel in his backbone would want her to know he's moved on," he said just as slowly.

Brianna sat back against the imitation leather seat. "You catch on fast."

"Not fast enough to keep my wife from running off."

Brianna refrained from pointing out that if she could be lured away, he didn't need her. When she finally found that special man to marry, a woman could dance naked in his face and he'd choose to come home to his wife. "How fast are you going to catch on this time?"

He poured a dollop of cream into the coffee, stirred. "My church has a singles bingo tournament every Thursday night, but I never thought about going. Didn't want to go alone." His head sank lower between his shoulders. "Everybody knows what happens. People would talk."

"So what?" Brianna leaned over the table and pinned him with the kind of look that made witnesses squirm and fellow lawyers on the opposite side uneasy. "You're there to find a woman lucky and smart enough to know a good man when she sees one."

"Will you go with me, and help me find her?"

Her shoulders snapped back. "What?"

Down went his head again. "That's all right. Why should a pretty young woman like you want to go out with a guy like me?"

Brianna stared at the shiny bald spot, the unsteady hands around the mug. She'd always been a sucker for the underdog. She'd volunteered with legal aid since she'd graduated from law school. "Suppose I go with you, and a woman tries to hit on you. Is that the kind of woman you want?"

"Suppose not." He glanced away, then back at her. "But at least they'd know that I could get a date."

His ex had taken more than their life savings; she'd taken a sledgehammer to his self-respect and manhood. "I'll meet you there. You had better be sober and cleaned up."

His head came up so fast that he should have injured himself. "You will?"

She arched a brow. "Against my better judgment."

Jumping up from the booth, he pulled her to her feet. She lost the indulgent smile when he grabbed her around the waist and lifted her easily off the floor. "Thank you! Thank you!"

"Harold. Mr. Hinson." Brianna gasped for breath and pushed against his chest. "You're squeezing me to death."

"That would be a pity."

Mr. Hinson stopped squeezing. Brianna stopped pushing. Both stared at Patrick, one long leg crossed over the other as he propped his arm over the back of Brianna's booth.

Brianna scrambled out of Mr. Hinson's hold and straightened her black cropped jacket. "What are you doing here?"

He grinned. She had to be the most gorgeous no-nonsense woman he'd ever had the pleasure of meeting. He couldn't believe his luck when he saw her crossing the street. After she'd ditched him last night, he had despaired of seeing her any time soon. He had actually been considering staking out the complex. "Visiting friends at the police station," he finally answered.

Her eyes narrowed in suspicion. "The police station is across the street."

"It is, isn't it."

Her beautiful eyes went lethal. She'd like to get him by the short hairs. His grin broadened. He couldn't resist, she was such a pleasure to tease, but he could think of other things that they could do to pleasure each other.

As if she could read his mind, her lips pursed. "This is a private conversation."

"And here I thought I was rescuing you."

"That will be the day," she scoffed. "Now leave."

Patrick smiled. "I told you why I'm here. What about you?"

"None—"

"Helping me," the man with her said. "She's my lawyer."

Patrick never took his gaze from the fuming Brianna. "You date your clients, Brianna?"

"That's also none—"

"She's helping me put steel in my spine." The man, who appeared to be in his middle to late fifties, stood straighter. "You wouldn't have trouble finding a date, but it's different for me."

"Brianna turned me down flat," Patrick admitted ruefully. "Twice."

"Don't even think of going for a third," she warned.

The older man's gaze flickered between the two. "That's not like her. She's always ready to help people. Her father talks nonstop about how sweet she is and how proud he and his wife are of her. She came back to Charleston to take over his law practice after his heart attack. That's why she came instead of him."

"Mr. Hinson, that's enough." Brianna caught her client's arm.

"I met her father when he was helping her move in." Patrick already understood why she couldn't allow her father to carry the heavy luggage. She was a good daughter. "Nice man."

"The best. His office is on First Street."

"Mr. Hinson, I said, that's enough. We should be going." Brianna tugged on his arm again, but the man didn't move.

"If you stay in the same place, you must know each other," Mr. Hinson commented.

"Not as well as we're going to." Ignoring Brianna's annoyed gasp, Patrick held out his hand. "Patrick Dunlap."

"Harold Hinson."

"Pleased to meet you. Maybe you'll share your secret."

Patrick glanced at Brianna. "I can't get her to go out with me."

Mr. Hinson pulled out a business card from his pocket and handed it to Patrick. "I can't help you with that but, if you ever need a lawyer, Brianna and her father are the best in the city."

"Thank you." Patrick slipped the card into his shirt pocket. Brianna looked as if she wanted to tackle him and wrestle it from his hand.

"This has gone on long enough." She sat down in the booth to retrieve her attaché case, then stood, once again taking her client's arm. "We're leaving."

"You want your bill now?" the waitress asked.

Brianna flushed. Placing the attaché case on the table, she opened her purse. "I'm sorry."

"She meant me." Patrick handed the waitress a ten. "I asked her to add your tab to mine."

"Thank you," Mr. Hinson said, then briefly tucked his head. "I'm tapped out after last night."

"No problem." Patrick looked at Brianna. "She wouldn't go out for drinks with me the other night, but I can at least pay for her coffee."

"You should come to bingo at the Greater Emmanuel on Thursday. Maybe you can get a date there."

"There's only one woman I want to date. See you around."

"Not if I see you first," Brianna told him.

Patrick acted as if he hadn't heard Brianna. She might have escaped him last night, but he had another chance now, and a plan. Whistling, he strolled from the coffee shop.

Ten

Dalton wrestled with himself all the way to Buckhead. He hadn't wanted to leave Justine, but he was too aware that his feelings for her deepened each time they were together.

Activating the garage door, he pulled into the three-car bay beside the '67 Corvette. The vintage car was one of the toys he'd recklessly bought. He'd kept it because of the resale value.

If his writing ever went stale, he could always sell the thing. The thought brought him back to his looming problem.

If he didn't finish *Sudden Prey* within the week he might be closer to that day than he wanted. Getting out of the Jeep, he grabbed his laptop case and went inside. He halted abruptly when he didn't hear the warning sound of the alarm, then shook his head.

He hadn't set the thing. He'd stayed up all night, then piled things into the car, and left shortly after seven in the morning. He honestly couldn't say if his absentmindedness was due to the stalled book or the woman he couldn't seem to get out of his mind.

Continuing to his office, he placed the case on his perpetually cluttered desk, then went back outside for his overnight case and garment bag. Returning, he dumped both on his king-size bed, then went to the kitchen for a drink. He wanted a beer, but chose a Pepsi instead. He'd spent enough time drinking to forget.

Taking a long swallow, he stared out the window. He'd call his sisters later to let them know he was home. They'd want to know if he'd made a decision about the house—he hadn't—but they would let him have his space to finish the book.

Perhaps by letting Brock Jernigan in *Sudden Prey* face his demons of the past and the woman he wanted and couldn't have, Dalton could confront his own demons and finally put them to rest. Until he did, he wasn't any good to Justine. No matter how his mind ran from the idea, she was important to him and, if it was humanly possible, he intended to learn what had taken the smile from her eyes and somehow, someway help put it back.

Tossing the empty can in the trash, Dalton went to his office and unzipped the laptop case and removed the portable flash drive. Soon he was staring at Chapter Twenty-six and the blinking cursor.

At the hotel in Charleston he hadn't even bothered to take the laptop out of the case. What would have been the use? His mind wasn't on the book.

Now with his hands poised over the keys, he realized that he faced the same dilemma as Brock. Dalton also realized something else. He'd transferred his own tumultuous feelings to the lead protagonist. A definite no-no.

Brock had never thought of Janice's husband dying and giving him an unexpected chance with his widow. He'd come back to his hometown at the request of the sheriff, an old high school buddy, to help solve the sadistic killings. His return had brought him face-to-face with the woman he'd left, a woman he could never have. But more than anything he wanted to see her happy. Her happiness, even if that meant he would never be a part of her life, was paramount.

Losing a spouse you loved would shatter the strongest person. Dalton had long since fallen out of love with his ex-wife, Gloria, but her deception and betrayal had almost crushed him.

The high, piercing scream came out of nowhere, agony mixed with rage. Janice flew at Brock. Her bare hands hooked like claws. "You killed him! You killed him!"

Brock wrapped his arms around her, trying to keep her from hurting herself as she kicked and fought to be free, not caring if she were hurt, only that she hurt him. "Janice, I didn't kill him."

"Liar!" she screamed. "You wanted me, and you killed him to get me."

Everything in him went still. There was nothing he could say in his defense. He could only hold her as her struggles grew weaker and weaker.

"Charles is dead, and I might as well be," she moaned.

Brock flinched, the words inflicting more anguish than he could have imagined. "I know, and that's why I couldn't have killed him. I'd never put you through this."

She was crying so hard he wasn't sure if she heard him or not. He only knew that he wouldn't rest until the person re-

sponsible was caught. The killer wouldn't destroy any more lives.

Dalton's blunt-tipped fingers raced across the computer keys. He knew where the story was heading, knew what Brock wanted more than anything. Justice and retribution, for the victims, their family and friends, and for himself.

"He is the most insufferable, pushy man I have ever met, and that's saying a lot."

Justine stood back as Brianna, carrying two large sacks, stalked inside her house a little after seven that night. "Anyone in particular?"

"Patrick Dunlap," she answered over her shoulder, never stopping on her way to the kitchen.

Closing the door, Justine followed. By the time she reached the kitchen, Brianna had the plates on the table and was removing the flatware from the drawer. Brianna on a roll was something to see. It was always best to stay out of her way. "Tea, lemonade, or cola?"

Brianna glanced up from removing the take-out containers of Chinese food. "A double bourbon."

"Lemonade." Brianna wasn't any more of a drinker than Justine. "I'll get the glasses, and you can tell me what Patrick did."

"The man is a menace," Brianna grumbled as she set several white cartons between the two plates. "If I didn't know better, I'd think he was following me."

Frowning, Justine took the pitcher out of the refrigerator. "Are you serious or just annoyed?"

Brianna made a face, then washed her hands at the double sink. "Annoyed."

Justine studied her agitated friend closely as she came to the table and they took their seats. "Men have been persistent where you're concerned before, and you've brushed them off without a backward glance. Why is Patrick different?"

"I don't know; he just is." Picking up the chopsticks, she filled Justine's plate, then her own.

Deciding not to comment on the amount of food on her plate, Justine picked up her chopsticks as well. "Is that an evasive answer, counselor?"

Brianna's hand paused, her head lifted. "What's that supposed to mean?"

"That of all the people I know, you are the most self-assured, self-aware person I know." Justine picked up a bit of noodles. "So, is Patrick making you rethink your plan to stay clear of men?"

Brianna scoffed, "I just met the man."

Justine's chopsticks wavered. "The moment Andrew came into the bookstore looking for a Walter Mosley title, I knew."

Brianna's chopsticks clattered on her plate. "Justine, I'm sorry. Here I am going on and on about me when you have so much to contend with."

"Don't be. If I have to think about what's going on in my own life all the time, I'll go crazy." Justine finally brought the food to her mouth. "Patrick is good looking and built."

"I prefer a brilliant mind and integrity." Brianna picked up a box of rice and fried shrimp. "But a good set of pecs and a drop-dead face doesn't hurt."

"Of course not," Justine said, thinking of Dalton.

The box plopped back on the oak table. "I was attracted by Jackson's intelligence and, I thought, integrity. He didn't have the former and his conduct shows he didn't have the latter, either."

Justine took another bite. "We chose badly, but don't take it out on Patrick."

"He butted into a conversation when I was having coffee with a client this morning." Brianna told her everything. "I bet my car that he'll be at the bingo tournament Thursday night."

"And if he does show?" Justine picked up her food without glancing down.

"I'll ignore him and consider getting a restraining order," Brianna said, her eyes narrowed.

"That seems excessive for a man just trying to get a date."

Brianna straightened. "Why are you so in favor of this guy? You don't even know him."

Justine looked thoughtful. "I'm not sure, perhaps because he's the first guy I know of that pushes your buttons. With Jackson and the other men you were always kind of blasé."

Brianna opened her mouth, then snapped it shut.

"I rest my case." Justine's chopsticks clicked against the stoneware. Surprised, she glanced down at her empty plate, then at Brianna. "I ate the whole thing."

"Not yet, but we're going to." Brianna spooned more food on both their plates. "Now that we've discussed my love life, what about Dalton?"

"Dalton?"

Brianna rolled her eyes. "After everyone left the store, he couldn't keep his eyes off you."

"I'm married." Justine busied herself with closing the open tops on the containers. She hadn't been able to keep her eyes off him either. "Besides, he went back home this morning."

"The rat. He didn't call to say good-bye," Brianna said, but there was no heat in her voice.

"He said to tell you good-bye." For something else to do with her hands, Justine picked up the chopsticks and put a small portion of shrimp on her plate.

"Did you want him to go?" Brianna asked softly.

Justine glanced around the kitchen before meeting Brianna's patient stare. "No, but it was for the best."

"You don't deserve this." The anger was back in Brianna's voice.

"No woman does." Her appetite gone, she pushed the food around on her plate.

"It cuts both ways." Moving her plate aside, Brianna placed her elbows on the table. "Dalton's been a free man for some time now."

Justine couldn't help asking, "Do you know what happened?"

"The scuttlebutt isn't pleasant. I don't like repeating any of it." Standing, Brianna began picking up the cartons.

Without knowing the full story, Justine was sure of one thing: It hadn't been because Dalton had cheated. He had too much integrity.

"He'll tell you when he returns," Brianna said.

Surprised by Brianna's prediction, Justine came to her feet as well. "What makes you think he's coming back?"

Brianna, reaching beneath the sink, paused. "What makes you think he's not?"

Justine's unruly heart raced, then slowed as she remembered the other reason Dalton had for being in town besides the book signing. "I almost forgot. He has to see about his home place."

"That would be one motive." Putting the containers in the two bags, Brianna put them in the trash beneath the sink and straightened. "But I wouldn't bet that's his *only* motive."

Justine didn't like the way her heart had sped up again, how glad, then panicky she felt. "You're wrong."

"Justine," Brianna said, coming to her. "You've given up so much to keep Andrew's adultery a secret. Don't you think you've sacrificed enough?"

"In my heart, the instant I saw that woman go into the bathroom, my marriage was over. Andrew's illness hasn't changed that." Justine leaned against the counter and wrapped her arms around herself. "Dalton isn't the first man to send out signals."

"But he's the first man you're answering back, and it scares you. You're not the cheating kind."

"With Dalton, that could change. And you're right. That scares me and makes me ashamed," she whispered softly, voicing her fear.

"Don't you dare," Brianna said fiercely. "You couldn't have been a better wife to Andrew or a better daughter-in-law. If fate sends another man your way, grab him."

"But—"

"Grab him," she ordered, putting her face closer to Justine's to stress her point.

"Are you going to take the same advice?" Justine asked.

Brianna's shoulders snapped back. "Patrick means diddly squat to me."

"I meant men in general."

Brianna flushed. "Oh."

"We're a pair. Letting what one man did rule us." Justine shook her head. "I have always heard what's fair for the goose is fair for the gander. If I promise to try and keep an open mind *if* Dalton comes back, will you try and do the same with Patrick?"

"I'd rather drop him headfirst off the top of the condo." Brianna's eyes darkened.

"Is that a yes?" Justine wasn't backing down.

Brianna wrinkled her nose. "That's a maybe."

"Good enough."

The phone on the counter beside her rang. Justine glanced at her watch. 7:45. Her eyes shut tightly as she bowed her head.

"Beverly?" Brianna asked.

Justine's head came up, her eyes slowly opened. "Yes. She's calling for me to say good night to Andrew."

Brianna's lips flattened. "How can she put—"

"She's his mother," Justine interrupted. "This might take some time. I'll call you tomorrow."

"Just—"

"Please."

"You're one of the special ones. We'll talk tomorrow." Brianna briefly hugged Justine, then she was gone.

Swallowing, Justine picked up the phone. "Hello."

"Justine, I was worried that you weren't there," Beverly said.

Wrapping one arm around her waist, Justine leaned against the counter. "I was just saying good night to Brianna."

"Good, now you can tell Andrew about your day since you had to leave this morning."

Justine thought she heard criticism in her mother-in-law's voice. She was just tired enough to bite back. "I have to work, Beverly."

"I didn't mean anything, dear. You know how much I love you. Haven't I always been there for you?"

Justine was instantly contrite. Beverly had been a wonderful mother-in-law. They were closer than Justine was to her own mother. "I'm sorry."

"There's no need to apologize. I know how much you love Andrew. Now, I'm going to hold the phone to his ear. You don't mind if I listen, too, do you?"

What choice did she have? "No."

"You're such a good wife."

A good wife wouldn't have lustful thoughts about another man.

"Here's Andrew."

Shutting out thoughts of Dalton, Justine begin to talk about the day, the people who came by the bookstore, who asked about him, the ministerial luncheon, Marcus's plans to restart the men's seminars. She didn't mention Dalton's signing and wasn't sure why.

A draining twenty minutes later Beverly said a nurse was there to hang another bag of IV fluid and check his monitors. Relieved and trying not to feel horrible that she did, Justine hung up, then finished straightening the kitchen before reluctantly going to her room. She dreaded going to bed because she didn't want to think of Andrew.

But the moment she got under the covers and closed her eyes, images of Dalton appeared. She sat up in bed, not knowing if that was worse. Just as she threw back the covers to get up and find a book to read, the phone on the bedside table rang.

She tensed and glanced at the ringing phone. It was half past nine. No one called her this late since Andrew's accident, except his mother or the hospital. She didn't want to answer it, didn't want to check the caller ID. She couldn't take any more. Not tonight.

But neither could she ignore it. By the sixth ring the receiver was in her hand. "Hello."

"What do you think I should wear to make Patrick's eyes pop?"

Brianna. Her best friend was fond of giving advice but seldom asked for or accepted it. She was also loyal to a fault. "I'm fine."

"Sure you are, and you're going to stay that way," Brianna said. Justine could just imagine the furrowed brow, the narrowed gaze.

"I'm certainly going to try."

"Don't try. Do."

Justine almost smiled. "Yes ma'am."

"Sassy. It was your idea for me to give him a chance. I'm open for suggestions."

Justine scooted back against the ecru silk padded headboard. "You've never needed help picking out anything to wear."

"This is my first pickup date at the church. Ouch," she laughed. "That didn't come out right."

Justine reached down and pulled the covers up to her waist. "But apt. How about that white sundress you told me about. You can wear the jacket at church, then if Patrick is lucky enough to follow you home and walk you to your door, you can take the jacket off and leave him salivating."

"From the middle of the back to the shoulders the dress is completely out. I like the way you think. He won't know what hit him. Maybe I should have thought of this before."

"You don't play with people's emotions," Justine said softly.

"Do you want to talk about the phone call?" Brianna's voice turned serious.

"No, and you have to go to work in the morning, so you need your sleep. You don't have to baby-sit me. Good night."

"I'm not sleepy and neither work nor school nor our mothers' dire warnings of consequences if we didn't get off the phone has ever stopped us before. Remember the time we went to the Prince concert?"

"You know, I do. Somehow Dalton got us tickets for the sold-out show."

"Not just tickets. Front row. He said he would if you'd go out with him."

"I insisted that you come." Justine remembered shaking in her penny loafers at the time, thrilled and scared he was playing some type of joke on her.

"We had a blast." Brianna laughed out loud. "Dalton is a great guy."

"No argument here." Just not the guy for her. "You never did mention where the bingo game was being held?"

"Greater Emmanuel at seven. You want to come?"

"I didn't go back tonight for the last visiting hour. I have to tomorrow."

"What would happen if you didn't?"

"Sometimes I wonder, but not enough not to go. I've turned into a coward."

"I don't want to ever hear you say that. You're stronger than most. You just don't like confrontations."

"That's how Mama always had her way. Going against her wishes and opening the bookstore was the first and only time as an adult I've stood up to her." There were none growing up. "I cried, but I never said a word when she sent me to Grandma Jenkins to get me away from Dalton."

"You succeeded beyond your expectations with the bookstore," Brianna reminded her. "You like peace. I like shaking them up."

"That's an understatement. Patrick better watch out."

"For real. Now, how about a movie Saturday afternoon? Saying no is not an option."

She hadn't been to a movie in over a year. The bookstore and other obligations with Andrew kept her too busy. "I might surprise both of us and go."

"I'll hold you to that and hang up before you change your mind. Night."

"Have fun. Night." Justine placed the phone in the charger, turned off the light, and drew the covers over her shoulders. She drifted off to sleep with the melody of "Purple Rain" in her ear and the image of Dalton and her dancing.

Eleven

Justine woke with a smile on her lips. Before her lashes lifted, the reason came rushing back. Groaning, she shut her eyes, but that only intensified the forbidden image. "Brianna, you're the cause of this," she moaned, then rolled out of bed. Too many forbidden memories were there.

In the shower, she mentally made out a schedule to pick up clothes from the dry cleaners, call the sales reps, check stock for an author event, and try to put a dent in her e-mail. She kept her mind busy while getting dressed in a lightweight magenta-colored suit. By the time she walked into the kitchen, the dream didn't seem quite so vivid and erotic.

One thing she told herself as she opened the refrigerator looking for apple juice was that she wasn't going to beat herself up about it. She was a woman with normal desires.

Retrieving the juice, she poured herself a glass, drinking it before she moved away. She was surprised to find that she was hungry. Replacing the juice, she checked the contents of the refrigerator. Foil-wrapped containers and plasticware—she wasn't sure who they belonged to or what they contained—were on every shelf. Friends and associates had brought or delivered food almost every day until a few weeks ago, when she'd asked them not to. She felt guilty throwing away food with so many hungry people in the world.

The phone on the counter rang. She pushed "talk" and went back to the open refrigerator. "Just you wait until I see you."

There was a slight pause. "Justine?"

She gasped, coming upright and slamming the refrigerator's door shut. "Marcus?"

"I'm sorry if I caught you at a bad time," he said.

Thankful she hadn't mentioned her dream, Justine tried to regroup. "I thought you were Brianna."

"Your friend?" he said, a smile in his voice. "I remember her."

Most men did. "How are you today, Marcus?"

"Fine. Grateful that you were able to help us. I just called to remind you of the meeting today."

Justine rubbed her temple. Having It All's board meeting was scheduled for that afternoon. In a weak moment at the luncheon the other day she had said she'd attend.

"You've done so much already. I wouldn't ask if it wasn't important."

Once more she'd have to play the part of the loving wife. When would it end? "Is one all right?"

"I'll make it all right. I'm just holding the company for Andrew. He poured his life into this organization."

Justine wondered how many of them really knew the side of him that cheated and lied.

"I'll see you at one," Marcus said.

"Good-bye." Justine hung up the phone. For one day she'd just like for everyone to forget she existed, but that wasn't about to happen. She was no longer hungry. Grabbing her purse from the counter, she headed for the garage.

Patrick knew some things were hard from the jump start. As a police office for eighteen years and the third son of a second-generation police officer, he was used to hard. His Cuban grandfather always said it made accomplishing your goal that much sweeter. Brianna was certainly putting his grandfather's words to the test.

Sitting at the elongated table with Harold Hinson, and three other women who had attached themselves to them as soon as they had walked through the door, Patrick could only hope the seat they'd saved between them would be put to use. He'd met Harold in the parking lot. He liked the older man.

The three women certainly did. They openly flirted with him. Harold was enjoying every moment of it and grinning from ear to ear. His days of not finding a date were over.

Patrick wished he could say the same. Without even holding Brianna, he knew she would fit perfectly in his arms. Their lips had yet to touch, but he knew Brianna's would be sweet and seductive. But he might not ever get the chance to find—

His thoughts came to an abrupt halt as he spotted Brianna standing in the doorway of the church's fellowship hall. His fingers clenched around the black marker in his hand.

He'd half expected her not to show. She was intelligent

and crafty. Her disappearing act the other night after she'd left the bookstore had proven that. She was too smart not to have figured out he'd be at the bingo game. Either she was there to show him he meant less than nothing to her or she was considering giving him a break.

She wore a white sundress with a jacket that was waist-length in the back, but in the front the jacket curved upward and stopped just beneath her beautifully shaped breasts. The flared hem of the dress beckoned attention to a pair of killer legs that a man would have a hard time not imagining wrapped around him. Patrick clamped his teeth together to keep his tongue from hanging out.

"Brianna's here." Mr. Hinson stood and waved. "Over here."

Patrick watched her cross the room in sky-high heels that accentuated her walk and made her bottom sway. Brianna rounded the table. "Hello, Mr. Hinson. You look spiffy."

The older man brushed his hand over neatly combed black hair liberally sprinkled with gray. "Thank you. We saved you a seat."

Brianna eyed the metal folding chair between them. "That looks rather cramped. Perhaps we should find someplace else."

Hinson looked around the crowded hall. "I don't see three seats together anyplace."

"B-seventeen."

"Harold, you have that number," Patrick told him. One more on that line and the older man would bingo.

"Oh, my goodness." He turned to the table, then whirled back to Brianna. "You want us to move?"

Patrick could see her wrestle with herself. She wanted the older man to have a good time, but she didn't want to be around Patrick. Another guy would have excused himself and taken one of the single seats. Patrick marked out Harold's number.

"This is fine." Brianna took her seat, scooting it closer to Hinson.

"Hello, Brianna," Patrick greeted.

She glanced at him. "Patrick."

"I-twenty-five."

Patrick shoved one of the three bingo cards in front of him over and handed an extra marker to Brianna. "The cards cost five dollars and the money goes to the mission fund. If you win, we split the take."

Brianna opened her purse and reached for her billfold.

He placed his hand on hers, felt hers jerk. So did his heart. "You can buy the next one."

"B-nineteen."

He glanced down at the card. "You're one away from bingoing. Harold, she might beat you."

Brianna gave up trying to outstare Patrick and looked down at the card. She was too competitive to pass up the chance of winning. She marked the number. Besides, she didn't want his hand on hers. It made her skin heat, her body want. "I'll pay you back."

"G-fifteen."

"Bingo," Patrick called.

Groans sounded through the room. "There are more prizes," the man calling the numbers said into the microphone.

The woman standing by the announcer came to their

table and handed Patrick a gift certificate to North of Broad restaurant. "It's for two," she said, her tone bold and suggestive.

He smiled lazily. "I'll remember that. Thanks."

"Do that."

She walked away, her hips swaying. Before she had taken two steps, Patrick turned his attention back to Brianna. She was staring at him with her usual disapproval. He was honest enough to admit that he wished there was even a hint of jealousy in her gaze. "Yes?"

"You gave me a card that didn't win."

It would take a strong man to get past Brianna's defenses and her sharp tongue. "There's always next time."

She leaned so close to him he could see his reflection in her eyes, smell the exotic perfume that made him think of long moonlit nights and them both naked. "No, there won't be. Winning that bingo game is as lucky as you're going to get tonight." Standing, she went to the front and came back with three cards. She handed him one. "Now we're even."

Taking her seat, she twisted away from Patrick, giving her attention to Mr. Hinson and the game. She'd almost miscalculated by getting so close to him. There was something about that half-smile, those penetrating black eyes, and conditioned muscles that made her restless. If the fiasco with Jackson hadn't happened she was honest enough to admit that she might have gone out with Patrick. He was a hard man to resist. "How is everyone's luck running tonight?"

"Rotten except for Patrick," a woman in her mid-fifties across the table said. She wore a pretty yellow dress with spring flowers. "I bet he gets lucky a lot."

The people at the table roared with laughter. "Sarah, you'll have me blushing," Patrick said easily, then winked.

Laughing, she shook her graying head of hair. "Would that I could. Now, ten years ago I might have made you blush for real." She looked at Harold. "Time brings about a change and a woman sees things differently."

"Amen to that, Sarah," said the small-boned, dark-haired woman next to her. "Flash and dash are all right when you're young, but women our age need a man of character."

Brianna's lips twitched. They were hitting on Harold and from the wide grin on his face, he was enjoying every moment.

"Time for another game. The winner this time gets a seventy-five-dollar gift certificate to Bliss."

Women around the room yelled and applauded. Men groaned.

Brianna snapped to attention. She'd heard the name of the upscale bath and body shop during a divorce case she'd handled. Three friends owned and operated the store, which supplied candles to Midnight Dreams, the luxe linen boutique of her client. If the owners of Bliss would have come forth to testify about what they knew of an associate of her client, she would have certainly lost the case.

"You've heard of my niece's company?" Patrick asked.

"O-seventeen."

Brianna scanned her card and didn't see the number. "There was a write-up in the Charleston paper," she answered, which was the truth, but she had researched the company once she heard that the women might jeopardize her client's case. "Which one is your niece?"

Patrick's answer was slow in coming. "Brooke."

"The marketing guru who was keeping company with Randolph Peterson III?"

"I-nineteen."

Brianna kept her eyes on the unlucky card, but she was sure Patrick hadn't taken his eyes from her. Her senses reeled.

"I get the feeling your association with Bliss isn't as a customer," Patrick said, his voice carrying a slight edge.

She had already pegged him as the protective type. "I can't listen if you talk," she said, evasively.

"O-twenty-three."

Brianna spied the number and lifted her marker, but Patrick moved the card out of reach. She glared at him. He didn't bat an eyelash. So he didn't sweat as easily as most people. Neither did she. "You're going to owe me fifteen dollars."

"I'm usually a patient man. You're pushing it."

She showed him her hundred-watt smile, the result of wearing braces for two years. "It's what I do best."

"Not this time, and not with me."

She was suddenly aware of two things. The table had grown quiet and her pulse was racing with excitement. Damn. She did not want to be attracted to an annoying man like Patrick. Time to end this. "The matter is confidential, but there was no threat to your niece's company or the other women who owned the shop with her."

He studied her a while longer, then picked up her card and made three marks. "Looks like you're close again."

Brianna looked from the card to him. She had heard only one of the numbers he'd marked. She'd been too aware of him to concentrate.

"I-fifteen."

"Bingo," Sarah called, jumping up and down, clasping her hands. "Bingo! I won! I won!"

The same woman came over with the gift certificate. "Here you go, Sarah," she said, then leaned over and said, "I hear the Better Than Sex line is fabulous."

Harold's mouth gaped, then he smiled when Sarah looked at him. From Patrick there was nothing. Brianna was unable to keep from looking at him.

"You'll just have to find out for yourself," Patrick said, his deep, raspy voice filled with a seductive promise.

Hot shivers raced through her body. "That will be the day," she muttered.

"Night works for me."

Brianna gasped and thought of kicking him under the table, but she was too busy trying to calm her racing heart. She might have just met her match and there was no way she was spending any more time than necessary with this man.

Deep in thought, Patrick walked the trail surrounding the marina. Last night he'd been listening to Harold trying to decide which woman to ask out and had let Brianna slip away. By the time Harold had made his decision Patrick had looked around and Brianna was gone.

Today she wouldn't find it so easy. He smiled and waited for her to reach him. He'd caught sight of her from his balcony window and hurried down. "Good evening, Brianna."

She kept right on running. Her lips had a faint trace of raspberry-colored lipstick, but the rest of her exquisite face was bare of makeup. She didn't need any. She looked fantastic.

He fell into step beside her. "Nice weather we're having."

She increased her pace on the mile-long walking trail.

"I ran track in high school and college," he told her. He thought he saw her mouth kick up at the sides. "How about we go out on my boat, *Proud Mary*?"

"Go away, Patrick."

He liked the way she said his first name, and took her speaking to him as a good sign that he was wearing her down. Stepping off the trail, she jogged in place, then began her cooling down routine with stretches and lunges. He didn't know if he was happy or not that she'd worn navy blue sweats instead of shorts.

"It's the thirty-footer tied at the end of the pier. There's a cove near here where we could drop anchor and swim or just enjoy each other's company."

She glanced up and arched a delicate eyebrow at him. "Or we could stay in and have dinner on the terrace and watch the sunset. The view is spectacular from my place."

She stopped inches from touching her toes in running shoes. "Your place?"

"Top floor. Corner."

She straightened, her gaze intense. "When did you move in?"

He didn't see what difference that made, but at least she was talking to him. "A little over a month ago."

"You!" Her finger stabbed his chest. "You're the one who stole the unit I wanted."

He rubbed his chin. "That's a strong word and untrue. Brooke never intended to sell the place."

"That's not what the concierge said when I asked about a corner unit," she said, her small chin jutting out.

His gaze drifted lazily over her. "I have a feeling that most guys tell you what they think you want to hear."

She folded her arms over her breasts. "If that's true, why aren't you saying good-bye?"

He laughed out loud. "Brianna. You are something else."

Her arms came to her sides. "All right. I'll say it, good-bye." Without another word, she started toward the side door of the condo.

He'd never enjoyed a woman more, he thought as he caught up with her. "Wouldn't you like to see the unit?"

She stopped. "Are you planning on leaving?"

There was entirely too much hope in her beautiful eyes. "As my guest."

She started toward the side entrance again. "If you change your mind, just let the concierge know."

"If you change yours, you know where to find me." He opened the door.

"Wish I knew how to lose you." She started toward the elevator. The door opened and three people got off, greeting Patrick by name and nodding to Brianna as they did so. Patrick punched both their floors. Neither spoke on the short ride to the third floor. As soon as the elevator doors opened, Brianna moved to get off.

"I don't suppose you'll let me walk you to your door?" Patrick said from behind her.

She stepped off the elevator and turned. "No."

"Thought not. See you around." The door closed on his smiling face.

Turning, Brianna continued to her apartment. Removing the key from the pocket of her jacket, she let herself inside. Patrick might be a menace, but he certainly was a sexy one. Annoyed because his offer had been enticing, she pulled off her jacket and continued to her bedroom. She loved the water and boats. That was a big reason why she'd chosen to live at the condos.

In Dallas there had been ample opportunity for her to enjoy both at the lake home of her boss. However, she'd stayed with Jackson as he'd wooed their boss instead of enjoying herself on the lake. She'd lent Jackson her support and left the talking to him. She wasn't the brownnosing type.

Undressing, she ran a tub full of water and climbed in. Thinking of Jackson made her even more determined not to go out with Patrick. The "maybe" she'd given Justine would have to be a firm "no."

But it was going to be difficult to resist Patrick's beguiling smile, his warm laughter. His ability not to take himself too seriously was endearing. For the first time in her life, a man tested her self-control.

Twelve

Patrick was a strategist. He knew how to plan, how to wait for the right moment to spring his trap. He already knew Brianna was a worthy opponent. She couldn't be pushed or cajoled. After seeing the brief flare of interest in her eyes the other day, he hoped she could be tempted.

Since seeing Brianna at the coffee shop he'd gotten up early each morning and gone to the marina, which fortunately had a clear view of the entrance of the parking garage. Sipping coffee, he'd wait until Brianna barreled out of the garage in the baby Benz with the top up. In a little notebook he'd recorded the time. 8:09. 8:13.

This morning it was 8:33. He shot up from his chair when she recklessly went through the caution light. The owner of the car she'd cut off rightly laid on his or her horn. He wouldn't have thought she was the careless type. Being late was no excuse for taking chances.

"Care for a refill or something more substantial?"

"I'm fine, thanks, Pasha." Patrick retook his seat and

entered another notation in his little book, then flipped the pages. Her coming home was even more erratic. The time span was from 6:00 P.M. through 11:18 P.M. And always she'd have the top down.

That bothered him. It might be fun, but it also made her more vulnerable to being car-jacked.

Patrick hunched over the small wrought-iron table. Pointing that out to Brianna would get him a stay-out-of-my-business look at best, at worst a tongue lashing. That woman could cut a man down in record time.

He considered telling her father, then thought of his heart condition. He didn't need anything else to worry him. Standing, Patrick signaled he was going and that they should put the coffee on the tab he paid weekly. He started to the condo. Looked like it was left up to him.

No guts, no glory, he always thought.

Brianna was late again. The reason annoyed the hell out of her. Patrick Dunlap. She couldn't seem to stop thinking about him, his magnificent body or that dreamy voice of his. She whipped around a van and shot onto the freeway going seventy miles an hour.

She wasn't the type of woman to let a handsome face or a set of pecs get her hot and bothered. Jackson could hold a jury spellbound with his voice, was handsome and charismatic. She'd walked out on him and not looked back.

One thing her parents had taught her was that character counted more than anything. If a person didn't have integrity and honesty, they had nothing. Jackson was devoid of both. But thinking that he had in the beginning weighed heavily on her.

It bothered her that he'd been able to slip past her defenses, and that Justine might be right in pointing out Brianna's history with Jackson was interfering with her giving Patrick a fair shot. She didn't want her past with Jackson to matter in the least. The simple and plain fact was that with her workload she didn't have time for a man. End of story.

Exiting the freeway to downtown, she merged with the slow-moving traffic on King Street headed for First. She parked in the back of the single-story frame house that had been converted into her father's law office, then went through the back door. The house was neat, with a fresh coat of blue paint and white shutters. Her father had kept the kitchen intact and turned one of the two bedrooms into a law library; the other served as his office. The front room had become the reception area.

"Your first client is here."

What Matilda didn't point out, but her face did, was that Brianna was late again. If she hadn't been seventy if she was a day, Brianna might have told her the reason. As it was, Brianna accepted the unspoken reprimand. Another thing her parents had drilled into her head was to respect her elders. "I'm sorry."

"I'll send her in and get you a cup of coffee."

Matilda turned away before Brianna could nix the coffee. She shuddered just thinking of the sludge Matilda called coffee. It was chicory and as thick as tar. She also liked bringing sweets to the office and had a passion for fried foods. No wonder her father had clogged arteries. The amazing thing was that it hadn't happened sooner and that Matilda was in excellent health.

Turning, Brianna went to her office and sat behind her

father's desk. After a brisk knock, Matilda ushered a young woman inside and introduced her. The prospective client looked to be no more than twenty years old, and scared to death.

"Good morning," Sylvia Atkins said, glancing back as if she wanted to follow Matilda from the room.

Brianna rounded the desk and went to the woman, who was wringing her hands. "Good morning, Ms. Atkins. I'm here to help you in any way I can."

"I—I don't know if you can."

Brianna had already been filled in on the case. Her anger mounted again. Lawyers, like doctors, were supposed to remain impersonal, but sometimes you couldn't. "Sexual harassment is illegal."

The woman's large eyes darted around the room, looking anywhere but at Brianna. "He said no one would believe me. I—I need my job. It helps me pay my tuition."

"He probably knows that and is counting on you feeling scared with nowhere to turn."

The fresh-faced young woman finally looked at Brianna. "Your father came to speak to our paralegal class at the university. He talked about a sexual harassment case and said if we ever needed help he was there. I don't have much money—"

"We'll talk about money later." Brianna had never been prouder of her father. "What you have to decide is if you want to continue with this. I did a preliminary search on your boss. He's a twenty-year employee. He isn't going to roll over and admit guilt. He'll fight. It might get dirty."

The young woman's head fell. "I have a two-year-old daughter. I'm not married."

"Congratulations, and that has no bearing on this."

Her head lifted sharply, her brow furrowed. "He said—"

Brianna held up her hand. "If you decide to pursue this, the first thing I want you to do is promise to listen to me and not the scum who is harassing you. You have to put your complete trust in me. Period."

"You're not like your father."

Where had she heard that before? "I am where it counts. I'm a good lawyer. Am I going to be your lawyer?"

The woman didn't hesitate. "Yes."

Patrick entered Brianna's father's law office and saw one elderly man looking through papers in an attaché case on his lap. Good. Patrick went to the slender gray-haired woman typing at the computer behind the L-shaped desk. She wore a black suit and a white blouse with an onyx brooch pinned at the neck. "Good morning, I'd like to see Brianna Ireland."

"Good morning. Your name, please," she asked, swinging away from the computer.

"Patrick Dunlap."

She spoke without looking up. "Ms. Ireland has next Thursday at two open if that's acceptable?"

He guessed all the appointments for today must be returnees, but how did she know the schedule so well?

She smiled and tapped the pen to her hair in a neat bun. "I worked before we had the computer."

"I was hoping I could see her today. It's important."

Her gaze sharpened. "Can you explain a bit more?"

"I—"

Before Patrick could finish, Brianna emerged from an open doorway. A young woman was with her. Brianna paused the instant she saw him, her mouth tightening. True to form, she ignored him and walked the young woman to the door, then returned. "Why are you here?"

"I was trying to get an appointment to see you."

Brianna looked at the receptionist for confirmation. "He's telling the truth about that," Matilda said.

"I don't think I'm the lawyer to represent you."

"I'd probably disagree if that was what I came for, but I'm here for another reason. Keep your top up at night."

Her hands went to her breasts. She gasped and stepped back.

"The car top," he quickly clarified, feeling his face heat for some crazy reason. Probably because the elderly secretary and the older man were listening to every word. "It makes you too vulnerable to car jackers."

Her eyes narrowed. "Have you been watching me?"

"That would be an invasion of privacy, wouldn't it?"

She opened her mouth to blast him.

"Brianna, your next appointment, Mr. Shaw, is waiting," the receptionist interrupted.

"Good-bye, Patrick." Dismissing him, she went to the elderly man, who was still shuffling through his briefcase. "Mr. Shaw, Brianna Ireland. My father briefed me on your case."

He attempted to rise and then sank back down. When he attempted again, Brianna assisted him by taking his arm. "The sofa is too low to make getting up easy. I'm sorry."

"These old bones don't help. Your father said you were sharp and a good girl."

"He's supposed to because he's my father, but I wouldn't

like to make him out to be wrong. Please come into my office, and let's see how I can help you."

Patrick watched until they disappeared. "She's good with everyone except me."

"I wonder why?"

Patrick was a man who took advantage of opportunities. "Me too. I met her parents when she moved into my complex. Her father seemed to like me."

"You met Charles?"

"He introduced himself when he and his wife were helping Brianna move in. We shook hands."

Matilda studied him with sharp black eyes for a long time. "Charles is a good judge of character." She stood. "Care to join me for a cup of coffee?"

"There's nothing I'd like better."

Brianna came out of her office forty minutes later. Thankfully, Patrick was gone. Her body reacted too unpredictably around him. After showing Mr. Shaw out, she approached Matilda. "If he changes his mind about wanting an appointment, you're not to give him one."

"Seems like a nice young man." Matilda kept typing.

Brianna wrinkled her nose. "Looks can be deceiving. He's pushy."

"He didn't seem that way when we had coffee. He liked my snickerdoodles."

Brianna blinked, then placed her hands palm down on the desk. She couldn't believe her ears. "You fed him?"

Matilda saved the document, then swirled in her chair and met Brianna's gaze without flinching. "Like your father, I liked him."

"He met Daddy one time." She shoved her fingers through her hair. "He keeps feeding people that same line. Daddy probably doesn't even remember him."

"We both know that isn't true. We also know your father is a keen judge of character. He might speak, but a handshake is different." Her eyebrow lifted. "Take that Jackson Hewitt person."

Brianna snapped to attention. "What about Jackson?" she asked, but had a good idea what the answer would be.

Matilda's penciled brow shot upward. "You aren't dumb, Brianna, so why act that way?" she asked, then continued. "You know as well as I that neither your mother nor father liked him when they were in Dallas visiting you. Their opinion didn't change when he came down after Charles had his heart attack. Good riddance, I'd say."

"What's that supposed to mean?"

Folding her arms over her flat chest, Matilda leaned back in her chair. "You haven't mentioned him since you've been back. Neither has he called." Unfolding her arms, she began typing again. "I'd say you finally saw through all those caps and polished manner."

Brianna rounded the desk and twisted the receptionist's chair around. "If he was so bad, why didn't anyone let me in on it?"

"Because you're as stubborn as a Missouri mule. No one tells you what to do or how to do it." Matilda's voice softened. "Besides, when you learn a lesson yourself you never forget it. He caught you at a vulnerable time when you were worried about your father. Everyone is allowed one mistake."

Brianna hated being wrong, hated worse when someone pointed it out to her before she realized it. But she also never made excuses. "That's why I don't plan to make another one with Patrick."

"With all those muscles and that boyish smile, that is one mistake a lot of women wouldn't mind making." Matilda pointed toward the appointment book on the edge of the desk. "Your next appointment is due here in five minutes. Go grab a cup of coffee and a snickerdoodle."

Imagining Patrick drinking the unpalatable coffee and eating gooey sweet treats almost made Brianna smile. "You really fed him?"

Matilda smiled, showing the full set of the teeth she was born with. "He ate four and took some with him."

Her smile growing, Brianna went to the kitchen. As always she checked to ensure that Matilda was busy at her desk before pouring the cup of coffee down the sink. Not for anything would she hurt the older woman's feelings.

Picking up a snickerdoodle, she wrapped it in a napkin, then hid it behind a box of cereal until she could slip it out in her briefcase. There were only four left. There had been at least a dozen this morning. Brianna shuddered. She didn't see how Patrick had been able to eat the sugary treats. Matilda always used way too much sugar in her recipes. Her brownies were so sweet they made Brianna's teeth ache.

Pouring a cup of coffee to take back to her office and later dump in the bathroom sink, Brianna imagined Patrick's shocked face on his first sip. But it wasn't shock on his face when the image materialized, but hot desire, the same desire heating her blood.

"Damn!"

"You burn yourself?" Matilda called from the other room.

"No." And she didn't plan to.

"Why are sensible women attracted to the men who are bad for them?" Brianna asked the question, her feet tucked beneath her jean-clad hips as she lounged on Justine's sofa and sipped iced tea later than evening.

"For me, it was because Dalton was so sexy he made me shiver. He was a little wicked and don't forget he was reported to be the best kisser in school," Justine said as she studied Brianna's pensive expression.

She'd invited Brianna over for dinner and picked up carryout from one of their favorite seafood restaurants on the way home. Just thinking about cooking a full meal made her tired. "I take it Patrick isn't as easy to get rid of physically or emotionally."

"He's a pest." The glass hit the leather coaster on the oval-shaped coffee table with a thud. "I can't believe he came to the office, then had the nerve to try and spout law to me."

Justine sipped her tea before answering. "I say that showed initiative, determination, and intelligence."

Brianna's eyes narrowed. "He just better not come back."

"He scared you that much?" If there was one thing Brianna could handle, it was men.

Brianna picked up her glass and drained it before speaking. "Yes."

"Join the club."

"Dalton," Brianna said.

"One minute I want him to come back, the next I pray he won't." Setting her glass on the table, Justine leaned her head back on the tufted sofa and closed her eyes. "I feel as guilty as hell, then excited, then ashamed."

"Don't. You didn't break your vows, Andrew did."

"But if Dalton had come back before I discovered Andrew at the cabin, would I have been tempted?" she asked, adding yet another question to the growing list she'd never have an answer to. This newest one weighed even more heavily on her mind than the others. "I've always considered myself beyond temptation. It's rather disconcerting to discover I'm not."

"Let's look at this logically." Brianna waited until Justine opened her eyes and looked at her. "You've read Dalton's books. Seen his photo on the jacket, which I think is hot and sexy as hell. What did you feel? Don't analyze, just answer."

"That he was even better looking and sexier than in high school, but that I had a man who was just as handsome and sexy and how lucky I was," she answered, her voice growing quieter.

"I rest my case. You wouldn't have strayed." Brianna picked up her glass and shook it until a couple of ice cubes slid into her mouth.

"But why did Andrew?" Justine asked. "Why wasn't I enough?"

Brianna crunched and swallowed before answering. 'There's probably not one single answer. Don't torture yourself trying to find out why," Brianna advised and picked up Justine's glass. "I think we need to change this tea to wine."

"Having trouble sleeping, too?"

"I'm late every day to work. Patrick is like a bad rhyme that won't get out of my head." Brianna came to her feet.

Justine stood as well. "Dalton is in my head and in my bed. At least in my dreams."

Brianna laughed. "Hot damn! This definitely calls for wine."

"We're pitiful," Justine said, but she found herself smiling.

"We're survivors."

"Survivors. Let's go find that wine."

Thirteen

Determined to be on time, Brianna had taken the drastic measure of asking Matilda to call her. It worked. Almost. There was a traffic jam and she'd left without her coffee again. She wasn't sure how much longer she could go without her caffeine. Usually she drank two to three cups of the stuff in the morning. She might have to break down and beg Matilda to let her make the coffee herself.

Parking, she grabbed her briefcase and sprinted in three-inch heels to the back door. She'd had to cancel the movie date with Justine until she had made more of a dent in her father's caseload. She'd worked on Saturdays before and it wasn't a hardship. Going without her coffee was.

She smelled coffee the instant she opened the door. Her gaze zeroed in on the automatic pot in its usual place, but the aroma had never been this wonderful.

She sniffed again, then cautiously walked closer as if expecting the delicious aroma to disappear. It smelled divine.

Yesterday when she'd gone to her parents' house to

check on her father, Brianna had mentioned Matilda's un-drinkable coffee to her mother. Knowing how much she enjoyed coffee, her mother must have come over that morning.

"Thank God for loving mothers," Brianna murmured.

Grabbing a cup, Brianna filled it to the brim, inhaled again, then drank. She moaned. Heaven.

"Wait until you taste the cranberry-walnut coffee cake."

Brianna lowered the cup to see Matilda at the door. She was pointing to a round covered red tin near the coffeepot.

Not waiting for Brianna to lift the lid, Matilda opened it herself. "I might make myself sick on these if you don't take this into your office," Matilda said.

Having missed breakfast . . . again . . . Brianna grabbed a wedge of already sliced coffee cake crammed full of fruit and nuts and drizzled with cream cheese icing, and took a huge, unladylike bite. Her taste buds sighed with pleasure.

"Thought you might like it. Please hide it from me. I've got a deposition to type."

Her mouth full, Brianna nodded as Matilda left the small kitchen. Even before she finished, she wanted an-other slice. She was as bad as Matilda. With supreme will-power, she closed the lid, settled for a second cup of coffee, and headed to her office.

Brianna stopped in front of Matilda's desk. "Sorry. Good morning."

"Good morning." Matilda glanced up briefly and con-tinued to type. "Believe me, I understand."

Brianna sipped leisurely and enjoyed her coffee. Once she sat behind her desk she'd get lost in work and not re-member the coffee until it was cold. "I wish Mom would have stayed until I got here."

Matilda glanced up. "Your mother wasn't here."

Lines of confusion puckered Brianna's brow. "Then who dropped the coffee and coffee cake off for her?"

The front door opened and an old client who needed to add his latest grandchild to his will entered before Matilda could answer. "Good morning, Mr. Otis. Ms. Ireland will be with you as soon as she gets settled."

"Good morning, Mr. Otis." Brianna held up her almost empty cup. "If you'd like you can come back with me or have a cup of coffee and some coffee cake."

The man patted his stomach, which was a slight bulge beneath his white shirt and herringbone jacket. "As you can see, I never pass up good food."

All three of them laughed. "I'll show you the way, then we can get down to business."

It was almost lunch before Brianna had a break in clients so she could call her mother. She leaned back in her father's chair and looked at their degrees and accolades, which took up three-quarters of the wall. They'd both achieved a great deal.

The phone rang for the second time. Brianna finished off her second slice of coffee cake, which Matilda had left on her desk earlier. "Self-preservation," she'd said.

"Hello."

Brianna quickly cleaned her fingers and braced her elbows on the desk. "Hi, Mama. How are you and Daddy?"

"Fine. He's anxious to try out the golf cart you bought us. We're going today."

"You make sure he lets you drive," Brianna advised.

Her mother chuckled softly. "That'll be the day. He's so

proud of it, but we're both prouder of you. We know you gave—"

"Not a hundredth of all the things you and Daddy gave me. I love you both." She didn't miss the hectic pace of the firm as much as she'd imagined.

"We love you, too. I see your father beckoning to me through the window. Do you need to talk to him before we go?"

"No, you two go on. I just wanted to thank you for the coffee and coffee cake. I don't know when I've tasted better. You saved my life."

"What coffee and coffee cake?"

Brianna frowned. "The coffee and coffee cake that were here when I arrived this morning."

"I didn't bring them."

Brianna's brow puckered. "Then if you didn't, who did? I thought you had someone drop them off after Matilda said you hadn't been here."

"I don't know. Sorry I can't help. Your father keeps looking at his watch. I better go or he might go off and leave me. I can't wait to show off my new golf outfit. Thanks, Brianna."

"You'll be the jazziest couple there," she said absently, thinking of the coffee and coffee cake. "I'll talk to you later. Tell Daddy to shoot a sixty-eight."

"I will. 'Bye, honey."

Brianna hung up the phone, the lines between her brows deepening. If her mother hadn't sent the coffee and coffee cake, who had? Getting up from the desk, Brianna went to find Matilda. "So, who did it?"

The older woman stopped filing folders in the bottom drawer of her desk. "You're not going to like the answer."

"Why wouldn't I—" Brianna's eyes narrowed, her hands clenched. "You can't be about to say what I think you are."

Matilda closed the drawer and studied her manicured nails. "Depends on what you think I'm about to say."

"Cut it out, Matilda, and spill. Who?"

The secretary looked up through her lashes in an uncharacteristic stalling tactic. "You promise to remain calm?"

"The name," Brianna snapped.

"Patrick Dunlap."

The banging on his front door interrupted Patrick's cooking. Tonight it was sea bass he'd caught himself. The three-pound fish had put up a good fight, but in the end Patrick had been victorious. He would have liked to have cooked it over an open fire on the bank of the river, but the grill mounted next to the oven was the next best thing. There was also a green salad with walnuts, and fresh squash and mushrooms waiting in the refrigerator and a huge baked potato in the oven.

The noise grew louder. Turning the fillets over, he went to the door in his black T-shirt and faded denim cutoffs. He'd taken a shower after he'd returned, then dressed comfortably. He had thought about lounging near the pier to see Brianna when she came home, but had discarded the idea. She was too unpredictable and totally captivating.

The noise grew louder as he neared. Whoever it was hadn't even tried the doorbell. He knew it worked because Brooke and her family had been over the night before. He looked through the peephole from force of habit.

A slow grin spread over his face. He couldn't get the

door open fast enough. "Hello, Brianna. Change your mind about visiting?"

A slim finger tried to dig a hole in his chest as she stalked into the room. Since that was where he wanted her, he let her have her way . . . for now. "Stay away from my office and from me."

He had no intention of doing either. Stepping around her, he casually swung the door shut, but he was careful to keep an eye on her. She looked ready to blow and absolutely gorgeous.

Today she wore a little pink suit with large black buttons. The collar was cut in a V that displayed a tempting hint of her lush breasts. He'd like nothing better than to press his lips there. "Would you like something to drink?"

Hands on her small waist, Brianna glared at him. "I don't intend to have this conversation again. Understand?"

He hooked his thumbs into the pockets of his jeans. It was either that or hook his fingers into the vee of her jacket, pull her flush against him, and kiss her until she stopped spitting at him and purred. "Could you tell me why?"

She spluttered. "I don't need you cooking for me."

He rubbed his chin in a thoughtful manner. "There must be some mistake."

"Mistake!" she yelled. He had a feeling Brianna didn't lose her temper often. She must really be fighting the attraction between them. "Are you going to tell me you didn't bring coffee and a coffee cake to the office?"

"No. Matilda and I were talking yesterday and we got into foods. I decided to drop by this morning before I took the boat out and show her how my grandmother taught me to make coffee. She had fresh baked goods yesterday so I returned the favor." He frowned. "Did she say they were for you?"

No, she didn't. Brianna had been so sure that Patrick was trying to get to her that she had simmered all day, then driven straight from work. Her cheeks heated in embarrassment. "I—" The apology stuck in her throat. She felt like a fool. First Jackson, now Patrick.

"Excuse me, I smell my dinner." Patrick headed to the kitchen.

Brianna figured it was a good time to make her escape, but she'd been taught if you could dish it out you had better be able to take it when it was your turn. She'd apologize, then make sure to stay away from Patrick.

"This might take a moment," he called from the kitchen. "Can you please come in here?"

Her steps were slow as she passed through the great room, which was done in a tasteful mix of eye-popping red and sedate black. In the spotless kitchen, which was bigger than hers, Patrick was dishing up fish fillets on a red platter. The delicious smell made her mouth water.

"I caught it today. You like fishing?"

"I haven't been since I was a kid," she said, hoping her stomach didn't growl. She'd worked through lunch . . . which was becoming an everyday occurrence.

"Once a fisherman, always a fisherman." He grinned, causing the dimples in his face to deepen. Brianna felt her stomach clench. Time to get out of there. "I really—"

"We haven't finished. Please have a seat." Setting the platter on the table, he pulled out a chair in front of the single place setting of bamboo stainless and an abstract plate of black and white.

"I don't want to interrupt your dinner."

"I hate to play hardball, but, after your accusation, the least you can do is have dinner with me."

She eyed the fish. Her mouth watered.

"There's peach cobbler and ice cream for dessert," he coaxed.

She'd been known to eat a whole cobbler by herself. "Matilda tell you I liked peach cobbler?"

"As a lawyer, I'm sure you'll understand confidentiality."

She also knew when someone was evading answering the question. He and Matilda had that much in common. No wonder they had hit it off. Brianna sat. She couldn't say if it was because of her weakness for the peach cobbler with a thick lattice crust she'd caught a glimpse of on the black granite counter, hunger, or the dimpled smile.

Almost immediately, Patrick stepped away. In no time the table was set with another place setting, a baked potato, and a large green salad. The amazement must have shown on her face.

"I grew up with four brothers and we were always hungry. You didn't waste time setting the table." He sat, bowed his head, and said grace. "How is your father?"

Brianna hadn't expected the question and tried to figure out if he had an ulterior motive. "Shouldn't you know about your new best friend?"

He stopped halving the largest baked potato she'd ever seen. "In my previous profession, you learn to judge people quickly. I think your father is the same way. Sometimes you know a person in an instant. At other times you can be around someone for years and not know them."

Andrew and Jackson popped into her mind. Her mouth tightened.

"Seems like you've had the experience."

Her gaze lifted. A mouth-watering body, a heart-pounding smile, *and* perceptive. Trouble was sitting across from her. If she wasn't careful, she might succumb . . . but she always was careful, at least she had been. Besides, she was too busy to even think about a relationship. She picked up her fork. "What profession were you in?"

He grinned and placed the salad plate with the halved potato in front of her. "Almost forgot you are a lawyer. Policeman."

She couldn't have been more surprised. Her gaze ran over him again. "That's why you were at the police station?"

"And the book signing." He dug into the salad, which was liberally sprinkled with fat toasted croutons an inch thick, walnut slivers, and fresh bacon bits. "Dalton does policemen proud."

"You said *previous*."

His gaze slowly met hers. "I retired about six months ago and decided to do some of the things I always wanted to do."

There was something dark and tortured in his black eyes that made her want to soothe him and not push for answers. She'd been around enough policemen to know they lived with images that would haunt them for the rest of their lives. "Like fish."

"And boating. You want to come along sometime?"

He'd slipped that in nicely. He was as sharp as Justine thought he was. "I'm busy working."

"Since I own the boat and it's a two-minute walk from

where we both live, if you change your mind, please let me know."

Brianna was surprised he hadn't tried harder to talk her into going. Oddly peeved, she tucked her head and dug into her salad.

"The food all right?" he asked.

"It's delicious. Thank you."

"Food is enjoyed better with someone," he said easily. "It's chicken primavera tomorrow night if you'd care to stop by."

"I'm—"

"Busy," he said, but he smiled. "At the risk of being redundant and predictable, since we're in the same building, feel free to stop by anytime. You're always welcome."

"Thank you, but it gets busier by the day at the office," she told him.

He cut into his fish. "How about eating dessert on the balcony? We can watch the sun go down."

A tempting offer from a tempting man. "In here is fine."

"You don't know what you're missing." His voice deepened; his gaze lingered on her mouth.

Her body heated. She barely kept from squirming. She could well imagine what she was missing, but self-preservation came first.

Fourteen

Dalton was going home. No matter where he'd lived since he'd graduated from college and moved to Detroit, Charleston had always remained home. Now, turning into the Riverview shopping center, he finally admitted to himself why he'd left. *Justine.*

He'd been angry that she hadn't tried to contact him as he'd tried to contact her after her mother sent her to visit her grandmother. Her mother might have tossed him out, but his parents would have told her how to reach him. She hadn't and that hurt.

Dalton shook away the feeling that he probably should have followed her example of years ago, get back on the freeway and not stop until he'd reached the hotel where he'd rented a room. But it was too late. Across the street was It's a Mystery Bookstore.

He'd run from his emotions and confrontations with disastrous consequences in the past. If there was a way to help Justine, he was going to try and find it. Hopefully, while he was with her he'd do his best to keep his feelings for her under wraps.

Stopping in front of the bookstore, he got out and went inside. There had been enough hesitation on his part. The second he saw her shelving greeting cards, her face pale even from ten feet away, the dress hanging from her shoulders, he knew he'd been right to come. She'd lost weight. Although he hadn't said a word, she glanced around.

From the dark circles beneath her eyes, she hadn't been sleeping either. Her hand that was holding the card shook. He didn't know if that was a good thing or bad, but he wasn't leaving. Justine might be as aware of him as he was of her, but she wasn't going to act on it. And, so help him, neither was he. She didn't need another complication in her life.

"Hello, Justine."

"You're back." Her voice was hushed, raspy.

"I finished the book," he said, closing the door and advancing further into the bookstore.

The uneasiness in her eyes was quickly replaced by happiness. "Congratulations."

"Thanks." He stopped a safe distance away. "How about helping me celebrate?"

Wariness entered her eyes again. Although she didn't move, he had the impression that she had stepped away from him. "Thank you, but I have to work." She ran her hand through her shoulder-length auburn hair. "I've missed a lot of time here."

"I'm sure you have a competent staff. I promise to have you back in an hour."

She was shaking her head before he finished. "I'm sorry."

"Dalton, what a wonderful surprise," Iris cried as she joined them. "How is the book going?"

"Finished and on my editor's and agent's desks." He allowed his casual gaze to touch Justine. "I was just trying to get my old schoolmate to have an early dinner with me and celebrate." The last thing he wanted was for there to be gossip about his association with Justine. "But she's too busy."

"Not that busy." Iris took the cards from Justine's hands. "I'll finish this. You've been missing too many meals as it is."

Justine ran her hand over her pale green linen sheath. "Thanks, but I'm not hungry."

"You will be when you smell the food at Big Jumbo's," Dalton said.

Iris smacked her lips. "I'll say. I stuff myself every time I go there."

"I really—" Justine began.

"Please, help me celebrate. I was holed up at the house for two weeks." He didn't mind playing on her sympathy if it would get her to relax. It didn't seem like she had done much since the accident.

"I'll go get your purse," Iris offered and rushed to the back. She returned in no time, giving Justine the large drawstring bag. "Have fun."

Justine clutched the large handbag to her chest. "If Beverly calls—"

Iris patted her hand in reassurance. "I'll tell her to get you on your cell."

Dalton glanced at his watch. "I didn't make reservations because I wasn't sure you could make it. We better go if I want to keep my promise and get you back here in an hour." Not giving her a chance to delay anymore, Dalton took Justine's arm and led her to his Cherokee, then assisted her inside.

Rounding the vehicle, he got in and started the engine. Fastening his seat belt, he said, "Thanks for coming."

The corners of her soft mouth tilted upward. "I'm not sure I had much of a choice."

He backed out of the parking space. "Then I'll have to make doubly sure that you enjoy lunch and have a good time."

The melancholy expression returned. "I don't think you or anyone else can guarantee that."

Dalton heard her comment and chose not to say anything. The words had sounded heartrending, hopeless. He was more determined than ever to be there for her . . . even if she didn't want him.

Justine knew it was a mistake thirty seconds after she entered the popular soul-food restaurant. Andrew was well known in the community and so was she. Heads turned, whispers followed. She tensed.

"It will be all right."

She looked up into Dalton's calm gaze. There was something else there that she couldn't identify. Or so she tried to convince herself.

"Two old friends just having dinner."

Oddly she hadn't thought of the gossip or speculations as much as the dread of repeating Andrew's condition. Each time she did, his betrayal came back.

"I wonder if they still serve bread pudding with rum sauce."

Bread pudding had been one of her favorite desserts.

She'd mentioned it on one of their three dates. "You have a good memory."

"On some things," he said.

Not knowing how to take his comment, Justine didn't say anything.

The hostess came to the wooden podium and removed two menus from the built-in slot. "Two?"

"Yes," Dalton answered.

The young woman in her early twenties smiled at him with youthful appreciation. "Follow me."

Justine idly wondered if Dalton got that "I'm available look" all the time, then she cast a sideways glance up at his handsome bearded face and knew the answer. Most *definitely.*

Dalton released her arm, then held the cane chair out for her. Justine accepted the menu and hid behind it.

"What do you have a taste for?"

You. The wicked thought came from nowhere. She was flustered and flushed, and her hands trembled. "I'm not sure."

"Something must tempt your taste buds. I know they do mine."

She lowered the menu, sure he would be studying his. Instead she found his eyes trained on her. Desire was there, and so much more. Patience, kindness, caring.

"Hello. I'm Sally, your waitress. You folks ready?"

Justine lifted the menu. Time to stop acting like the awed teenager she used to be around Dalton. "I'll have the blackened red snapper, garden salad with house dressing, and iced tea."

"I'll have the same." Dalton handed the oversize menu to the waitress.

"I'll bring your drink order right out."

"Does your mother still live here?" Dalton asked as the waitress moved away.

If ever there was a question designed to snap Justine back to reality, it was that one. "Yes. She teaches second grade at a school near the house."

"I'm glad she's here to help you," he said quietly.

Justine couldn't keep the surprise from her face. She blinked.

"Your drinks," the waitress said. She sat them down and left.

"I might not have agreed with her method, but she was trying to help you when we were in high school. My rep was pretty bad," Dalton admitted.

"But you weren't like that," Justine defended him.

"She couldn't have known that," Dalton said. "Although, at the time, my thoughts weren't so forgiving."

"Mine either," Justine admitted.

"Your order." The waitress sat their food on the table, then withdrew. Justine blessed the food, then picked up her fork.

She didn't expect to enjoy the food. Had planned simply to go through the motions. It was easier than arguing. But after one bite, she discovered she was ravenous.

"How's the food?"

"Wonderful," Justine said. "Have you called Brianna yet?"

"On the way here, but she was in session with a client. I left a message with her receptionist."

"Have you made up your mind what you plan to do with your home place?"

Dalton sipped his tea. "Nothing beyond repairing it.

The place holds a lot of happy memories for me and my sisters."

Justine watched the play of muscles in his throat, the large calloused hands that could be so gentle, the flash of strong white teeth in his chocolate-hued face. He was so good looking and much too appealing.

"Hello, Justine."

Justine started and glanced up to see the wives of two of the ministers from the luncheon. Their husbands had been among the first to donate funds. "Hello, Mrs. King, Mrs. Carter."

Their gazes kept sliding to Dalton, who had stood. Justine quickly made the introductions. "Pleased to meet you, ladies. Besides owning the bookstore where I had a signing a couple of weeks ago, Justine is an old schoolmate of mine."

"I've read your book," Mrs. King said. She was in her mid-fifties and attractive. The aqua Lilian Ann suit fit her slim body well. "The church's book club considered reading it, but thought it had too much violence."

"Murder mysteries aren't for everyone," Dalton said easily. "I'm honored it was considered."

"Well, we have to be going," Mrs. Carter said, her gaze narrowed. "We're all praying for Andrew. Please say hello to his mother for us."

Justine was sure the comment also meant she was going to tell Beverly she had seen her dining out with a man while Andrew lay in a coma. "I'll tell her tonight when I see her at the hospital."

Dalton took his seat as the women walked away. He didn't speak until they were a good distance away. "Brianna said you go there in the morning and evening, plus working, and now you're becoming more involved with Andrew's firm. Don't you think you should take it a bit easy?"

"I can't." Her cell phone rang. She glanced sharply at her purse. She had the strangest urge to let it ring or to shut it off. People in the restaurant were shooting annoyed looks her way.

"Justine, are you all right?"

"Yes." She picked up the phone, knowing it wouldn't go to voice mail until after the tenth ring. "Hello."

"Justine, it's Andrew!" his mother cried. "His heart stopped again!"

Her own heart lurched. She began to tremble. "I'm on my way." She came unsteadily to her feet, swayed. Dalton quickly stood and took her arm to steady her.

"What is it?"

For a moment she couldn't get the words out. "He . . . he had another cardiac arrest."

Dalton's long fingers flexed on her bare arm. "I'll take you." Releasing her only long enough to throw enough money on the table to cover their food and a big tip, Dalton ushered her outside to his Jeep.

Her mind was in chaos the entire trip. How much more could his body take and continue to fight back? How much more could she and his mother take?

Justine was grateful Dalton didn't say anything on the way to the hospital or when they rode the elevator to the ICCU floor. Her thoughts were too scattered to carry on a conversation.

As soon as they entered the waiting area, Beverly spotted them. Her eyes narrowed with suspicion and speculation.

For a moment Justine thought how it must look, then decided she didn't care. She wasn't the one who had committed adultery. "How is he?"

"I don't know. I don't think we've met," Beverly said to Dalton, her voice without the least bit of the warmth it usually carried.

"Dalton Ramsey," Dalton greeted. "Justine and I went to school together."

"The author."

"Yes, ma'am. We got here as fast as we could. I didn't think it wise to let Justine drive."

"That was thoughtful of you." Beverly looked at the silent Justine. "You two were together?" There was no mistaking the accusation in her voice.

"We were having an early dinner," Justine told her, becoming more annoyed with Andrew's mother by the minute.

"Andrew needed you here."

Justine's lips tightened. The door behind them opened and Dr. Lane came out. "We got his heart going again."

"Thank God," Beverly breathed.

Justine swayed. Once again, it was Dalton who steadied her.

"Mrs. Crandall, I'd like to speak with you," Dr. Lane said, his thin face as austere as always.

"I'm going, too," Beverly said, stepping up beside Justine.

"I'll wait here," Dalton said.

With one last perturbed glance at Beverly, Dr. Lane reentered the ICCU. Both women had to drag their gazes away from the door to Andrew's room when Dr. Lane began to speak. "He's unstable. We ran another EEG after we got his heart going again and the brain activity is decreas-

ing. His pupils are unresponsive to light, there is no response to pain, and the respirator is breathing for him."

Justine knew he'd just ticked off the criteria to determine if a patient was brain dead. The heart had its own
pacemaker. It could continue to beat even though the
brain was dead as long as there was oxygen flowing to it. If
they disconnected the respirator—

"Have you thought of signing those papers, Mrs.
Crandall?"

"I can't. Not now." Not when she'd been having sexual
thoughts about another man.

The neurosurgeon's mouth flattened into a narrow line.
"All right. I have other patients to see. Good-bye."

"That man doesn't know anything. My baby is going to
be all right." Beverly hugged Justine. "I'm going to scold
Andrew for scaring us."

Justine followed Beverly back outside. Dalton, who had
been leaning against the wall, pushed away and came to
them. "His vital signs are unsteady," she told him.

"Can I get you anything?" Dalton asked, his voice and
face filled with sympathy.

"No. Thank you." What she wanted neither he nor
anyone else could give her. Peace.

"Dr. Lane left before I could ask him if we can still visit
Andrew. I wouldn't want to tax him," Beverly said. "I'm
going back inside and ask him."

"Sorry about your celebratory meal," Justine said as
Beverly went through the door.

"Don't feel guilty that you were at dinner with me,"
Dalton said softly.

Oddly she wasn't. "I won't."

Beverly came back out smiling. "We can go in now. He'll be so glad to see you."

Justine didn't want to go in, but she didn't have a choice.

"I'll be here waiting for you when you get back," Dalton told her.

Beverly sent him a look meant to intimidate. "Thank you, but that won't be necessary."

"You probably forgot. I drove her here," he said pleasantly.

"Thank you." Justine should send him away and call Brianna or take a taxi, but she didn't want to. For the first time in months, she was going to think of what she wanted. "I'd appreciate that."

"I can take Justine ho—"

"Andrew is waiting, Beverly," Justine said, cutting off her mother-in-law. Mentioning her son was the surest way to get her moving.

She brightened immediately. "Of course. Let's go in." Beverly took Justine by the elbow, ensuring that she went as well. Justine glanced over her shoulder at Dalton and took what comfort she could from his steady, patient gaze.

Brianna didn't second-guess herself or often change her mind. With Patrick she had done both.

There was no denying that he was a handsome rascal with a dimpled smile that made her mouth water and her body hum. Justine had been right. She might not be putting up such a hard fight if she hadn't been so wrong about Jackson, and the fact that she had sworn off men.

Blaming it on her heavy work schedule was an excuse.

She never made excuses and prided herself on facing any problem head-on. She was busy, but not *that* busy. So why couldn't she make up her mind about Patrick and make it stick?

She didn't like to think perhaps it was because she feared she couldn't handle him. She snorted at that idiotic notion. Hands in the pockets of her windbreaker, deep in thought, she continued her late afternoon stroll on the walking path around the marina.

"Care for some company?"

Brianna didn't have to glance up to know that Patrick had fallen into step beside her. Even if she hadn't recognized the deep voice that reminded her of aged bourbon, the sudden acceleration of her heart and the slow heat that rolled through her body would have alerted her. "Would it make any difference if I said no?"

"Probably not. How was your day?"

She threw a glance at him just as they passed the restaurant. He was looking at her with those fathomless eyes of his, dark and mysterious, black and full of promise. In any other guy she probably would have thought he was just making conversation. She was slowly learning that Patrick wasn't the type. "Hectic."

"When I want to relax, I take the boat out. How about it?"

The suggestion was appealing and that settled the answer for her. Until she figured our why she reacted so differently to Patrick than to other men she was steering clear of him. "No, thank you."

"I give a great massage."

"I'll just bet." The trouble was, she could already imagine his long, sexy fingers on her bare flesh, stroking, teasing, pleasing her. She hunched deeper into the lightweight jacket. The wind off the water was chilly today. "Don't you have anything better to do than harass me?"

He chuckled. "I've gone from stalking to harassing you. I wonder if a good lawyer would think I had a case for slander?"

She stopped abruptly. "Get lost, Patrick."

His smile did something crazy to her stomach. "I like the way you say my name."

She spun on her heels and started back the way she had come. "It will be the last time."

He easily caught up with her. "I'll leave you alone for tonight, if you'll answer one question."

She stopped abruptly. "A restraining order will do the same thing and last longer."

"Why are you trying so hard not to like me?"

He was too close to the crux of her problem and much too attractive. Turning away, she propped her arms on the wrought-iron rail that circled the marina and looked out into the choppy waters of the harbor. "You give yourself too much credit."

He stopped just behind her. "I wish I had my hand on the guy you're punishing me for."

There was such an underlying menace in his voice that Brianna spun around. She realized her mistake instantly. He was too close.

She could feel the disturbing heat of his body, smell the spicy aftershave he wore. She was trapped between him and the railing. So she did what came naturally. "You have five seconds to get lost."

He didn't move one glorious muscle. If anything, he seemed to edge closer. "Don't judge me by what he did."

"Three seconds."

"Answer my question."

She'd met few men who were as stubborn as she was, and even fewer who stood their ground when she challenged them. Patrick was a law unto himself. Dangerous at any time, but more so to her now. "If you won't leave, I will. Perhaps I'll see a security or police patrol car on the way."

Stepping around him, she started to the condo, very much aware that Patrick was watching her. She was surprised how much she wanted to look back. She wondered what his next move would be.

The shrill ring of the cell phone in her pocket interrupted her thoughts. She paused and hooked on her ear piece. "Hello."

"Brianna, this is Dalton. Andrew is fine now, but he arrested earlier. I'm at the hospital with Justine."

Before Dalton finished, she was running. "I'm on my way."

"Thank you. Justine and his mother haven't been out since they went in thirty minutes ago."

Brianna reached for the door, but a big hand reached it first. *Patrick.*

"Is your father all right?"

The concern and worry were evident in his deep voice. "Justine's husband had another cardiac arrest."

He muttered an expletive and took her arm with one hand while pulling out his car keys with the other. "If you don't need to go back up, I can drive you."

Her car keys and purse were upstairs. She didn't want to wait that long. "Thank you." Together they raced to the elevator to get to the underground parking garage.

Fifteen

Dalton didn't like feeling helpless, but he'd learned the hard way that you couldn't control every aspect of your life and that when those times came all you could do was pray and hold on. Seeing Brianna hurrying toward him with the man from the book signing, Dalton met them halfway.

"How is she?"

Dalton had known Brianna's first thought would be of Justine. Just as his had been. "I'm not sure. She still hasn't come out."

Brianna wrapped her arms around herself, her gaze glued to the doors leading into ICCU. "I wish there was something I could do."

"You're here," Dalton said.

"He's right," the man with her agreed.

Brianna didn't say a word, just wrapped her arms tighter around herself. The wide-shouldered man standing by her side curved one long arm around her shoulders and extended his hand. "Patrick Dunlap."

"Dalton Ramsey, but I guess you already knew that."

"Do you know what happened?" Brianna asked.

Dalton shook his head and explained that they were having dinner when Justine received the phone call. "They got his heart going, but the doctor still seemed concerned. He talked with Justine and his mother in private."

"He wants—" Brianna began, then clamped her lips shut.

Dalton's gaze narrowed. "What? What does he want?"

Brianna glanced away. "Nothing. I wonder if I can just peek in? Sometimes they let more than two people in at a time." Her arms came to her sides. "I can't stand this waiting. They can put me out, but at least Justine would know I'm here."

Dalton's hard stare followed Brianna into ICCU. She was hiding something.

"Whatever she was about to say, you won't get it out of her," Patrick said, staring after her as well. "If she hadn't been so concerned about Justine you wouldn't have gotten that much."

Dalton's attention snapped back to Patrick. His assessment of Brianna was dead on. "I thought you two just met."

Patrick slid his long-fingered hands into the pockets of his jeans. "We did, but it didn't take long for me to realize that Brianna is a woman of integrity and she could give lessons in stubbornness to a Missouri mule."

"She's giving you a hard time, huh?" Dalton asked. The corner of his mouth tilted upward.

"That's putting it mildly. She was doing a good job of brushing me off when she received your phone call." Patrick's hands came out of his pockets. "I hope you don't mind my being here. I didn't want her driving herself."

"No. Thank you. She and Brianna are closer than sisters." Dalton faced the double doors. "Whatever it takes for Justine to get through this, I'm all for it."

Justine glanced up as the door to Andrew's room eased open. Brianna, her brows drawn in worry, hesitated at the door. The lump in Justine's throat thickened. Brianna crossed to her and hugged her. "I'm here."

"Andrew needs peace and quiet," Beverly said, irritation in her voice.

Both women straightened and turned. Justine saw the angry glint in Brianna's eyes and shook her head.

Dalton had to have called her. Her hair was in a ponytail, her face free of makeup. Brianna wasn't fussy, but she'd never venture far from her house without looking her best. "Thank you for coming, but you can go home."

"Is he all right?" Brianna whispered.

"His vitals signs are stable . . . for now, at least," Justine told her.

"Justine," Beverly called impatiently.

"Please go home, and tell Dalton to please do the same." Justine steered Brianna back to the door. "Thanks for coming."

Brianna hesitated. "Do you want me to call your mother?"

"No, she'd just worry. Good night."

"Good night." Brianna closed the door, then stopped by the nurse's station to thank them for letting her visit. She stepped into the waiting area, and immediately Patrick and Dalton rushed to her.

"She's tired, but determined. Andrew is stable, but I got

the impression that that might change." She ran a shaky hand over her hair. "Dalton, she said for you to go home."

"I'm staying." Dalton folded his arms over his chest.

"I thought that might be your answer." Brianna touched his steady shoulder. "She needs us more than you could ever imagine."

Dalton's eyes narrowed, but she had moved on to Patrick. "We can go."

"You're sure? I don't mind staying if Justine needs you."

She couldn't imagine Jackson being willing to wait. In fact, he'd always come when visiting hours were almost over when her father was in the hospital. "If I thought it would help for me to stay, you couldn't drag me away with a team of horses."

Patrick briefly curved his hand around her neck. "You're some woman, but then I always knew that."

Shaken by the brief contact, a contact that she found much too pleasing, she hastily turned to Dalton. "I'm glad you're back. Good night."

"Me too. Night."

"I'll see that she gets home safely, Dalton." Patrick cupped Brianna's elbow.

"Thanks." Dalton sat down on the lumpy couch, his thoughts troubled. He'd been right. There was more to the haunted look Justine wore than just Andrew's accident. But what? It was going to be a long night, but he wasn't leaving unless it was with Justine.

"Home or do you need to drop by your parents' house?"

Brianna stopped staring out the window and finally

looked at Patrick, something she had refused to do since she had gotten into his truck. He continued to amaze her. How had he known that she wanted to see her parents, especially her father.

Despite the heavy traffic, he threw her a quick glance. "It was easy to see how close you are to your parents that day in the elevator. Seeing Justine's husband had to remind you how blessed you were to still have your father. Wanting to see him to reassure yourself he is all right is perfectly understandable."

"How would you know that?"

If she hadn't been watching him, she might not have seen his jaw clench. "I know."

Brianna recalled his early retirement and wondered again about the circumstances. The hospital had shaken him up as well, yet he was willing to help her. He was a good man. She'd just met him at the wrong time.

She gave him her parents' address. "Do you know where that is?"

"Yes. Brooke's business partner, Claire, and her husband divide their time between his grandmother's home on East Bay and a home on Sullivan Island."

"You're very close to your niece," she said.

"To know Brooke is to love her, as the saying goes." He turned onto King Street. "Perhaps you'll get to meet her or at least visit Bliss and try some of their products."

The way Patrick said the last word made Brianna think of the "Better Than Sex" claim. Despite herself, her body heated. There wasn't a shred of doubt in her mind that Patrick would rise to the occasion and prove the claim false. She groaned at her choice of word.

"You all right?"

Instead of answering his question she said, "It's the third house on the right."

Patrick pulled into the driveway of a three-story yellow-brick mansion surrounded by black wrought-iron grill-work. Directly in front of the house was the ocean. "It's beautiful. No wonder you like the water so much."

"Thanks." Brianna got out of the door he held open and looked across the concrete barrier. A cruise ship was coming into the port located a few blocks away. "For a long time I didn't think I'd ever want to live anyplace else."

"Why did you leave?"

"I didn't want to be daddy's little girl. I wanted to make my own way." She answered without thinking about it or guarding her words, something she never did with anyone other than her parents or Justine.

He closed the door. "I don't have to ask if you succeeded."

She stared up at him. People usually couldn't read her. With Patrick she was an open book, which didn't bode well for her.

At her silence he continued. "You don't back down, and you can't be manipulated. You're your own woman. It takes time for a person to be that way and be comfortable with themselves."

"Then why can't I get rid of you?" she asked without heat.

Patrick tilted his head to one side. "You sure you want the answer?"

"No, I just talk to hear myself talk." She braced her hands on her hips.

He leaned so close she could see her own reflection in his mesmerizing eyes. "Because deep down, you really don't want to."

Shock rendered her speechless. How could he have figured it out when she was just beginning to?

"Brianna?"

She whirled to see her parents coming down the street, which was lined with palmetto trees. As usual, they walked hand in hand as if they were newlyweds instead of about to celebrate their forty-second anniversary in a month. They'd almost given up hope of having children when her mother had become pregnant with her. There weren't better parents in the world.

She quickly closed the distance between them and threw one arm around each. It was easier with her mother, who matched her in height. Her father was several inches taller. Their arms closed securely around her.

"What's the matter?"

"Are you all right?"

"It's Andrew." She stepped back. "He's all right now, but he arrested again."

"Do you want us to go to the hospital with you?" her mother asked, smoothing stray ringlets of hair behind her daughter's ear.

"We just left," Brianna answered.

Finally their gaze went beyond her to the man standing quietly on the sidewalk in front of their house. Brianna hadn't thought through what having Patrick meet her parents would infer. "I was out walking when I got the call. Patrick took me."

Patrick stepped forward and offered his hand. "Patrick Dunlap. We met when Brianna was moving in."

"I remember. Charles Ireland, and this beautiful woman is my wife, Susan."

"Brianna takes after her," Patrick said.

Brianna made a strangling sound. Her father laughed. "Thanks for taking her."

Before answering, Patrick glanced at Brianna with her arm still around her mother's waist and blood in her eyes. "I didn't want her driving alone."

"Rightly so. Would you like to come inside for coffee? I just baked a lemon cake," her mother said.

"It's with artificial and low-fat everything, but it still tastes good," her father commented. "Maybe if you're around you'll distract them while I have a cup of real coffee. They watch what I eat like a hawk."

"Because we love you," Mrs. Ireland said. "Please join us."

"If Brianna doesn't mind?"

She arched a delicate brow. "Thank you for taking me to the hospital, but don't get any bright ideas."

Patrick laughed. "I'm trying to wear her down and get her to go out with me. I wouldn't want her to think I'm taking unfair advantage."

Brianna wrinkled her nose. She and her parents had always talked openly about dating. "Mama invited you. But don't think this will make me change my mind about you."

Patrick slid his hands into the pockets of his jeans. "Never thought it would."

Her mother's mouth twitched. "Now that that's settled, we can go inside."

Mr. Ireland opened the gate. "Do you play golf?"

"Not very well, but I have a thirty-foot boat."

"You do? I had to sell my boat when my wife pointed

out I hadn't been on it in a year." Unlocking the leaded glass front door, he stepped aside. "That was over five years ago."

"I'll take you out anytime you want." Patrick followed them inside and down the knotty pine hallway. "The other day, I caught a three-pound sea bass."

"There's nothing like the taste of fresh fish. That I can have. Baked or broiled, of course." Mr. Ireland entered the kitchen, which had high ceilings and a breakfast nook that looked out over a fish pond. Mrs. Ireland and Brianna busied themselves preparing a tray for the coffee and cake.

"I'll bring you some of my next catch," Patrick said. "Your home is spectacular."

"Thank you. It's been in the family for over seventy years."

Mrs. Ireland picked up the tray from the counter and turned. Three pairs of hands reached for the heavy silver tray. Patrick's were fastest. "Where should I set this?"

"In the library. I'll show you," Mr. Ireland said, walking from the room with Patrick following.

"You know I never interfere, but why won't you go out with him?" her mother asked when they were alone.

"Because I've sworn off men for the time being," Brianna said. Which was the truth. Dating a man as perceptive and as titillating as Patrick could cause a woman a lot of grief.

"Pity," her mother said as they left the kitchen to join the men. "I like his honesty. Your father likes him, too."

Brianna could tell. Her parents didn't invite just any-one into their home. Her father was downright picky about his golfing buddy. Patrick might have charmed her parents, but she still wasn't going out with him.

An hour later Brianna and Patrick stepped into the elevator at their condo. "I'll say good night now."

"I promised your parents that I'd see you safely to your door."

Brianna said nothing. Her parents had been very specific. If she didn't know better, she'd think they were trying to matchmake. "They liked you."

"Most people do."

If he was asking in a roundabout way why she didn't, she wasn't answering. The elevator door opened and she stepped off. She didn't stop until she stood in front of her unit. Unlocking the door, she turned. "Thank you for—"

Her startled gasp was cut short as he pulled her into his arms, his lips brushing across hers. She stiffened, then the tip of his tongue stroked her lips. Hunger splintered through her. His tongue slid into her mouth.

Pleasure rushed through her, banishing the thought of slugging him. With a helpless whimper, she pressed against his hard length. Heat raced through her veins. Her hands slid up his muscular chest and circled his neck, bringing him closer. She couldn't get enough of his hot mouth. She didn't want the kiss to end.

When he finally lifted his head, they were both breathing hard. Releasing her, he stepped back. She couldn't tell if it was because he feared she might retaliate or to keep from grabbing her again. "I've wanted to do that since I first saw you."

She should knee him where it would hurt the most, or at least give him a good tongue-lashing. She would do both—just as soon as her brain started functioning again.

"Justine is lucky to have a friend like you. I hope one day you'll consider me a friend as well." Leaning over, he placed a tender kiss on her forehead. "If you want to stop by for breakfast around eight in the morning and sample my renowned blueberry pancakes, the door will be open. Night, beautiful." Turning, he walked away.

Still a bit dazed, Brianna finally went inside and closed the door behind her. In her bedroom she happened to glance at the tri-fold mirror over the dresser as she passed. She stopped dead in her tracks. Her eyes were glazed with passion and unquenched need, her lips pouty and moist.

Squeezing her eyes shut, she turned away. Patrick was more of a threat than she'd imagined. His kiss had left her reeling and in danger of losing herself to a man for the first time. Somehow she had known all along that Patrick would test her on every level and so she had instinctively tried to steer clear of him. He hadn't let her. He was a man who went after what he wanted. He wanted her and he planned to have her.

The realization was scary, an emotion she'd never experienced regarding a man. But her body grew hot, her breast heavy at the thought of them making love.

If he hadn't pulled away, she wasn't sure she would have had the presence of mind to do so. The smart way to handle this was to stick to her original plan and stay away from him.

But could she?

Shortly after midnight the ICCU charge nurse asked Justine and Beverly to leave. Her mother-in-law's eyelids were drooping. The coffee Justine had gotten for her from the nurse's station to keep her awake hadn't helped. The true gauge of how worn out Beverly was came when she didn't protest too long. Justine wanted to weep with relief. The muscles of her legs cramped from standing so long. Beverly had stood by Andrew's bedside, so Justine had as well.

"Please call if there is any change," Beverly told the charge nurse, who followed them to the entrance to ICCU. "We'll be back first thing, won't we, Justine?"

"Yes."

"You know I will, but now his vitals are stable," Nurse Hopkins said. She was a full-figured woman with a warm smile and a soothing manner. "Get some rest."

Justine thought she saw pity in the other woman's eyes. "Thank you." Pushing open the door, she faltered on seeing Dalton, his dark head bowed, his attention on the Blackberry in his hand.

As if he knew she were there, he lifted his head. For a long moment their gazes clung. Standing, he made a couple of notations in the handheld, then put it in the inside pocket of his jacket. In four long strides, he stood in front of her. "He must be resting."

"He is, but the charge nurse wouldn't let us stay," Beverly told him, glancing back at the closed door.

"When my mother was in ICCU, it was difficult for us to leave, but doing so gave us the strength to come back the next day and be with her," he told Beverly.

Justine had gone to his parents' funeral, but didn't think Dalton had seen her. She'd left as soon as the services were over. "I'm sorry to hear of your mother's death. She was a wonderful woman."

"They're together now. I never thanked you for coming," he said.

Justine's brow lifted in surprise. The church had been packed. How had he seen her with all the people there?

"Andrew will come back to us. He'll live," Beverly said, her voice unsteady.

Justine put her arm around Andrew's mother and started toward the elevator. She couldn't imagine the feeling of helplessness or the pain of losing a child. "You need to go home and get some rest."

"I'll drive both of you." Dalton fished his keys from his pocket.

"My car is here," Beverly said.

"Not a problem." Dalton punched the call button of the elevator. "I'll be happy to pick you up in the morning and bring you back."

"Thank you. I am rather tired," Beverly admitted. "What about your car, Justine? If you were dining out, your car is still at the shopping center."

"I'd forgotten." She raked her fingers through her hair. "Dalton, if you could drop me off I'd appreciate it."

"No problem. Let me take Mrs. Crandall home, then I'll take you to your bookstore and follow you home. You're dead on your feet." Dalton took Andrew's mother's arm, then Justine's, and stepped on the elevator. "You both must be. Andrew is a lucky man to have you two."

Justine flinched and hoped he didn't notice.

"We're the lucky ones. Andrew is the best there is. Isn't he, Justine?"

"Yes." She was discovering that lies became easy after a while. They certainly had for Andrew.

Justine pulled into the garage, then went to the front door and opened it. Dalton was almost to the door. The neighborhood was dark except for a few front porch security lights. She didn't think she'd ever felt as drained.

"Go to bed," he ordered.

"I wi—" That was as far as she got. Tears clogged her throat. She didn't want Andrew to die, but neither did she want to keep up the charade.

"Honey, don't." Coming inside, Dalton closed the door behind him and took Justine in his arms. "He'll be all right. Please don't cry. Please."

The tears fell faster. Great sobs erupted from her. "Nothing will ever be right again."

"Shhh. Please." He kissed her forehead, her cheek, her lips. Instead of moving on as he intended, his lips clung. Heat and need built. With a muttered curse, Dalton gathered Justine in his arms, his hungry mouth devouring hers, giving her the reassurance she needed.

With a moan of pure pleasure she went into his arms, her body pressed against his muscled warmth, the hard length of him. She didn't want to think. She wanted to feed off this emotion where she wasn't hurt, where she wasn't betrayed, where she was wanted, desired.

Dalton suddenly realized what he was doing. With all his willpower, he broke away. Transfixed, he stared down at her moist trembling lips. There was dazed confusion in her eyes. Had she been kissing him or Andrew? Either way he felt lower than a snake's belly. "I'm sorry; you'll never know how sorry."

Justine realized what she had been doing, her body plastered to Dalton while her husband lay in a coma and fought for his life. Shame hit her like a balled fist. "Please leave."

"Jus—"

"Please."

His hands came to his sides. "There's no excuse for what I did, but I want you to know that it wasn't easy for me to pull away. This was my fault, not yours. Good night."

Justine stared at the closed door, then went to her room and lay down on the bed. She could still feel the softness of Dalton's beard, the heat of his lips, the hunger. She curled tighter. She was as wrong as Andrew had been. If Dalton hadn't stopped, she wouldn't have. Worse, she wanted to kiss him again.

Trembling fingers covered her face. "What am I going to do?"

The next morning Dalton picked Beverly up from her home, an elegant house that reminded him of the many antebellum mansions in Atlanta. He'd read up on Andrew after his accident. Brianna's parents had a mansion as well, but it had been in the family for a number of years. The two-story house with its four stately Doric columns seemed too much space for the small, almost reserved woman sitting beside him.

"Your home is beautiful."

"Thank you. Andrew purchased it for me last year. It has twenty rooms."

His parents had been happy raising three children in six. "You must be proud of him."

She smiled. "I am. He was building something few men in their lives ever accomplish. Once he's out of the hospital, he'll continue."

Dalton did a double take. He believed in prayer and positive thinking as much as the next person but, after last night, the chances of Andrew's recovery weren't good.

The disbelief must have shown on his face because Mrs. Crandall said, "You are just like the rest that don't believe. Except Justine, of course."

"The important thing is that you believe."

Ten minutes later Dalton pulled into the underground parking garage. They rode the elevator to the sixth floor in silence. He stepped off, but he didn't follow her down the hallway. Linen and breakfast carts lined the hallway.

Mrs. Crandall stopped and faced him. "You aren't coming in to say hello to Justine?"

He was positive the question wasn't an idle one. "No."

A pleased smile spread across her face. "Justine and Andrew were the perfect loving couple. Nothing could separate them. Andrew will recover and they'll make me a grandmother."

She was warning him off. "Justine deserves every happiness."

"She does, and she'll have it with Andrew."

"I want only the best for Justine."

"On that we both agree. Good-bye."

Dalton watched her walk off. Had she sensed the undercurrents between him and Justine or was she just being protective? His cop instincts were kicking in again. Something more was going on than met the eye. Andrew's mother might not know it, but she'd made him even more determined to find out what it was.

Sixteen

Brianna stood in front of Patrick's door the next morning, her hand clenched around the handle of her attaché case, her lips pressed together in a thin line. "It's just breakfast."

She closed her eyes. Not only did he have her talking to herself, she was lying to herself as well. How could a man turn her to mush after she'd just gotten out of a relationship? She wasn't the flighty type. She certainly didn't sleep around.

She could count the men she'd been intimate with on one hand and have fingers to spare. Intimacy wasn't something she took lightly. The debacle with Jackson still pissed her off.

Yet, here she stood, knowing that sooner or later she'd be horizontal with Patrick. After that kiss last night he knew it, too. Somehow that galled her the most. That he somehow had known all along that he'd break through her resistance. She could really dislike him for that.

She gave the doorbell a sharp punch. If she stayed angry she might get through this.

The door swung open. Patrick wore a white T-shirt that delineated the hard muscles of his impressive chest, the awe-inspiring biceps, the flat stomach, and soft, faded jeans that defined his long, muscular legs. Damn him again.

"Morning. Great timing. The first batch of pancakes is ready."

She just stood there.

"I won't bite."

Somehow that excited her. "I don't like this."

The teasing smile left his face. He brushed his hand gently across her cheek. "I know. Just trust your instincts."

"If I did, I wouldn't be here."

He stared at her. "Are you sure that's your instincts talking and not something else?"

Her gaze narrowed. "You calling me a liar?"

"Nope. I like my body in one piece. I better go rescue the pancakes."

Brianna came inside and closed the door. It was that or else stand in the entryway like an idiot, and she had acted like that enough around Patrick. Her eyes somehow zeroed in on his Grade-A butt.

"Coming?" he said over one broad shoulder.

Close to it, she thought. Muttering under her breath, she followed him into the kitchen. On the table was a cut flower arrangement in a white wicker basket that hadn't been there the last time. Otherwise, things were the same. "Put your briefcase in one of those chairs and take a seat. I don't want to get on Matilda's bad side if you're late."

"That makes two of us."

Patrick placed a four-inch stack of pancakes in front of her with Canadian bacon, an omelet, cheese grits, and freshly squeezed orange juice. She'd seen the peels on the counter.

The coffee was in a mug, not a cup. He took his seat and blessed the food. "What's on the agenda for today?"

She picked up a fork. She had to eat and she was hungry. Logical. "Briefs and appointments until late afternoon."

"You want to unwind with a quick sail around the marina?"

"Don't you ever give up?"

"If it was something that mattered to you, would you?"

"No." She tasted the pancakes. Light and delicious. "What are your plans?"

"Besides strategizing how to get a date with you?"

She lifted a brow, and he smiled. "Taking Mark and Amy to the zoo."

Her shoulders snapped back. "You have children!"

"I've never been married."

She simply stared.

"Right, but I hope I'm more responsible. Mark and Amy are Brooke's children. Stepchildren actually, but none of us think of them that way. Amy is a riot and Mark is the smartest nine-year-old you'll ever meet."

She heard the pride in his voice. All that going for him, and he liked children as well. She was sinking deeper and deeper over her head.

Justine was purposefully thirty minutes late going to the hospital. Beverly might be upset, but she could take that. It occurred to her that she had been doing just that, "taking it" a lot these days. What she didn't want to do was face Dalton. Despite what he'd said, the kiss was as much her fault as it had been his. More so—knowing how vulnerable she was, she should have never let him hug her.

She didn't want to use the word "needy," but it also came to mind. Not very good for a woman who, although not very assertive, hadn't let people step on her—unless she counted her mother. And she didn't plan to.

Justine entered the room to see Beverly in her usual position, standing over Andrew's bed, doing her usual thing, talking to him. She was five feet to Justine's five-six. Perhaps that was why she didn't have back problems.

"She's here, Andrew. I told you she might be a few minutes late."

Justine frowned. "How did you know?"

She smiled, but it lacked warmth. "I know a lot of things, don't I, Andrew?"

Justine thought of one thing she didn't know, and worried about the rest of what she did.

Justine woke up three days after Andrew's last cardiac arrest and didn't want to get out of bed. She was wise enough to know it was the first sign of depression. Facing Beverly and her nonstop talk *of* Andrew and *to* Andrew was taking its toll on her. It annoyed the hell out of Dr. Lane.

He and Beverly butted heads on every issue. More than once he had come in the room, seen her, and paused as if he seriously considered leaving. Beverly acted as if she didn't notice. They were at war over Andrew. Justine wasn't going to get into it or let them drag her into it.

She still didn't know what decision to make. She couldn't even decide whether to get up or not. How could she decide to sign the papers to disconnect life support?

The doorbell rang and she ignored it, just as she planned to ignore the ringing phone. At least she planned to until her purse started playing "Hungry Like the Wolf."

Throwing back the covers, she crawled to the foot of the bed and emptied the hobo purse out on the bench where she'd left it last night. "Brianna."

"We have a movie date."

Justine plopped back on the bed, running her hand through her tangled curls.

"No buts and no excuses. Come and let me in. While you're showering I'll pick you out something to wear."

"You wouldn't take a rain check, would you?"

"Would you take one from me?"

Justine blew out a breath. Through good times and bad they were always there for each other. "No."

"Exactly. Now hurry up. I'm starved." The phone went dead.

That was one way to win an argument. Justine placed the cell phone on the nightstand and went to open the door.

Breakfast was at a family restaurant chain near the edge of town. Blessedly, no one approached Justine. Afterward, when Brianna asked where to, Justine suggested a drive to Summerville, a quaint nearby city known for its antiques, small-town charm, and hospitality. There would be less chance of her being recognized.

"Let's go. I need to put the car on the road since it's only been in the city." Brianna lowered the top of the convertible and headed for the freeway.

"You still drive fast," Justine commented later as she glanced at the speedometer.

"But competently." Brianna winked, checked traffic, and accelerated to pass another car.

"You're also impatient," Justine noted as the speedometer climbed another five miles per hour until they were going seventy. "Patrick seems just the opposite."

Brianna made a face and said nothing.

Justine straightened. "What was that look for?"

"We kissed."

"And?"

"If he hadn't stopped, I'm not sure I would have." Brianna passed another car. "Men are supposed to be off my list. What is wrong with me? Why can't I tell him to get lost and make it stick?"

"Probably because you really don't want to," Justine said quietly.

"Same thing he said," Brianna told her, her annoyance obvious.

"At least the both of you are single. Dalton and I can't say that." Justine briefly tucked her head when Brianna's gaze whipped to her.

"What happened when he took you home?"

Justine clasped her hands in her lap. "Let's just say Dalton's techniques in kissing have greatly improved since high school. I was clinging to him like cellophane. He called a halt to things and apologized."

"But knowing you, you feel guilty," Brianna correctly guessed.

"My husband is fighting for his life."

"That same husband cheated on you and brought this on himself." Brianna took the highway to Summerville and slowed to the posted speed limit. "Don't beat yourself up because you accepted a little comfort and want to move on."

Justine briefly tucked her bottom lip between her teeth. "I want that more than anything. I'd settle for one day of peace."

"And I aim to help you find both. Starting now."

Less than five minutes later Brianna had parked, put up the convertible top, and together they strolled the downtown streets, which offered a wide variety of retail stores that catered to everyone's budget.

"First stop," Brianna said, looking in the window of an upscale clothing boutique. "You'd look sensational in that apricot pantsuit."

"I—"

"I'm not hearing an argument." Grasping Justine's arm, Brianna literally dragged her into the spacious store. "You're getting a new outfit and that's that."

Thirty minutes later, they both came out with clothes. Of course, they had to shop for shoes for Justine's three-piece apricot-colored pantsuit and Brianna's coral dress with a ballet collar. They hit pay dirt a couple of stores farther down.

"I'd forgotten how much fun this can be," Justine said as they stored their packages in the trunk of Brianna's Benz.

"There's nothing like shopping to give a woman a second wind." Brianna closed the trunk. "Or make her hungry. How about we grab a waffle ice cream cone with fixings?"

"I want mine with strawberries and pecans." Justine turned and saw a man in a wheelchair with a portable oxygen unit. Her smile froze.

"Don't you dare start feeling guilty about taking some time for yourself," Brianna ordered.

"I won't, but I do need to call." Justine reached in her purse for her cell phone.

Brianna folded her arms and tapped her lavender and yellow slingback sandals. The shoes perfectly matched her shoulder purse, scooped neck silk top, and floral print jeans. "If I knew you wouldn't just worry anyway, I'd take it from you."

Justine held up her finger as Beverly answered. "Good morning, Beverly. How's Andrew?"

"Improving by the hour," was Beverly's happy reply.

Justine doubted that statement, but decided not to contradict her mother-in-law. No amount of talking would change her mind. "I just wanted you to know that I'm with Brianna. We're running errands." She moistened her lips. "I might not make it back today."

Brianna gave Justine a thumb's-up sign.

There was a long pause, then Beverly said, "Perhaps you need this time away. Andrew and I will be fine."

Surprised and relieved, Justine repeated Brianna's sign. The other woman pumped her fist. "I'll see you tomorrow. Good-bye."

"Yes!" Brianna said. "Now for that ice cream."

After they gorged themselves on ice cream, they decided to take in a movie, a legal spoof that was light enough to make them both laugh. It was after six when Brianna pulled up in front of Justine's house behind a floral delivery van.

"More flowers for Andrew," Justine reasoned and got out.

"I sure hope you're Mrs. Crandall," the delivery man said, nearing the car with a huge arrangement of cut flowers.

"I am."

"Great. I've been by here twice, but I thought I'd try one more time." He handed the arrangement to Brianna, who reached for it. "The customer specifically asked that the delivery be made today."

Justine signed and tipped the man. "Thank you."

"Enjoy." He bounded back to the van and drove off.

"He still gets flowers?"

Opening the door, Justine looked over her shoulder at Brianna. "Yes. I spoke to his mother about the waste, but she said people wanted to do something, and once Andrew wakes up he'll know how much people admired him."

"Talk about a snow job." Brianna entered and went into the great room to set the flowers on the round glass coffee table. "If he doesn't come through this, she is going to need grief counseling big time."

Justine sighed and picked up the envelope. "I know and I worry about her, but there's nothing I can do. She—" Justine gasped.

"What?" Brianna asked, rushing over.

Silently Justine handed her the card with one word written on it. *Sorry.* There was no signature.

"Dalton," Brianna said, handing her back the card. "So, what do you plan to do?"

With the card clutched in her hand, Justine took a seat

in front of the lush arrangement and stared. "He gets to me. I'm not sure if it's because we were sweethearts in high school or because I'm attracted to the new Dalton as much as I was to the old Dalton."

"A good kisser always makes it more difficult." Brianna sat beside her. "Throw in sensitive, handsome, and a great body, and you're in real trouble."

"Dalton and Patrick have certainly made us rethink our plans."

Brianna leaned forward to sniff a blood red rose. "Speak for yourself. I'm still resisting."

"Are you happy about it?"

Brianna scrunched up her face. "No."

"Neither am I, and I want to be happy again." She looked at Brianna. "Is he staying at the same hotel?"

"You're going over there?" Brianna asked.

"Calling." Justine rose to her feet and went to the kitchen to look under the cabinet for the phone directory. Brianna was a step behind her. "The least I can do is thank him for the flowers."

Less than two minutes later she hung up the phone, disappointed. "He wasn't there."

"There's one place he might be."

"Where?"

"His family place."

Dalton positioned another pine board in place to repair the rotten porch at his family place. The six-room frame house sat in the middle of two acres surrounded by oak and pine trees. He'd decided this was top priority since he'd almost fallen through it that morning. It would have served him right if he had. His mind should be on repairing the house and not on another man's wife.

Hearing the motor of a powerful engine, he glanced over his shoulder. He wasn't expecting anyone. His grip on the hammer tightened when he saw the passenger in Brianna's Mercedes. *Justine.* No matter how he'd tried, he couldn't shake her from his thoughts. He hoped her visit meant he was forgiven, and not that she was there to ask him to stay out of her life. He wasn't sure he could.

Laying the hammer by his bag of nails, he straightened and went to meet them. Brianna stopped behind his Jeep, which was parked beneath the heavy branches of a fifty-year-old oak tree. "Hello, Justine, Brianna."

"Hi," they greeted in unison. Brianna's was as warm as always. It was Justine who had his body tense and whom he kept his gaze on. She met his hopeful gaze, and he mentally gave a sigh of relief. There was no recrimination in her eyes. He was forgiven.

Opening the passenger door, he stepped back. He didn't plan on making the same mistake of getting too close. The consequences were too great.

She stood. "Thank you. The flowers you sent were beautiful."

So are you, he thought. I wish I knew how to make you happy. "I'm glad you like them." A woman didn't usually drive twenty miles with her life in turmoil to thank a man for flowers unless there was more going on. His family had lived just inside the city limits. "You want to get out and see what I've done to the place? Perhaps give me some ideas?"

Her smile was tentative, but it was there. "I'd like that."

As soon as he closed the door Brianna started the car. "I've got an errand to run. I'll be back in an hour."

This time he did see panic on Justine's face. "You're not staying?"

"Wish I could," Brianna said, and put the car in reverse.

Dalton wanted this time with Justine, but only if *she* wanted it. "Brianna, wait." The car immediately stopped. He faced Justine. "We can do this another time."

She stared at him a long time, then shook her head. "No, it's all right." Turning, she waved to Brianna. "Go do your errand."

"I'll bring her back," Dalton said.

"Make sure you feed her," Brianna ordered.

"I will," Dalton called.

Her hands wrapped around her waist, Justine watched Brianna turn her car around and drive off.

The last thing Dalton wanted was to lay another problem on Justine's already overloaded shoulders. "You're safe but, if you're uneasy, I'll take you back now."

"No, I don't want to go back."

There was such desperation in her voice he reached out to touch her, just her arm, and then only briefly. "I started on the kitchen first. Come on, I'll show you."

"Lead the way."

"Careful on the porch. A couple of the boards need replacing." Side by side, they walked up the driveway, which until four days ago had been full of weeds, and entered the wood frame house. "This is the living room, which I plan to turn into a great room. The dated wallpaper comes down. I'm toying with the idea of taking out the narrow windows on either side of the door and putting in larger ones. The ceilings in every room are ten feet high so I'll probably install ceiling fans all over. What do you think?"

"It's a good idea, but be sure the hardware on the fans

matches whatever is in the room." Her arms came to her side, her fingers fidgeting with the leather strap of her purse. "Windows would bring more light into the room and a mirror across from the sitting area would make it appear bigger. What colors do you plan to use?"

Dalton rubbed the back of his neck. "I hadn't thought that far."

"When you do, get the biggest sample possible." She looked around the dim room. "Some colors look fine until you get them in the room or add upholstered furniture that introduces more color and causes the hues to change. When Andr—" she stopped abruptly and her face became shadowed.

Dalton's gut knotted. She looked as if someone had sucker-punched her. "Maybe this wasn't such a good idea. I'll get my keys."

"I don't want to go." The words were whispered, but he heard them and stopped. "You were going to show me the kitchen."

Before he thought better of it, his hands reached out to circle her forearms. Her eyes were wide. He felt her tremble. "You don't have to be brave with me. Friends. Remember?"

"That's why I'm staying. I've run enough." She stepped out of his hold.

Dalton didn't know what to make of her statement, but instinctively knew now was not the time to push. He took her to the only finished room in the house, and that was because of a minor miracle.

Gone were the copper-tone appliances in the small kitchen, the cracked linoleum flooring, and pressed wood cabinets painted brown. Instead, pristine white appliances and cabinets gleamed. Five-inch mahogany molding was around the top of the walls, giving the kitchen a casual yet elegant look.

The counter was sand-colored limestone. Track lighting marched down the center of the ceiling and a white ceiling fan with a copper light fixture hung over a butcher block table. Four cane-back chairs sat around it.

"It's wonderful." She turned in a full circle. Beneath her feet was buff-colored tile. "How did you do this so fast?"

"Luck. I was browsing in the store and overheard the salesman talking about a customer who had backed out on a kitchen remodeling job. I introduced myself, handed him my measurements, and asked if we could work a deal with some of the orders." Dalton ran his hand across the shimmering backsplash, which was made of small iridescent tile. "We ended up helping each other out since I wanted this fast and he had merchandise he couldn't use."

"You don't need my help," she said, and he thought he heard regret.

"Don't you believe it." He leaned against the counter. "This was already picked out. All I did was hand the man my credit card. My sisters helped me with my house in Buckhead, but both work and can't take off to drive down here. You are needed."

"You're sure?"

"You saw the living room. I'd like to move out of the hotel next week, so the bathroom is the next big project. If I can decide what to do, the same firm can start next week." He pressed his point. "I'd like it to be a house Mama and Daddy would be proud of. This place meant a lot to them and to me and my sisters."

"Roots are important." She opened her purse and took out a pen and paper. "I'll help in any way I can."

"Thank you."

"Keep that thought when I ask you to make decisions on paint, wallpaper, and a dozen other things."

"I will." He went into the small bathroom, then the bedroom. "This was my parents' room. I rented a bed and purchased some bedding until I can decide what to do." Before she could get nervous again, he said, "Let's go back to the kitchen. Would you like something to drink?"

"Yes."

Waving her to a seat, he pulled a couple of Pepsis from the refrigerator, grabbed a couple of paper towels, and took a seat in front of her. She didn't reach for the drink. "I went by your house the first Thanksgiving I came home from college."

That brought her head up. "You did?"

"Your mother told me if I came back she'd send you to live with your grandmother permanently." He reached over and opened her drink, then his. "I'd spoken to Brianna a couple of times and knew that although you liked your grandmother, you hadn't liked it in Mississippi."

Her hands circled the can. "Brianna only said you called once."

"I asked her not to tell you about the rest." He took a long swallow.

"Why?" she questioned, her brows furrowed.

"You weren't the type to go against your mother, and that's what it would have come down to." They'd met in secret a couple of times, but it had bothered Justine, so he had picked her up at home with disastrous consequences.

She sat back in her chair and stared down at her drink. "I was a coward then and now," she said, utter misery in her quiet voice.

He desperately wanted to reach out to her. "You aren't. You care too deeply. You'd rather be hurt than hurt others."

Her head slowly lifted. His gaze went to her mouth, soft and trembling. His grip tightened on the can. "You game on helping me finish the porch?"

"I'll try."

"Let's go."

Justine didn't have any knowledge or experience repairing anything. Her mother always hired professionals. She also knew being in close proximity to Dalton when her emotions were so erratic was asking for trouble. Brianna knew this, and it was her none-too-subtle way of pushing Justine into facing the problem head-on.

"Another one." Dalton held his strong brown hand palm up and she placed a nail in it. "Thanks."

"Why didn't you hire someone to do this as well?"

"Because I get satisfaction out of knowing I helped bring this place back to life," Dalton said, hammering the nail.

Andrew had hired an architect to design the cabin. She'd given her input, picked out fixtures, appliances, and all the rest, but didn't actually see the cabin until it was almost finished. Andrew said that was what they were paying the builder for. They had a house built. Dalton wanted to keep alive the home that meant love and devotion to his family.

Justine handed Dalton another nail without his asking. He grinned up at her. "You're getting good at this."

She watched the play of muscles on his back as he worked. Brianna was right, he was built. She remembered too clearly the ripple beneath her fingertips when they'd kissed. Justine moistened her lips. It was time to get her mind off Dalton and what his heated skin would feel like. "I don't remember your sisters."

"They both have two kids, a boy and a girl each, about the same age. All of them are at Duke in premed."

She clasped the box of nails to her. She'd wanted children.

He looked up at her and frowned. "What's bothering you? I want to help," he told her.

She shook her head and handed him another nail. "No one can."

Accepting the nail, he began to hammer it in, then stopped and came to his feet. "Take this hammer and get out your frustrations. I know it worked wonders for me."

She shook her head. "No."

"Yes." Taking her hand, he pulled her off the porch so she didn't have to kneel. When she didn't move, he took her hand, closed it around the hammer, and hit the nail a couple of times.

By the third nail she was crying. She couldn't seem to stop. Dalton muttered something, then pulled her into his arms. Resistance never entered her mind. She just burrowed closer to his strength, his warmth. Picking her up, he sat down on the steps with her in his arms.

"Let it go, Justine. Let it go."

As if being given permission, the muffled sounds became loud, gut-wrenching sobs. He continued to hold her in his arms, not asking questions, just rocking her as if she were a small child.

Brianna stepped off the elevator and saw Patrick, his arms folded, leaning against the wall by her door. Her pulse skipped. He straightened, his dark gaze watching her intently as she continued down the hall.

She stopped a few safe feet away. "This stops now." She meant the words to be stern, but they were soft and underlined with yearning.

"I agree." He closed the distance between them. Heat and desire arced between them like an electric current. His eyes darkened, his nostrils flared.

"Back off."

"I don't seem to be able to do that. Have you ever wondered how I show up where you are?"

Her eyes widened. "You've been following me?"

"Occasionally, but I also asked the security guard to let me know when you came home."

Brianna's mouth tightened. "I don't like being spied on."

He gave one curt nod. "I disliked asking Toni those leading questions even more. She had no idea. Time for truth or consequences."

"You got that right," Brianna said. Toni was the security guard in the afternoon when Brianna came home. She was pretty, single, funny. Brianna didn't imagine Patrick would have much difficulty getting her to help him with his plan. She liked her. "You tricked her, but that doesn't mean I shouldn't tell the management."

"I'm counting on that compassionate heart of yours,

and that deep down you know I'd never do anything to hurt you."

"I wouldn't be so sure about that."

His thumb grazed her lower lip, causing her to shiver. "I would."

Batting his hand away, fighting the sudden heat in her belly and the desire in her body, she whirled and unlocked the door. "Good-bye."

The flat of his hand stopped the door from closing in his face. "I have dinner reservations for eight at Circa 1886. Before you answer, I want you to know that if the answer is no, I won't ask again."

Disappointment hit her. Her chin lifted. "That's good to hear."

"If I thought you meant that I would have given up long ago. I don't."

"That doesn't excuse what you've done."

His eyes hardened for the first time. "If you need to be angry with anyone, let it be me." His hand fell and he straightened. "If you change your mind, I'll be at the restaurant waiting."

She closed the door. Patrick was out of her life for good. She just wished she felt happier about it.

Seventeen

Brianna tried to keep from looking at the mantel clock in the great room, but couldn't quite pull it off. She'd called Justine's home and gotten the machine. A call to her cell went into voice mail. A short time later she'd gotten a strange call from Dalton saying Justine was all right and not to worry. He'd hung up before she could ask anything else.

At 7:35 her phone rang again. She just knew it was Patrick. He was too persistent to give up. Her heart thumped pleasantly. Perhaps she'd let him talk her into going out with him. What could dinner hurt?

"Hello."

"Hello, Ms. Ireland. This is Toni."

"Toni?"

"Yes, ma'am. Patrick left ten minutes ago by himself. He came by to apologize."

Apologizing wasn't high on the list of most men. It

gave Patrick a point, but it didn't excuse him, Brianna thought.

"With all the women after him, you're the first one since he's been here that he's taken an interest in."

"How would you know that?" Brianna asked, aware that she'd gone from being indignant to edging close to being jealous.

Toni laughed. "Because my fiancé is a policeman. Patrick has had us up to his place for dinner and taken us out on his boat. You'd be surprised at the things women have done to get him to notice them. One even stowed away on his boat. Most nights, if he's not at his niece's, he's at home."

"So why did you give him information on me?"

There was a long pause. "My fiancé is always telling me I talk too much, but, as I said, you're the first woman Patrick has showed any interest in since he left the force. Any of us would have done anything to help after what happened to him."

A chill raced down Brianna's spine. "What happened to him?"

Another pause. "He didn't tell you?"

"No."

"Oh, my bad. I told you I talked too much. Ronnie always says I do. I have to run. I just wanted you to know that Patrick is a stand-up kind of man. Good night."

Brianna was left listening to a dial tone with a lot of questions. There was one place she could get the answers. By leaving Justine with Dalton, Brianna had forced her best friend to face her fears. Could she do the same?

At 8:38 Patrick accepted the truth, Brianna wasn't coming. The restaurant stopped serving at nine. He had gam-
bled and lost. Getting help from Toni hadn't set well with
either of them. He was the straightforward type and admired honesty and truthfulness. Obtaining information
behind Brianna's back wasn't the way to handle things. But
what was?

Sitting at the table in the posh restaurant, he felt as if
he were on display. Around him couples were dining and
happily chatting. He'd glanced surreptitiously at the other
tables and wanted to sink lower in his chair. He was the
only one alone.

The waiter for his table was probably tired of coming
up and asking if he were ready to order or wanted to continue to wait for his guest. There had been compassion in
the older man's gaze, as if to say she's not coming, you poor
fool, so order already and stop embarrassing yourself.

He lifted his hand to signal the waiter for the check
and saw Brianna. She looked stunning in a little black
dress that clung to her glorious body as if it had been
poured on. The creation stopped a good five inches
above the knees, the backs of which he had dreamed of
kissing. Her hair was piled on top of her head in flirta-
tious curls that made his hands itch to let down and to
run his fingers through.

The waiter reached the table a few steps in front of her.
"The check, or are you ready to order?"

"White wine."

The waiter jerked his head around. His jaw became un-
hinged. Patrick couldn't keep the smile off his face as he

got up from the table to hold Brianna's chair. "Please bring the lady her drink, then give us a few minutes."

Brianna sat, placing her small jeweled clutch on top of the table covered with white linen. "Thank you."

"Thank you." Patrick took his seat, then grew serious. "I want to apologize for invading your privacy. It won't happen again."

"If I didn't believe that I wouldn't be here."

"Your drink," the waiter said, gushing for all he was worth.

Patrick shook his head as the smitten man moved away. "Before you came, he was ready to toss me out."

"Then you owe me one." She picked up the menu.

"I'm more than willing to pay," he said, his voice dropping lower.

Brianna lowered the menu. "I just bet you are."

Patrick laughed. He didn't know what had gotten her to change her mind, but he was grateful she had. The waiter came and took their orders. Life had certainly taken a marvelous upswing.

Brianna had a wonderful time at dinner, and later dancing at a small club. Besides liking the water, they both liked old movies, shared similar taste in music. They both agreed that Louis Armstrong was the greatest trumpet player who ever lived.

Back at her place, Brianna unlocked her door. "Thank you for a wonderful time."

Patrick braced his hand on the doorjamb above her head. "I'll pick you up at nine for brunch at the marina restaurant, then we'll take the boat out."

"Nine it is." She was actually looking forward to it, but not as much as the good-night kiss she knew was coming when Patrick's head descended.

The first touch set her body afire. She went from simmer to explosive. She heard the door close as if from a distance.

"Brianna," Patrick breathed. "I can't get enough of you."

She felt the same way. Her mouth sought him. His large hand cupped her breast, then his fingers plucked the pebbled nipple. She whimpered as need pulsed through her.

She felt herself falling and clutched Patrick closer. Her back pressed against something soft, the mattress. Her mind said "wait," but when his hand cupped her hips, pressing her against his rock-hard arousal, her body was of an entirely different response. *Enjoy.*

She did as he loved her with equal parts of tenderness and ferocity. She was caught up in a whirlwind of passion. Clothes were hastily stripped away. After he sheathed himself, he brought them together with one powerful thrust. Her body arched, her legs wrapped around him.

The rhythm was fast as he measured the hot length of her, wringing cries of pleasure from her lips. He took her to a place she had never been before, pure passion, pure ecstasy. She felt herself spinning out of control, hurtling toward release.

She buckled, cried out his name when she came. Before she could come down, he was sliding in and out of her body, taking her up once again.

"Come with me, Brianna." She would have followed him anyplace, her body his to command, to pleasure. This time they came together. Sated, she curled against him and slept.

When Brianna surfaced from the sensual haze, she was curled up against the muscled warmth and hardness of Patrick's body. She stiffened as shock swept through her. She'd never acted so irresponsibly.

Angry at herself, she tried to push out of his arms. His hold tightened; his lips brushed against her damp forehead.

"Get up and get out."

"No. I'm not leaving. This was quick for both of us, but it's been coming for a long time."

Brianna didn't want to listen to him. But she too had suspected from almost the first that he'd be one man who would change the rules. "Let me go." She pushed against his chest, his stomach, then stilled as she felt the rough ridge beneath her hand.

His body momentarily stiffened, then he released her. Brianna quickly sat up and stared at the place her hand had been. The scar was very long and ugly. Her stomach rolled.

"W-what happened?"

"I got in the way of a drug dealer's bullet."

Her head snapped up. He'd said the words so calmly, but his eyes weren't. They were dark with painful memories. She couldn't imagine, didn't want to imagine what he had gone through.

"The doctor was ticked about the scar tissue forming. Messed up his work, he said."

Brianna's gaze helplessly drifted back to the scar.

"If it bothers you, I'll put my shirt on."

All she could think of was the pain he must have endured. "You could have died," she said, her voice hushed and strained.

221

"No, I couldn't, because I hadn't met you yet."

With a cry, Brianna hugged and kissed his face. "I've never heard anything so beautiful."

"That's what I thought when I first saw you."

She lifted her head and stared into his eyes. His large hand brushed her hair from her face. "That I'd never seen anyone as beautiful as you."

"Patrick." She melted in his arms, then trailed kisses over his chest, his taut stomach, the scar.

With a hiss, he rolled her over. His dark eyes stared into hers. "My turn."

Justine awakened the next morning in a strange bed and room. There was a brass ceiling fan in the guest room, not a bare bulb. Sunlight came through windows with old-fashioned shades and not custom swag draperies. The mattress beneath her was firmer. She was still wearing her sleeveless blouse and cropped pants.

Slowly sitting up, she saw Dalton asleep in an easy chair with his feet propped up on one of the kitchen chairs. He looked uncomfortable and oddly adorable with his fingers laced on his flat abdomen. He'd given up his bed to her, and a lot more.

Yesterday he'd held her as she cried, demanding nothing, giving her the freedom to let go. She wished she could crawl back into his lap. Only this time she wouldn't be seeking only comfort.

Dalton's eyes opened. Justine knew that the desire she felt was clearly visible on her face, and she made no attempt to hide it. The same desire shone back at her, causing her body to warm, her stomach muscles to tighten.

His feet hit the floor when he stood. "Morning, what would you like for breakfast?"

Instead of answering, Justine's eyelids flickered downward. How could she have forgotten a man who always put her needs before his own? How could she have chosen a man who only thought of self-gratification?

Her eyes opened. Dalton was standing by the bed, patient and understanding. "I need to tell you something."

Taking her hands, he hunkered down in front of her. "I'm listening."

With her hands trembling as much as her body, she told him of surprising Andrew with another woman. She told him about the accident and admitted what she had not even confessed to Brianna. "I blame myself for the accident. Maybe if I hadn't blown the horn, the deer would have crossed the road before Andrew rounded the curve."

"The accident was not your fault," Dalton said tightly. "You only had seconds to react. Deer crossing signs were clearly posted. Andrew knew the dangers."

"But—"

"His actions set him on that path, not you," Dalton talked over her. "From what I've heard and read, your quick actions saved his life. If you hadn't been there his car might not have been discovered until after the explosion." His hands flexed on hers. "Blame Andrew. Not yourself."

So far she hadn't been able to do that. "How about we go get takeout? My treat." She didn't want to talk about Andrew any longer.

Dalton's brow arched as if he was aware that she hadn't answered his question. "Deal. Let's go," he said.

Thirty minutes later, Justine and Dalton were back at the house eating breakfast when they heard a car. Fear leaped into Justine's startled gaze.

"Wait here. I'll see who it is." Dalton surged to his feet. Although they had done nothing wrong, Justine was still married to Andrew, a man many admired.

"I'd rather go with you." She rose to her feet just as a knock on the door sounded.

Justine tensed. Dalton reached to brush his hand gently down her arm. "You don't have anything to be ashamed of."

"We both know that's not entirely true."

His dark eyes narrowed, then he spun on his heels and started for the front room with Justine following. Through the faded sheers at the window they saw a black truck. "I've seen that truck before. It's Patrick."

"Patrick? Why would—?" Justine beat Dalton to the front door and swung it open. "Is it Andrew?" she asked as Brianna emerged from the truck.

"No," Brianna quickly assured her. "Your mother couldn't get you on your cell. I told her you were in the shower and would call."

Charging her cell was usually the last thing she did before she went to bed. Last night she had gone to sleep in Dalton's arms and slept better than she had in months. Justine's cheeks heated. "The battery is probably dead."

"Use mine."

Justine's hands closed around the phone Brianna gave her. "Thank you. Excuse me." She dialed the phone as she stepped onto the porch.

"Come in and have a cup of coffee," Dalton said before closing the door to give Justine some privacy.

"Good morning, Mama."

"You should have let me know you weren't going to be at home."

Justine's fingers clenched on the porch column. "I'm sorry."

"I like Brianna, but I'm not sure it's such a good idea to spend so much time with her."

Justine's brows knitted. "Why?"

"She's single and attractive. Men are bound to approach her. You don't want to give people the wrong idea about you."

Her mother was always worried about what other people thought more than the welfare of her daughter or what she wanted. "Let them think what they want. Was there something else?"

Her mother's sigh was one of long suffering. "Why didn't you tell me Andrew had another cardiac arrest?"

The accusatory tone was clear. "I didn't want to worry you."

"Do you know how stupid I felt when Shirley Hightower asked me about it last night at the bridge party and I didn't have a clue as to what she was talking about? It was so embarrassing."

Justine rubbed her temple. So the real reason for the call was finally coming out. "I'm sorry."

"You should be. I don't know what gets into you at times."

"I'm sorry," she repeated, not knowing what else to say.

"I have to get ready for church."

Thank God. "Good-bye, Mother."

"Good-bye."

Justine deactivated the cell and called the nurse's station. "This is Mrs. Crandall. How is Andrew?"

"There has been no change."

Justine rubbed her temple again. "Thank you. Is his mother there?" By this time, all the staff was familiar with them.

"She hasn't arrived yet, but she didn't leave until almost after one this morning. The eleven-to-seven shift had to run her out as usual."

While his wife had been sleeping in another man's bed. "Thank you."

Hanging up the phone, she called Beverly, hoping to catch her before she left for the hospital. The phone was picked up on the third ring. "Hello."

"It's Justine, Beverly. Andrew is fine. I just spoke with the charge nurse."

A relieved sign echoed through the phone. "You sound strange. Is everything all right?"

Why couldn't her mother care as much? "I'm fine. I forgot to charge my phone last night and thought you might have called."

"No, I thought you needed the day off. I explained to Andrew. You're coming today, aren't you?"

"This afternoon." She desperately needed a few more hours during which she could just be herself.

"All right. I'll tell Andrew. I better go. I don't want to be late."

Justine couldn't help but wish that her mother would

have been that faithful and diligent in caring for her. "All right. I'm using Brianna's cell. You have the phone number if you need me."

"We'll be fine. Reverend Harding and Pastor Bird are coming by to have prayer before they go to their churches. We almost have our Andrew back. I can feel it."

"All right." She was beginning to sound like a parrot. "Good-bye."

"Good-bye."

Feeling like a fraud, Justine disconnected the phone.

Dalton, who had one eye on the entrance to the kitchen, stood the moment Justine appeared. His fist clenched in fury and helplessness. The guilt was back on her face. He had hoped she had put that behind her.

"Dalton, I see you got some work done on the porch."

He looked briefly at Brianna. She was trying to help Justine as well. Lecturing wouldn't do any good. Maybe work would. "Justine was my assistant. I'm hoping she'll pitch in today."

"Count me in too if you need an extra hand," Patrick said easily. "I'm pretty handy with a hammer."

"I'm game," Brianna put in, a wide smile on her face.

Justine eased into her chair. "I'm not sure what I can do, but I'd like to try."

"I work better if I have company," Dalton said. "Besides, as we talked about yesterday, the inside of the house needs as much work as the outside. I don't want to mess up with colors either. Maybe you could help. I think I'll keep the hardwood floors throughout the house and just have them stained. Once I seal them, they shouldn't be that difficult for me to keep up."

"You're keeping the house?" Justine asked.

He thought he heard hope in her voice, or was it wishful thinking on his part? "Yes."

"Woo-hoo!" Brianna yelled, and pumped her fist. "It'll be great having you around again."

Justine said nothing and stared down into her coffee cup as if it held the secrets to the universe. He'd give anything to know how she felt about his staying. "Finish your breakfast, and we'll get started."

"I'm finished." She closed the Styrofoam lid of her food container. "We can start whenever you're ready."

Her breakfast was practically untouched. Before Brianna and Patrick had arrived, Justine had been trying to grill Dalton for information on *Sudden Prey*. She'd been smiling. Now the shadows were back in her eyes. "Then we'll clean up the kitchen and get started." He turned to Patrick. "Ever hang Sheetrock before?"

"I was a volunteer with Habitat for Humanity for the past five years before I moved here." Patrick glanced at Brianna. "I look great with a tool belt hanging from my waist."

Brianna sent him a sexy smile. "He's also not the modest type."

"I can use all the help I can get," Dalton said. It was clear that Patrick had finally broken through Brianna's resistance.

Patrick pushed to his feet and reached for Brianna's chair. "Then let's get started. I'll go outside and give Brianna a few lessens on what not to do with the hammer."

"Wonder what I could give you lessons on," she tossed.

Chuckling, he curved his arm around her waist and kissed her lightly on the forehead. "It boggles the mind."

Dalton waited until the door closed behind them. "You all right?"

The corners of Justine's mouth briefly quirked upward as if she wanted to smile but was too tired to pull it off. "Yes. Reality just caught up with me."

"Jus—"

"Please." She lightly touched his arm, then let her hand fall. "Let's just concentrate on fixing your house."

He'd push if he thought it would do any good. "All right. Don't forget I need your help. It will take a lot of work to get this place together."

"Most things do." With those words, she started clearing the table.

Feeling helpless, Dalton began picking up cups. What he wouldn't give to see Justine happy again.

Eighteen

That afternoon Dalton stood by the back passenger door of Patrick's truck, his hands curled over the window frame. "If you ever feel like hammering again, you know where to come," he told Justine.

Everyone needs a sanctuary. Dalton had helped her find hers. For a little while, she'd been able to forget. "I might take you up on the offer," she said.

"Any time. I want to move out here permanently in a few days. The phone company is coming next week."

"I'll remember that. Good-bye."

His fingertips tenderly brushed her cheek. "'Bye."

Warmth rushed through her. Justine sat in the backseat and turned her gaze straight ahead instead of at Dalton. The more she looked, the more she wished things were different.

Patrick pulled away and Brianna twisted around in the passenger seat. "Take one day at a time."

"I'm try—I'm going to." It was time she stopped trying and did. She certainly had reasons to. She glanced back to see Dalton still standing there looking after them. She straightened in her seat as the truck pulled onto the highway, watching as the dense trees gave way to office buildings and shops.

Patrick entered the underground parking garage of the hospital. "Brianna said you planned to come by, and I thought you might want to stop now."

"Thank you."

"Don't mention it." He pulled into a vacant spot near the elevator and cut the motor.

"He definitely has his moments," Brianna said.

"Shucks," Patrick said. "Praise like that will go to my head."

"Can't have that." Brianna opened her door. "Your head is big enough all ready."

Justine emerged from the car and stuck her hands into the pockets of her pants. Brianna had faced her fears and won. She just hoped and prayed she could do the same.

"We're here with you," Brianna said.

Justine glanced from Brianna on one side to Patrick on the left. "Patrick, you haven't said anything about today."

"I trust Brianna, and she's solidly in your corner. That's all I need to know."

So simple, and it meant so much. "I'm glad you wore her down."

"Me too." Patrick pushed the elevator button.

In a matter of minutes they were walking down the hallway to ICCU. At the entrance to the waiting room, she turned. "Thank you again. I can get a cab home."

Brianna shook her head. "No way."

"Don't be stubborn," Justine said. "I'm not sure how long I'll be here."

"Then Patrick can take me home and I can drive back and wait with you."

"I can also wait with you," Patrick said.

"This isn't the time to be stubborn," Brianna told him.

He faced Justine. "I'd feel better if I knew neither of you had to go outside at night by yourself."

"I've been doing this for over three months. I'll be fine." She hugged Brianna and stepped back. "Thanks for today." She glanced at the closed door. "This might take awhile."

Brianna proved Patrick wasn't the only one who could be stubborn. "I don't like leaving you."

Justine nodded her head in Patrick's direction. "Go home and enjoy yourself. I want all the details tomorrow."

Brianna flushed. Patrick suddenly found something interesting on the wall.

Justine hugged her best friend again, then went through the door.

"Justine, oh, my goodness!" Beverly said, excitement ringing in her voice. "I thought I saw his fingers move just now."

Justine's startled gaze went first to her mother-in-law, then to the nurse changing the IV solution. The amber-haired woman shook her head once.

Justine put her arm around Beverly. If by sheer will and love you were able to bring a person out of a coma, Beverly's absolute love could do it. "The bond you and Andrew share is very special."

"So is the love you two share." Beverly put her hand on Andrew's leg. "He'll come back to us."

Not to her . . . if he woke up. "Have you eaten?"

"Earlier," Beverly said, moving to Andrew's side as the nurse finished hanging the IV and left. "It's important that he knows we're here."

"He'd want you to take care of yourself."

"Being with Andrew is better than anything."

If only that were true. "It won't take long for us to go get a cup of coffee and a sandwich, then we'll come back."

Beverly looked at Andrew a long moment, as if seeking his permission or looking for something. "We won't be long."

On the drive home, Brianna had debated whether she should invite Patrick in for a drink. That would surely lead to more. This morning she had awakened in his arms. No man had ever spent the night before. One look into his eyes and heat had begun to build, and her body to tingle with want. He'd gently kissed her, then had taken her on a long, slow journey of lovemaking, making her cry out with her release. He was turning her into a screaming nut.

She stopped in front of her door and turned without unlocking it. Patrick was too old-fashioned to let her get away with leaving him at the elevator. "Thanks for today, and especially being so nice to Justine."

His hand swept the curls behind her ear, then lingered. "I like Justine."

"I better go in."

"Yes, we better."

Time to set the ground rules. "I don't let men spend the night."

"Never thought you did." Taking the key out of her hand, he opened the door.

"I'm not going to start now."

"Sounds reasonable." Catching her around the waist, he lifted her and took the necessary steps to enter the condo, then kicked the door shut behind them.

She braced her hands on his wide shoulders. "Patrick, you're not listening to me."

He nibbled her ear and kept heading to her bedroom. "You don't let men spend the night."

He nipped her neck. Her fingers flexed on his shoulders. She arched her neck to allow him greater freedom. Her feet touched the floor. The knit top she wore followed.

"You're the most exquisite thing I've ever seen." His fingers trailed across her skin. "Your skin is so soft I could kiss every inch of you."

"You have," she said, her voice shaky.

"I plan to do it again." He began at her forehead. By the time he reached the valley between her breasts she was naked in bed and trembling with need. She'd send him home . . . later.

Justine and her mother-in-law stayed at the hospital until after ten, long past the posted visiting hours. Expecting to see the empty waiting room, she was surprised to see Dalton, long legs crossed at the ankle, his BlackBerry in his hand. Just as before, the moment they stepped into the area he looked up, hit something on the BlackBerry, and stood. "Evening, ladies. You ready to go home?"

"How long have you been here?" Beverly asked.

"Not long," he said, not flinching at the lie as he joined them. "I spoke with Brianna, and she said she had dropped Justine off. The hospital is on the way back to the hotel from my place. I thought I'd stop by just in case you needed a lift."

"That's very considerate of you, Mr. Ramsey," Beverly said.

"Please call me Dalton, and not at all. I can bring you back in the morning like last time."

"I am rather tired." She turned to her daughter-in-law. "Justine?"

"I'd feel better knowing you got home safely and didn't have to drop me off," she said.

"We accept your offer." Beverly smiled and started toward the elevator. "It's nice meeting an honorable man, just like my Andrew."

Dalton didn't dare look at Justine when he said, "Yes, ma'am."

Parents were supposed to love their children. The bond between them was strong. Although as a youngster Dalton had tried to take wild to a new level with fast driving, underage drinking, and girls, Dalton and his parents were close.

Before he was sixteen his father had taken him on a fishing trip for their "heart-to-heart" about sex and responsibility. Dalton had been too scared and finally ashamed to tell him that he was about two years too late. One of his sister's girlfriends had seen to that.

But sometimes love was destructive. Perhaps if Gloria's parents had loved her more they would have sought help for her violent mood swings before it was too late. He wondered if Mrs. Crandall had given in to Andrew as well.

"Where are you staying?" Mrs. Crandall asked. She sat in the front passenger seat beside him.

"Charleston Place," he answered, pulling into the traffic.

"What a coincidence. Andrew and Justine had their reception there in the Gazebo and Grand Hall. The day was simply spectacular. Light shone through the twelve-foot picture windows as if the angels were smiling down on them."

A thick silence descended in the vehicle. Dalton wanted to look in the rearview mirror to see Justine's reaction, but her mother-in-law was watching him too closely.

"The Thoroughbred Club there serves the most divine tea. Andrew and I went there numerous times. They have scrumptious desserts," Beverly told him.

"So I've heard."

"Could you do me a huge favor?" she asked. "It's an imposition, but I just have to ask."

It wasn't hard to guess what she was about to ask. "If I can."

"Please drop Justine off first, then take me by the hotel. I want to get one of their delicious strawberry tarts before I go home. The lobby lounge is open until eleven. That is, if Justine doesn't want any."

"No, thank you," came the answer from the back.

"Strawberry tarts are one of Andrew's favorite desserts."

Dalton finally gave in to temptation and glanced in the

mirror. Justine was looking out the window. His heart clutched at the sight. She looked lost. "Are you sure? I could swing by now."

She spoke without turning. "Yes, I'm sure."

Dalton's attention returned to driving. There didn't seem to be any more he could say. They both knew Mrs. Crandall was trying to make sure they weren't alone. She could have saved her breath.

Justine walked ahead of Dalton on the curved brick path to her front door. She couldn't help but recall the last time they were there together, the searing kiss they'd shared, the almost overwhelming need she'd felt. If she was honest with herself she wished he could take her in his arms again, wished she could tell him to come back later. Two things held her back: She was married and she remained a coward.

Opening the door, she turned and stuck out her hand. "Thank you. For everything."

His large hand closed around hers, causing her heart to speed up. "For you, I'd do anything."

The whispered words curled through her like mulled wine. Dalton wasn't a man to talk to hear himself talk. He meant every word. "I know, and that means a lot. Good night."

Lightly squeezing her hand, he went back to his car. Continuing inside, Justine locked the door, then went to her room and sat on the side of the bed. She might be tired, but her brain wasn't foggy enough to have missed Beverly's none-too-subtle reminder to her and Dalton of her marriage to Andrew.

Justine might have been worried if Beverly hadn't acted the same way on a number of occasions when she thought a man might be interested in her daughter-in-law. She fiercely protected what was Andrew's.

In the past Justine had taken pride in knowing that a woman she respected and loved warned off men. Now, Justine saw it for what it was, possessiveness and distrust. Andrew was the one his mother should have been watching.

Standing, Justine pulled a nightgown from the lingerie drawer and went to take her bath. Beverly thought Andrew almost a saint. Justine reluctantly admitted she had as well as she sank into the tub brimming with scented bubbles. Looking back on their marriage, she couldn't think of one single incident that indicated he was cheating. Even when he'd been on out-of-town trips, he called every morning and every night before he went to bed.

In hindsight she could see the possibility that he might have regulated the calls so there would be less chance for her to call at an inopportune time. The wife is often the last to know. She'd heard the old saying often, and always felt sorry for the poor, gullible wives. She had preened like a silly peacock that she was one of the lucky ones, glad that she wouldn't be like her mother or Andrew's mother.

Climbing out of the tub, Justine dried, lotioned, then slipped on the gown. As the heavy silk slithered over her body her thoughts went not to Andrew, but to Dalton. She was aware that she was beginning to think of him more, and that she was walking a thin line between friendship and something more perilous. His attentiveness soothed the hurt caused by Andrew's deception, but was it fair to Dalton?

Did she care about him or was she simply trying to

prove to herself that she remained desirable, that Andrew's betrayal wasn't because of a lack in her. She just didn't know.

Turning off the light, she sat on the side of the bed. She was tired, but not sleepy. Her thoughts immediately went to the previous night, when she had slept soundly because of Dalton. If she wasn't careful, she'd start to rely on him, and that could lead to disastrous consequences.

Her mother had preached to her from an early age that just because someone did something wrong, it didn't give her an excuse to do the same thing.

The ringing telephone intruded on her chaotic thoughts. She reached for it immediately. "Hello."

"Did I wake you?" Dalton asked.

Her heart thumped even more. No matter how wrong it was, she couldn't stop thinking of him, didn't want to. "No."

"Having trouble sleeping?"

"A bit," she said. "I'll just read a book until I fall asleep."

"Hope it's not one of mine that you're considering reading," he teased.

"No." She glanced at the suspense book of a new author on the bedside.

"Good. If you don't mind company, I can be at the back door in five minutes."

The front door wasn't an option. "The fence is six feet tall."

"It won't be the first time I've scaled a fence to see you. Make that four minutes."

Justine replaced the phone in the cradle and remembered that other time, the night before she left to stay with her grandmother in Mississippi. Dalton had climbed the six-foot wooden fence in the backyard. Brianna had come by to tell her he was coming to say good-bye. She'd waited an hour for him to come, afraid something might keep him away.

Part of Justine had desperately wanted to see him, the other, insecure, part hadn't because her eyes were red, the lids puffy. Since the night her mother had decided to send her away, Justine had done nothing but cry. Her mother was unmoved.

"All that boy wants is sex. You're pretty, but not as pretty as Brianna or some of the other girls. You have to ask yourself why he'd go after you, and face the hard facts. He's too good-looking to be content with one woman. I'm just keeping you from going through what I went through."

Then and now Justine had known her mother was thinking of Justine's father, a handsome man whom women chased and flirted with right in front of her mother. The sad part was, he'd chased and flirted right back. Still, the words had hurt. There were few occasions in Justine's life when her mother had approved of her. Marrying Andrew was at the top of that list.

Her mother had been wrong about Dalton and wrong about Andrew. The phone rang, causing her to jump. "Hello."

"I'm here."

Justine came to her feet, started toward the back door, then realized she was wearing her nightgown. "Just a minute." Hanging up the phone, Justine tossed the nightgown on the bed, then quickly dressed in a pair of jeans that sagged at the waist and a black pullover top. Finished, she rushed to the back of the house and opened the double doors leading to the dimly lit portico.

"Sorry it took so long. Come on in."

"That's all right." Dalton's gaze gently touched her, from her bare feet to her tousled head of hair.

Self-consciously, Justine raked her hand through her hair. "I must look—"

His large hand closed over hers, sending shock waves from her palm up her arm. "You could never look anything but beautiful."

She didn't want to feel the warm curl of pleasure, but it was there nonetheless. Then she was free of his touch, and she felt oddly bereft. "Come in."

"It's a pretty night and nice out here. Why don't you come out?"

She hadn't paid that much attention to the backyard or for that matter much about the house since Andrew's accident. She glanced around the covered structure, as if seeing it for the first time. Huge pots of blooming pink hibiscus were on either side of the steps leading from the house. Trailing vines covered the four white columns of the portico.

"All right." She closed the door behind her.

Dalton sat down on the top step and waited until she sat beside him before he spoke. "Mrs. Crandall decided she didn't want the strawberry tart after all."

"We both know she never did. She's always been that way. I'm sorry if she embarrassed you."

Dalton faced her. "Justine, do me a favor?"

She frowned. "What?"

"Stop apologizing. You aren't responsible for the actions of others, and Andrew's are at the top of the list."

"I know, but I . . ."

"Just hurt, feel stupid. I've been there."

Her mouth gaped. "Your wife cheated."

"Yes." He stood, walked a few steps away.

"I'm sorry. Here I am feeling sorry for myself when you've been through the same thing."

He returned to sit beside her and picked up her hand. "With one difference. My wife's affair made the five o'clock news and newspapers around the country. It wasn't pretty."

Justine heard the pain and the disillusion in his voice and ached for him. So that was what Brianna had alluded to. In feeling sorry for herself, she'd never considered how she'd feel if anyone else knew. She could just imagine the whispers, the sly comments that he had had to put up with. "She shouldn't have cheated."

"Neither should Andrew. Their fault, not ours."

"Yes, but we pay."

His thumb stroked the top of her hand. "That we do."

"I can't imagine how horrible that must have been for you."

"It was rough." He faced her more. Their knees bumped. "I don't want you going through what I went through, the sleepless nights, the blame, the questions that had no answers."

She had been through all that, was still trying to get her life back together. "How did you move on?"

"One hour, one day at a time, by finally accepting what I couldn't change and realizing if I didn't accept it, it would destroy me. My family and writing helped."

Her hand fisted in his. "Mother would probably blame me, but I have Brianna and the bookstore."

He took her other hand in his. "You also have me."

The way he said the words and the look in his eyes caused a ball of heat to roll through her. "Dalton—" She didn't know what she wanted to say.

"I've kept you from resting long enough." He came to his feet, bringing her with him. As soon as she was upright, he released her and opened the door leading into the house. "Get some sleep. Good night."

She wanted him to stay, but realized it was wiser for him to go. Both of them were too vulnerable and dealing with too many emotions.

"Good night, Dalton." As soon as she was inside, he closed the door. For a long time they simply stared at each other through the glass, then he walked away, disappearing into the murky darkness of her backyard.

No matter how wrong it was, she wished she could have gone with him.

Nineteen

The next morning, Justine heard the loud voice as she neared the double doors leading into the ICCU unit. She noticed even more the stares from the people in the waiting area. Some of their faces were sympathetic, others bordered on hostile. She hit the door almost running. She heard a nurse call out her name, but she didn't stop. Over all the voices was Beverly's, filled with rage.

Justine burst through the door, her frantic gaze going immediately to Andrew, expecting to see the worst. Instead, his respirator continued to wheeze, his IVs dripped, his various monitors functioned as always.

"Justine, I'm glad you're here."

She jerked around. At first she couldn't see Beverly because of the people surrounding her. One Justine recognized as Dr. Thomas, the chief of staff and a friend of Beverly's, the second was Andrew's doctor, the third a woman she didn't recognize. Neither did she recognize the fourth person, a man.

"Tell them I'm not crazy."

"No one said you were, Beverly," Dr. Thomas said sooth-ingly. "We just think you should spend less time here."

"Andrew needs me." Beverly pushed through the peo-ple surrounding her and rounded the bed to stand by An-drew's side and place her hand on his shoulder. "My son needs to know I'm here."

Dr. Thomas looked at Dr. Lane, whose lips pursed. "I've told you. Your son is unaware of what is going on."

Beverly's eyes narrowed angrily. For a moment Justine was afraid she might rush across the room and attack the neurosurgeon. "I want you off this case. You're fired."

Andrew's doctor merely lifted a bushy eyebrow. "Your daughter-in-law is the only one who can do that."

"Tell him, Justine. Tell him!"

"Please." The unknown woman held up her hands. "I'm aware that feelings are running high, but this is a critical care unit. This can't be good for Mr. Crandall, the other patients, or their families."

Dr. Lane shot her a sharp look, but said nothing.

"Could someone please tell me what is going on?" Jus-tine asked.

"They're trying to keep me away from Andrew." Beverly edged closer to the bed. "I won't allow that to happen."

"Mrs. Crandall, I'm sorry if it appears that way." The woman turned to Justine and extended her hand. "I'm Eliz-abeth Lancaster, head of Social Service." She indicated the man on the left. "Chaplain Hall."

"Mrs. Crandall, I'm sure this is confusing, but we're all here to help you get through these difficult periods," Chaplain Hall said as he shook Justine's hand.

Justine's confusion didn't clear. She looked from the

middle-aged chaplain with his shock of white hair and light blue eyes to the social worker, fashionably thin and attractive in a pink suit that shouted designer. "I don't understand."

Dr. Thomas stepped forward. "We've gotten reports that Beverly keeps insisting that Andrew is waking up."

"He is!" Beverly hissed.

Justine went to her. She'd never known her mother-in-law to raise her voice. "Just let him finish, please."

"No one is making me leave my son!" Beverly insisted.

Dr. Thomas spoke to Justine as if he realized that Beverly's mind was closed to anything he might want to say. "While it's not unusual for close family members to feel this way, it can lead to problems later on. It's the consensus that the prolonged visiting hours might not be the best thing for either of you, given Andrew's condition."

"The nurses told you what I said," Beverly accused.

"Who the information came from is unimportant," Dr. Lane said. "It's not healthy."

The social worker looked as if she wanted to throttle Andrew's doctor. "Our concern is for the patient and the family."

"Exactly," Dr. Thomas quickly agreed. "That is why I might have been remiss in allowing the family extended visiting privileges."

"We're getting complaints," Dr. Lane said.

"Complaints?" Justine repeated, trying to make sense of everything.

"Unfortunately, other families have voiced their concerns that we're giving you special treatment," the social worker said, sympathy in her voice.

"The families of patients on this unit are often thrust unexpectantly into painful situations. Trying to come to terms with them is difficult," the chaplain told them.

Justine recalled the faces outside. How would she have felt if others were given special privileges and not her? She understood, but feared Beverly wouldn't.

"Andrew needs us to help him wake up," Beverly said, tenderly stroking Andrew's face.

"He loves you both," the social worker said.

"More than anything," Beverly said as she continued to gently stroke her son's cheek.

"Then he'd want you both to take care of yourselves. Mrs. Crandall, I'm told, has lost considerable weight and obviously needs rest. Andrew would want to see you both at your best."

Justine didn't need to have taken psychology to know where the social worker was leading Andrew's mother. Beverly looked at her, and it was all Justine could do to keep from squirming. The navy blue suit hung on her. There were dark circles beneath her eyes that she no longer tried to hide with concealer.

"Unfortunately, it can be more draining on visitors than patients because the patient is resting, and doesn't have to deal with all the issues going on outside of the hospital," she went on to say. "If you left at the posted time you both could rest more. I understand you both were here until after ten, two hours after the posted visiting hours were over."

"I'll make sure Justine goes home from now on," Beverly said.

"Do you think she'd rest, knowing you're still here?"

The social worker looked at Justine. "From what I've heard about your daughter-in-law, she is a very loyal and brave woman. She cares about you just as much as her husband."

Beverly reached out her other hand to briefly run it down Justine's arm. "She saved Andrew's life."

Justine stared down at her feet. She hated the attention then, hated it now. She wasn't brave. She proved that daily by continuing to live a lie.

"Justine," Beverly said. "I need to be here."

Justine's head came up. She knew what it was to live with regrets. She spoke to the social worker, who seemed to be the most understanding. "Can't you make an exception? They were extremely close. What if she came back an hour after visiting hours were over so the other families wouldn't know?"

"This stops today. Now. Ms. Lancaster has pointed out that the other families are already complaining. I'm sorry," Dr. Thomas said. "You both will have to adhere to regular visiting hours from now on."

"The nurses and Dr. Lane will take excellent care of Mr. Crandall," Chaplain Hall said.

Beverly stared at Dr. Lane with hate in her eyes. "There will be no more talk of signing any papers to shut off his machines or not to resuscitate him."

"I don't—"

"Dr. Lane," Ms. Lancaster said, cutting him off. "If that is Mrs. Crandall's wish, and it would make this easier for his mother, perhaps it would be best to wait a few days. What do you think, Chaplain Hall?"

"I agree that the family needs time."

"Mrs. Crandall?" Andrew's doctor prompted.

Justine knew she held the key. "I agree with Andrew's mother."

"As you wish," Dr. Lane said tightly. "I have patients to see."

"Sorry, Beverly, but this is for the best." Dr. Thomas nodded and followed Dr. Lane out the door.

The chaplain came to them. "If you ever need to talk, just have the operator page me. If I'm not here, one of my associates will be."

All three men left. The social worker glanced at the clock on the wall. Seven fifty-one. "You can stay a few more minutes, but then you'll have to leave and come back at ten. You can page me as well if you want to talk. You're not alone in this."

"Thank you," Justine said, very much aware that from Beverly there was nothing. The door swung closed after the social worker left. They were alone.

"You'll show them all, won't you, Andrew?"

Justine searched her mind for something to help Beverly, and tried not to feel guilty because all she could think of was what it meant to her. She was freer than she had been since the accident.

Brianna woke up to the smell of coffee. Her eyelids shot up. Abruptly she sat up in bed as the night came crashing back.

Patrick had spent the night, and what a glorious night it had been. At times their lovemaking had been achingly gentle, then fast and furious, whipping them both into a frantic fury. She'd never felt more exhilarated then or more frightened now.

No man had ever touched her so deeply or wrung so much from her body. She'd been helpless in giving him all that he asked for, helpless to demand from him as well. He'd given, seemingly as helpless as she was to hold back.

The door opened and Patrick stood there with a smile on his lips that did marvelous, naughty things to her body. "Morning, beautiful."

A woman's heart shouldn't race when a man called her beautiful; shouldn't want a man she barely knew to crawl back in bed with her and take her on a slow ride to paradise.

"Breakfast will be served in ten minutes. You better get a move on, or you'll be late for work."

"Wait," she called when he started to leave. She'd never been the insecure or needy type, but she was in bed with only a sheet covering her. He should have some reaction. "Is that all you have to say?"

His head tilted as if in deep thought. "I can't think of another thing." He turned, took a couple of steps, then came back to the door. "On second thought, if you don't get a move on, I might join you. Then you wouldn't make it to work until it's very late, but we'd both be wearing big smiles."

For a moment, just a moment, she considered being late and wearing that smile, letting him take her where only he could. He must have read her surrender, because he took a decisive step toward her, then stopped. "You tempt me like no other. Ten minutes and counting."

Brianna let out a breath. She'd known from the first that Patrick would touch her in ways that she didn't want to deal with. She'd never fished for compliments. The man was a menace to her peace of mind.

"Brianna, are you moving?"

He also seemed to have an uncanny instinct where she was concerned. "Just don't burn the pancakes."

His answering chuckle warmed her as she threw back the covers and headed for the bathroom. No man had ever cooked for her or tended to her so sweetly except her father. Patrick genuinely cared about people.

He hadn't asked yesterday or last night about Justine and Dalton. Men didn't gossip as much as women, but there had to be questions on his mind. Instead he'd helped Dalton with his remodeling tasks, and taken Justine to see Andrew.

She frowned as she dumped perfumed bath salts beneath the hot running water in the oversized bathtub. When Justine's mother had called Sunday morning and she couldn't find Justine, she hadn't hesitated to let Patrick drive her to Dalton's house. On some level she trusted him. Her parents and Dalton and Justine liked Patrick. They trusted him.

Brianna stepped into the tub, picked up a bath sponge, and began to wash her arm. If she was honest with herself, and she wanted to be, she shared their opinion. She was fighting the attraction because of the quickness of finding someone after she broke up with Jackson.

She moved the sponge to her other arm, then stilled as realization struck her. She was punishing herself instead of moving on. She'd accused Justine of doing the same thing. No more, she told herself as she resumed bathing.

Patrick made life interesting, and for as long as it lasted, she was going to take full advantage and enjoy him.

Shortly after six that day, Brianna stepped off the elevator on the fourth floor of her condo building with a huge smile on her face. Patrick was the reason and this time she was going to pamper him. Shifting the bag of groceries in her arm, she rang his doorbell.

The door opened. Her heart did a quick dance at the first glimpse of Patrick's gorgeous face. He smiled, causing her to sigh inwardly. Taking the bag with one hand, he wrapped his other arm around her waist and drew her to him. His dark head descended, his mouth settling on hers. The kiss heated her blood and made her body tingle.

"Hi, beautiful," he greeted, his lips just above hers.

"Hello, handsome," she answered when she had the presence of mind to do so. "Tonight, I'm taking care of you."

Desire flared in his eyes, telling her exactly how she could take care of him. Her breasts grew heavy. Maybe they could put off eating for a bit.

"Perhaps you'd like to introduce me?"

At the sound of the teasing male voice, Patrick's arm around her waist tightened. Disappointment hit Brianna. "I'm sorry, I didn't know you had company. You can call me later."

"You're not leaving. He is." Patrick kissed her on the nose, then drew her inside and closed the door.

Several feet away stood an angelically beautiful, broad-shouldered man with a wicked smile to match the glint in his black eyes. He was dressed in a black polo shirt and tight jeans that molded to his long, muscular thighs.

"Brianna Ireland, my kid brother, Rafael."

"Hello, Rafael."

Rafael grinned, charm and mischief mixed together in one sinful package. Brianna could imagine his smile brought women by the droves. He crossed to her in a walk just shy of being a swagger and reached for the hand she extended.

"Brianna," Rafael greeted, his voice deep and velvety smooth.

Patrick drew her back before their hands touched. "You're not pulling that kissing her hand crap."

Rafael's grin widened. "Can't say I blame you. No wonder you didn't want to go out with me on the boat."

"You have the key. Don't rush back on my account," Patrick told him.

"Brianna, if you get tired of the old man, just look me up."

Brianna looked up at Patrick. Her heart swelled with an emotion she had yet to put a name to. She couldn't imagine being with anyone else. "That's not about to happen."

Patrick kissed her on the mouth, then said to his brother, "She told you."

"She sure did." Rafael opened the door, then looked back, his face serious. "I'm really glad to meet you. He's one of the best. Good-bye." The door closed after him.

"You could have gone with him," Brianna said.

"I enjoy being with you more."

Pleasure coursed through her. "Patrick."

He sat the bag on the floor and drew her fully into his arms. "What do you say we go enjoy each other and eat later?" he asked, nibbling on her ear.

Her answer was a soft moan of surrender. "Enjoy now, eat later."

Picking her up in his arms, he strode to the bedroom.

Brianna thought of the thick porterhouse steaks in the bag on the floor until his hand cupped her breast, his mouth covered her. They could always order takeout. Right now they were going to take care of and enjoy each other.

She reached for the snap on his jeans.

Twenty

Justine had her life back. Almost.

The next morning when she woke up she didn't have to think too hard on what she wanted to do with the reprieve she'd been given. For too long she had thought of others first and herself not at all. That was about to change. She'd quickly bathed, dressed, and left the house.

A short while later, she flicked on her signal and turned into Dalton's driveway. She parked behind his Jeep and got out of her van. She felt better already.

She didn't want to think of the time she had sought to surprise Andrew and had received the shock of her life. Dalton had proved time and time again that he wanted the best for her. And, at the moment, she wanted the peace of the sanctuary he offered so selflessly.

The sound of hammering reached her ear as she knocked on the door. When the noise continued, she twisted the knob and let herself in, and followed the sound. Dalton was bent from the waist nailing molding in the bathroom.

Justine almost sighed. The man had a nice backside.

She wasn't aware of making a sound, but he went still, then straightened and spun. His eyes lit up, and the mouth she had dreamed about curved into the most beautiful smile she had ever seen.

"Justine."

Just hearing the sweet, almost reverent way he said her name confirmed her decision to see him. She lifted the handled bag in her hand. "Breakfast."

Placing the hammer on the commode top, he studied her face as he walked to her. "What's different?"

He'd always been able to read her emotions. Briefly she explained the new restrictions on the visiting hours and finished by saying, "I want my life back. I want to do the things I want to do, not have to do." She wiggled the bag in her hand. "Like share breakfast with a good friend."

"You deserve that and more."

She breathed an inward sigh of relief. Although they both knew the attraction they shared, she'd purposefully used the word "friend." She hadn't decided if she wanted to build on those feelings. "The food is getting cold. I told Iris I'd only be gone a couple of hours."

"Then let's not waste another minute." Taking the bag in one hand and her arm in the other, Dalton steered her into the kitchen. Once there he released her, set the bag on the table, and washed his hands. "There are paper plates in the cabinet."

Justine prepared their plates. "The kitchen is as neat as it was the other day."

"I had cooking and clean-up duties just like my sisters."

Grinning, he took a seat next to her. "Housekeeping chores were the one thing I couldn't talk them into doing for me. Now I'm glad. My office might be a mess, but I don't want the house to be the same way."

"It shows." Justine pulled out two large foam cups. "Coffee for you and hot chocolate for me."

He blessed their food, then sipped the coffee and sighed. "One thing I've never learned is to make good coffee." He nodded toward the automatic coffeemaker on the counter. "It's top of the line, but the results are the same."

"If you have the coffee, I'll fix you a pot before I go." Justine buttered her biscuit.

"I do, and thanks." He bit into his pan-fried sausage. "Yesterday I picked up some paint samples and a lot of books at the home improvement store. If you have time I'd appreciate it if you'd look them over."

"I have time. Tell me what else you've done since I was here last."

"I painted the master bedroom and finished the crown molding around the ceiling as well." He sipped his coffee, his gaze on her. "When we finish, you can see it."

"I'd like that. What else do you plan?" she asked, enjoying a normal conversation and realizing how much she'd missed the everyday things. Her life had been tied to Andrew's. As she listened to Dalton, she felt freer than she had in months. She planned for it to continue.

In the days that followed, more than one person commented that Justine had a new sparkle in her eyes. She thanked them and changed the conversation. Beverly even noticed and commented. Justine explained she was getting more rest. Although her mother-in-law had studied her for a long time, she said nothing further on the matter.

Brianna, in her usual straightforward manner, had said the attention of the right man could do that to a woman. She'd had a dreamy expression on her face at the time. Patrick's doing. They'd giggled like they were in high school. Life had taken an upswing for both of them.

Each time Justine was with Dalton, she became further and further removed from Andrew. She continued to visit him in the morning and afternoon, but she did it out of respect and courtesy for Beverly, to support her. On one of those visits Dr. Lane had met Justine in the hallway and told her flatly that Andrew was not going to recover and to prepare herself.

She'd kept the emotions contained until she was at Dalton's house that night, and then cried in his arms. She'd cried for Andrew, for his mother, for those who loved him. Dalton had held her as he had the day she'd first come to see him at his house. She'd mourned the loss, then given Andrew up.

Sunday, a few days after she'd spoken with the doctor, she'd driven to Dalton's house after church. She caught herself humming and smiled. Life certainly had turned. Brianna was happy with Patrick. Justine had teased her about being tired lately. Patrick's fault, she'd said and grinned.

The right man could do that and a whole lot more.

Pulling up behind Dalton's Jeep, Justine got out. By the time she closed the door Dalton was there, a huge grin on his face.

"Good morning." He caught her hand. "I finished the master bedroom and bath. Come on."

Laughing at his enthusiasm, she allowed herself to be pulled up the steps and into the house. They'd shopped online to build around the antique mahogany four-poster and armoire of his maternal great-grandmother, which had been stored at his sister's house.

"Ready?" he asked.

"Ready."

Opening the door, he stepped back. "What do you think?"

At first sight she palmed her face. Masculine. Elegant. They'd chosen a bold floral print over a chocolate background with persimmon accents. It had meant redoing the walls in a rich paneling, but the results were worth it. "It's beautiful."

"The mantel looks great over the fireplace." He rubbed his hand over the detailed hardwood with antique pewter highlights. Gas logs burned behind the black metal hinged fire screen.

Justine fingered the striped chocolate silk draperies that framed the two elongated windows. "Everything came out perfect."

Relief shone in his eyes. "Your doing." He rubbed his chin and glanced at the bed. "Although I'm not so sure about all those pillows."

There were at least ten. Justine laughed. "You can put some in the great room on the chocolate leather sofa you ordered."

"Will do." He went to her. "Thank you for helping me make it home. Mama would have liked it. Daddy would have liked it because she did."

"When two people love each other they learn to compromise," she said softly.

"Yes, they do," he said just as softly.

Justine felt her body heat. Her world narrowed to the man standing in front of her. She recalled the soft texture of his beard, the searing kiss. Her breathing hitched.

One finger, just one finger, curved from her chin to across her lower lip. "I want you, Justine. More than I've ever wanted another woman."

She gulped in air as her body quivered.

"It won't go away." He stepped closer, tempting her. "I want your friendship and you to be happy just as much. Walk out of this room and this conversation won't come up again."

"I can't," she whispered. "I want you, too."

"Thank goodness." His mouth fastened on hers, pleasing her. She kissed him back with all the pent-up need and passion she'd been holding inside. The kiss seemed to go on forever.

His fingers went to her blouse. Hers tugged his T-shirt over his head. He was as awed by her breasts as she was with his bare, muscled chest. He trembled, then hissed as she freely ran her hand over the warm, muscled flesh.

"Justine."

The needy way he said her name made her feel powerful, an emotion she had thought never to feel again. She stood before him naked to the waist and unashamed.

She started to lower her head to kiss his muscled chest, but he stepped back. Her head lifted, questions formed in her eyes.

"Bed," he gritted out. Locking one powerful arm around her waist, he grabbed the top of the comforter and jerked. Pillows flew in every direction.

Justine's laughter at his exuberance was short-lived as she

found herself in bed with Dalton towering over her. The intensity in his eyes shocked and delighted her. His head lowered to her nipple. She watched the slow descent, her breath held. At the first hot, wet touch, she quivered inside.

His hands and mouth pleasured her, driving her closer to the point of no return, and he had yet to bring them together. When he did, she arched up, her arms and legs wrapped around him.

"Heaven. Sweet heaven," he murmured as he stroked her, loved her. His mouth fastened on hers, his hands cupping her hips. She was helpless in his arms and wanted it no other way. Pleasure mounted until it was almost unbearable. She lost herself in his loving, then went over. He followed.

Afterward, her breathing labored, she opened her eyes to find his trained on her, searching. Without words she knew what he wanted—to know if she felt guilty. Lifting her hand, she palmed his bearded cheek. "That life is over, this one has just begun."

His forehead lowered to hers. Once again she felt his body tremble against hers. "I don't want to lose you again."

"That's not going to happen." Wanting to reassure him, she kissed him, reached for that part of him that had given her so much pleasure, felt it surge to life in her hand.

"You read my mind." His voice was hoarse, strained. He slipped inside of her, then took them both on a slow ride to paradise again.

Brianna woke up Tuesday deliciously satiated. Patrick hadn't left her bed until early that morning. He'd been as reluctant as she to leave, but he wanted to get an early start on getting the boat ready for their outing after she came home from work today. Besides, she'd been feeling tired lately, and he wanted her to rest.

Both knew that with him there it wasn't likely to happen. She'd teased him that it was his fault for keeping her up at night. He'd said he'd make—

Her thoughts abruptly halted as an intense wave of nausea hit. With one hand over her mouth, the other on her churning stomach, she raced to the bathroom. She made it just in time.

Finished, she went to the vanity, stared at her reflection, and shuddered. She looked awful with her pale face and droopy eyelids. She was glad Patrick hadn't seen her this way. Men hated to be around sick women. Her father, who dearly adored her mother, was the same way. He'd said it was because it made him feel helpless that he couldn't ease her discomfort and make her feel better.

Bracing herself with one hand on the cold marble, she rinsed her mouth and brushed her teeth. Thank goodness the nausea was gone, but she couldn't remember ever feeling this drained. Every movement was an effort.

Going into her lingerie drawer, she picked up the first things she touched. Today matching from the skin out didn't matter. In fact, if she didn't have a full schedule she'd call Matilda and cancel all of her appointments and crawl back in bed.

In the bathroom, she grabbed her shower cap and adjusted the multiple sprays. She didn't feel like standing, but she needed the bracing effect of the jets. As worn as she felt, she'd probably go to sleep if she got in the Roman tub.

Once she showered, she dressed, feeling as if every move was an effort. Picking up her attaché case, she left to catch the elevator to the fourth floor. She and Patrick had easily gotten into the habit of him cooking for her every morning and some nights. A couple of times, Dalton and Justine had joined them.

Getting off the elevator, she slowly walked to Patrick's unit and rang the doorbell, hoping he'd get there before she slid to the floor. She swept her hand over her face. She must have picked up a mean bug. She never got sick.

The door swung open. Patrick took one look at her and the playful smile on his face vanished. "What's—"

Nausea hit without warning. Dropping the attaché case, she pushed him aside and rushed to the bathroom. When it was over, she brushed her teeth, glad Patrick had had the foresight to buy her a toothbrush. He'd also picked up a comb and other toiletries for her that he kept in his bathroom. She made a couple of half-hearted swipes through her hair, but found it too much of an effort, and put the silver-plated comb back in the cabinet and left the room.

Patrick was waiting just outside the bathroom. For once he was silent and simply stared at her. "I must have the summer flu. I hope I don't give it to you."

"I don't think you will."

The way he said it had her frown matching his. She was too tired to try and figure it out.

"Come on in the other room and sit down." As if she were fragile, he led her into the great room and sat her on the sofa.

The moment her bottom touched the supple leather her eyes closed. Calling Matilda and canceling was becoming more and more appealing by the minute.

"Brianna, you were sick yesterday morning as well," Patrick said as he held her hand.

"Please don't remind me. I just hope this passes soon."

"I don't think it will."

Her eyes blinked open. He was staring at her again with those intense eyes of his, but this time they made her feel uneasy. She hadn't seen him look so serious since he thought she might be a threat to his niece.

"There is no flu or virus that affects a person just in the morning."

She started to tell him she must have a new strain, then felt her world tilt. The implication of what he was getting at slowly sank in. She was good with facts and figures. It was no trouble to think back to the last time she and Jackson had been intimate. They'd used a condom. She hadn't been on the pill because she hadn't expected to be in a relationship. Since she'd been with Patrick she'd already been to Justine's ob/gyn for her well-woman's checkup. She'd planned on starting the pills after her period started.

The reason she was late had nothing to do with job-related stress, as she and her gynecologist had thought.

Tears clogged her throat and filled her eyes. "Oh, God."

"Sweetheart, don't cry," Patrick said, taking her into his arms and holding her tightly. "Don't cry."

She couldn't help it. She'd seen the stunned expression on his face. He was just as shocked as she was. What was she going to do? She was pregnant with Jackson's baby.

"Brianna, please stop crying and tell me what is the matter so I can help," Justine said, sitting on the coffee table in front of Brianna, who was curled up in a ball on the sofa. Justine had come as soon as Brianna called. "I know it's not your parents, because I called to check on them before I came over here."

Brianna stopped crying long enough to ask, "You didn't mention anything, did you?"

"Of course not." Justine brushed Brianna's hair from her face. "After all this time I know how to keep quiet. Now, please. Is it Patrick?"

That set Brianna back on another crying jag. Standing, Justine pushed the coffee table aside and knelt by Brianna's head. "Did you have a fight? That—"

"I'm pregnant."

The two words left Justine momentarily at a loss for words. "That can't be. You and Patrick haven't been together long enough for you to know that."

Brianna sniffed and looked miserable. "Jackson."

"Are you sure?" Justine asked.

Brianna bit her lip before answering. "I've been nauseous two mornings in a row, and I'm tired all the time." She swallowed. "You said the other night that I was moving slower than usual."

"And you pointed out that it was because of Patrick."

Brianna flushed. "What have I done? I'm pregnant with one man's child and having an affair with another."

"You had no way of knowing," Justine said sensibly. "All ties with Jackson had been severed."

"Except one." Brianna's hand cupped her stomach.

She looked so miserable that Justine wanted to help as Brianna'd helped her. "Perhaps the pregnancy test was faulty."

"I haven't taken one yet."

Justine was up and grabbing her purse from the end

table. "There's a drugstore at the corner. I'll be back with one as soon as I can."

Hope shone in Brianna's eyes. "You—you think it might be a virus?"

Justine wanted to say yes, but she didn't want to give Brianna false hope. "Let's just be sure." Opening the door, she was gone.

The stick turned blue in three seconds. Positive. So did the stick on the second test of another brand. Brianna stared at the proof of her carelessness and felt tears sting her eyes again. "I can't be pregnant. I have too much to do."

"You'll find a way." Justine put her arms around Brianna and led her back to the bed to sit down. "You're getting undressed and under the covers. I'll call Matilda and tell her you're not coming in."

Tears streamed down Brianna's cheeks. "What will Mama and Daddy think of me?"

"They love you, Brianna," Justine said, sure of that if nothing else. She picked up the phone on the bedside table and called Brianna's office. "Matilda. Good morning. Brianna isn't feeling her best today and is taking off for a couple of days. Could you please reschedule her appointments? Yes, I knew you'd take care of it. Yes, I'll tell her. Good-bye." Justine hung up the phone. "She sends her best, and said for you to get well soon."

"Some women have morning sickness through their entire pregnancy," Brianna whispered. "I can't do this. I simply can't."

Justine sat on the bed and hugged her. "Take one day at a time."

"It sounded better when I was telling that to you." Brianna laid her head on Justine's shoulder.

"If you can joke, you'll be all right. I'll get a gown." Justine searched until she found a long gown with cap sleeves, and then came back to the bed.

Brianna let Justine help her undress, and then crawled under the covers, silently wishing she were dreaming. "You can go now."

"I'm not going anywhere." Justine tucked the covers around Brianna's neck. "I'm going to fix you some soup and the Seven-Up I picked up at the store."

"You knew it would be positive?" Brianna asked.

"It's best being prepared." She patted Brianna on the shoulder. "First the soup, then I'll call our gynecologist and get you an appointment."

Miserable, Brianna scooted down in bed. "I don't want anyone to know."

"You know Dr. Woodson and his nurses can keep a confidence. If not, you can take them to court," Justine said.

Brianna knew she was expected to smile, but couldn't. "He must hate me."

"Jackson?"

"Patrick," Brianna clarified. "It wasn't just sex. I care about him. What must he think of me? You should have seen his face."

"He cares about you, too." Justine sat back down on the side of the bed. "Give him some time."

"All the time in the world won't fix this, and we both know it," Brianna said, misery in each word.

"You never know," Justine said. "I thought my life was over when I caught Andrew cheating. Then after his accident, when I was trapped into playing the loving wife, I was even more miserable. Now, I have Dalton in my life."

Tears formed in Brianna's eyes. "I used to have Patrick."

"Don't throw what you had away until you two can talk about this," Justine suggested.

Brianna wiped the tears from her eyes. "There's nothing to talk about. It's over."

Justine stood. "You're too stubborn to try to change your mind. I'll go get the food and make you a doctor's appointment."

As soon as Justine left the room, Brianna reached for the phone and dialed a number she had hoped never to use again.

"Jackson Hewitt."

Her hand clamped on the phone. "Jackson, this is Brianna."

There was a long pause, giving her the opportunity to speak again. "It's urgent that you come to Charleston as soon as possible. It concerns our future."

"You're coming back? Elton talks about you all the time. You could score that partnership, and we could go places," he said, excitement in his voice.

How could she have been so wrong about a man? "Can you come today or tomorrow? The sooner we talk, the better."

"I'm headed to meet a client whose firm will bring millions to us, but I'll call my secretary as soon as I hang up and have her get me tickets." He laughed. "Barring that, if I tell Elton that you're coming back, he'll let me have the company jet. He's that gone on you."

"I admire him, too." *And wish I could say the same thing about you.*

"Meeting with Günter and your call makes my day. I'll have my secretary call and let you know when to expect me. 'Bye."

" 'Bye." Brianna put the phone back in the charger. She had been seconds behind a client. At least neither of them had lied and said they had missed each other. That had to count for something. She just wished she knew what.

Although she had been expecting Jackson, Brianna jumped when the doorbell rang. His secretary had called less than thirty minutes after he'd hung up to say she had booked him a flight out after his last appointment the following day. A car service would have him at her place no later than nine that night.

Brianna glanced at the clock on the end table as she passed on the way to the door. Eight fifty-eight. "Hello, Jackson."

"Brianna, honey." His arms opened wide; he reached for her. She stepped out of his reach. He frowned and came inside. "What's the matter?" His frown deepened. "Are you sick?"

"No." She waved him to a chair.

He didn't take it. "I was hoping you can be on board next week. Günter is resisting. With you on the team, he'll sign on the dotted line and make us both shoo-ins for that junior partnership."

Since he wasn't wasting time presenting his case, neither was she. "I'm pregnant."

His head jerked back. Shock reflected in his face. "You're kidding?"

She folded her arms. How had she ever thought he was intelligent? "No, I'm not kidding."

"You're not going to pin this kid on me. We only slept together a couple of times!" he shouted, loosening his silk tie.

"Haven't you heard, once is enough?"

"Damn!" He paced away, then whirled back. "This is your fault. You're probably one of those scattered women who forget to take her pills."

Her arms came to her sides. "I can understand shock and anger, but I won't take you calling me names. This is your baby, so get over yourself."

He stared at her, his chest heaving in anger. "Have you thought of an ab—"

"Don't even think of saying it," she said, her body vibrating with anger.

He held up his hands in submission. "All right, I'll support it, but that's all. If you think you can trap me into marriage, think again. I'm going to the top and I won't be hampered by a clinging wife and a rug rat."

Brianna took a menacing step toward him. Rage almost consumed her. He took a step back, but she kept coming until they were inches apart. "You're right. You won't be bothered by a clinging wife or a rug rat because my baby and I are neither of those things. But listen and listen well." She punctuated each word with a sharp jab of her finger to his chest. "You'll set up a trust fund compensatory with your salary, the amount I know very well, or we'll see each other in court. A paternity suit would not help your climb."

"You—"

"I dare you to say it," she challenged.

Whirling, he muttered an expletive halfway out the slamming door.

Brianna's hand cupped her stomach. "Sorry I didn't choose you a better father." Sighing, she picked up her purse from the end of the sofa. There were two more people she had to tell.

All the way to her parents' house she debated on the best way to tell them, but as soon as her mother opened the door, the tears began to fall. Her father rushed out of his study to see what the commotion was.

"Are you hurt?"

"Did you have a fight with Patrick?"

"If only I had," she gulped, trying not to think of what might have been. The pregnancy was unplanned, but she'd give her baby all the love a child deserved.

"Let's go into the den," her father said, his arm around her waist. He stopped when he felt resistance.

The most difficult thing in her life was looking at them when she said, "I let you down."

"With a case?" her father wanted to know.

Her mother said nothing, just briefly shut her eyes. She knew.

"A man. I'm pregnant with Jackson's baby, and there won't be a wedding." Tears started falling again. "I'm so sorry. Sorrier than you'll ever know. If you want me to leave—"

"Hush that nonsense," her mother said, hugging her. "Things happen for a reason."

Her eyes sought her father, her idol. It would kill her if he thought less of her, less of the innocent baby she carried. "Mother is right as usual." He wrapped his long arms around her. "I won't lie and say I don't wish the wedding had come first, but things do happen for a reason. We love you, and I don't want you to ever think differently."

Too full to speak, she nodded.

"Have you been to the doctor?" Her mother was always practical.

"This morning. I'm seven weeks," she said. "I'm due in March."

"You look tired. You're spending the night. Go on upstairs, and get dressed for bed. I'll bring you a tray," her mother told her.

Her room hadn't changed since she'd moved out after she'd graduated from college. "I'd rather stay down here with you and Daddy for a while, if I could?" she asked. Perhaps if she wasn't alone her fears wouldn't be so great. She wanted her baby, but she didn't want to be an unwed mother.

"Come on into the den, and you can tell me the parts of *Perry Mason* I miss when I fall asleep." His arm still around her, they headed down the wide polished hallway.

"You've seen them so many times, you know the script by heart," her mother teased.

Brianna almost smiled at the running joke. She'd been raised with love by two exceptional parents. She wished she could have given that to her child.

"Sit here with me, Pumpkin." Her father patted the couch beside him.

"I'll get you some decaffeinated tea." Her mother palmed her cheek, and then she was gone.

Like she had as a little girl, Brianna curled up beside her father. "Thanks, Daddy."

"We love you. Just remember that," he said, his voice gruff with emotions.

"I will, and I'm sorry I disappointed you," she whispered.

He stared down at her. "You could never do that. You're still the best in my book, and I'll defy anyone who says differently."

She did smile that time, then put her head back on his shoulder. She had her family and Justine. She'd make it. She just wished she hadn't lost Patrick.

Twenty-one

Justine heard the ringing as if from a distance. When she roused enough to tell it was her cell phone, Dalton was already handing it to her. Their eyes met. They'd fallen asleep after making love and left the light on.

Sitting and pulling the sheet up to cover her breasts, Justine glanced at the caller ID, then answered. The euphoric feeling of moments ago disappeared. "Hello, Beverly."

"Justine, you have to come! You have to come now!" Beverly said, excitement in her whispering voice.

"Come where?" The clock on the bedside read 1:16 A.M.

"The hospital!"

"The hospital," Justine repeated as dread slithered down her spine.

Dalton sat on the bed and curved his arm around her shoulders, silently giving her his support.

"Is—"

"Just come! I hid in the bathroom, so they wouldn't put me out. I'll be waiting." The line went dead.

Justine cut the phone off, and turned to Dalton. "Beverly hid in Andrew's room and wants me to come."

"I don't suppose you'd consider calling the nurse's station, and letting them handle this?" Dalton asked.

"She loves him."

Dalton tenderly touched her cheek. "Love has a way of making people do strange things."

Justine's heart thudded. They'd never talked about love.

"We have a lot to talk about when you return," he said.

She turned her head to kiss his palm. "I don't want to go."

"But you will." He kissed the top of her head. "You care, sometimes too much." Dalton came to his feet.

Justine watched him in all of his naked splendor, then began gathering and putting on her clothes. When she was almost finished, she saw Dalton had done the same. "You can't go with me, and you know it."

His lips flattened into a thin line. "Yeah, but I don't like it."

"I'll call." Stuffing her blouse into her pants, she snagged her purse on the way out of Dalton's bedroom and hurried to her car.

"Drive safely, and call when you get there." Dalton leaned into the open window on the driver's side.

"I will," Justine promised, then backed up and headed for the hospital, trying to decide the best way to get Beverly to leave.

Justine expected the night nurse to go ballistic and even understood her wanting to call security. It had taken some fast talking to get her to let Justine handle it, and promise that this would never happen again.

"It had better not."

With that ominous warning prodding her, Justine eased open the door to Andrew's room. The light from the open door illuminated the bed. The rest of the room was in shadows. "Beverly?"

"I'm here." Beverly popped out of the bathroom. "I'm so glad you're here. I called you at home and got the machine."

Justine had no intention of explaining. "Beverly, you can't do this. They'll bar you from visiting all together."

She smiled. "Not after tonight." Catching Justine's hand, she dragged her to the bedside. "I wanted you to be the first to see after me."

"Beverly, please."

Beverly pointed toward Andrew's face. "Just look. That's all I ask."

"We'll leave afterward."

"If you want me to," she answered. "Andrew, dear, Justine is here."

Justine looked at Beverly, who put on the light over the bed and waved her hand toward Andrew. Justine slowly turned toward Andrew, her concern for Beverly growing.

"Look closely. Look at his eyes. Andrew."

Justine decided she had wasted enough time. The charge nurse had probably already called security. She was about to straighten when she thought she saw a movement. Unconsciously, she gasped, then gave a startled cry. Andrew's eyelashes, always long, flickered.

"I told you! I told you all!" Beverly cried happily. "My baby is waking up."

Dalton prowled his house. He hadn't gone back to sleep after Justine left. He was too worried about her. Despite what Andrew had done to her, she'd still blame herself if something happened to him. Dalton prayed the bastard would wake up; then, when he was well, he could beat the crap out of him, then thank him for being such an ass.

Swiping his hand over his face, Dalton poured himself a cup of coffee and sipped. He didn't have to drink his own brew anymore. Justine always got things ready before she left. She'd put homey touches around the place. With her presence, she had made his house a home. Now if he could just get her to make it permanent and legal.

Dalton looked at the silent phone. She'd called when she reached the hospital, but he hadn't heard from her since and that worried him. He glanced at the clock on the wall. Eight-thirteen. Since they had to adhere to strict visiting hours, he'd expected her call long ago. He might be jumping the gun, but they had things to discuss.

He'd seen her eyes that morning when he'd mentioned love, he'd seen surprise, but also, he hoped, happiness. Dalton glanced at his watch again. He'd called the store once already, disguising his voice like a teenager.

He went to the sink. The radio was on, but he wasn't paying much attention to it. Even when the announcer said there'd been a miracle . . . until he heard Andrew's name. Rushing across the room, he increased the volume.

"You heard me right, audience. This morning a miracle happened right here in Charleston when Andrew Crandall showed his first voluntary movements after being in a coma for over four months. Doctors had given up hope for his recovery, my sources tell me, but not those who loved and admired the great motivational speaker, especially his wife and mother. There will be a news conference in about thirty minutes at the hospital. This is big and welcome news indeed. Now back to our regular broadcast program."

Dalton grabbed his keys and sprinted for his Jeep. He drove as fast as he could in the early morning traffic. Parking, he raced to the elevator. He would have paced in the elevator, but it was too crowded. As it was, he tried to keep his displeasure from showing as the elevator stopped at every floor before reaching six. Getting off, he saw the crowd that reached into the non-ICCU area of the floor. Somewhere in there was Justine.

"Excuse me, please." Some people looked at him with annoyance; others readily moved aside. Dalton kept pushing through the crowd until he gained his objective.

Cameras flashed, microphones were thrust in front of Beverly's face. She seemed to take it all in with aplomb. Justine, standing between her mother and her mother-in-law, who fielded questions like a pro, looked shattered.

He'd been afraid of this. She didn't want Andrew to die; she just didn't want to be his wife. Brianna, looking a bit off, was on the other side of Justine's mother. Her left hand, as was Justine's right, was behind her back. They were holding hands while her mother did nothing to support her.

A woman stepped forward and hushed the crowd. "I'm Sue Watkins, head of public relations for the hospital. I'm sure we're all pleased to see Mr. Crandall's recovery, but this is a hospital. Once this news conference is over, we'd like for you to quietly disperse," she told them.

"If you need further information on Mr. Crandall's recovery, please go through the regular channels. I'm sure you can understand that, while the family is pleased, they also need time. Ten minutes, and that's it." She stepped back.

Immediately, microphones were thrust back into Beverly's face. "What are you feeling now, Mrs. Crandall?"

"Pure happiness. Our Andrew is coming back to us, to the world. Others, like his doctor, might have given up, but Justine and I never did." She briefly turned to Justine and hugged her. Cameras flashed. "Thank you for loving Andrew as much as he loves you, for being the kind of wife any man would cherish, for keeping the faith."

"The doctors had given up hope, you say?" asked another reporter.

Beverly's face hardened. "He even badgered my daughter-in-law to sign papers to disconnect his life support."

The woman who had spoken earlier stepped up to the mike when the crowd began to grumble. "It is the hospital's standard procedure to ask a family member to sign the papers. The doctor wants to know the family's wishes when there is no living will."

"Mrs. Crandall, do you have anything to say?"

Dalton wanted to snatch the microphone out of the reporter's hand and bash him over the head with it. He'd have to have been blind not to see how stricken Justine was.

"I—"

"I'll handle that." Brianna stepped in front of Justine. "Brianna Ireland, family friend and lawyer. Mrs. Crandall is, of course, overjoyed with her husband's recovery, and is naturally still trying to process it. I'm sure you understand that, while good news, it has been a shock. She'll issue a formal statement later today." Brianna moved back to where she had been standing

"Justine has been the best possible wife to Andrew. When I called her this morning to see for herself she didn't hesitate to come here. We're blessed to have her," Beverly continued.

A reporter asked the doctor, who had just arrived and looked upset, about the papers and Andrew's recovery. "Ms. Watkins explained it is hospital procedure when there is no living will. As for the length of recovery, that's unknown at this time. Mr. Crandall can response to stimuli with flickers of his eyelashes; his pupils react to light. Given the three prolonged cardiac arrests he sustained, we are unable to determine how this will affect his recovery or if he sustained any neurological damage."

"I know. He'll be fine. Won't he, Justine?" Beverly declared.

The focus shifted to her. Justine numbly nodded, then glanced away to look straight at Dalton. Her eyes widened in surprise and lit up for a brief second before reality hit. Her eyes dimmed, her head lowered.

When a reporter asked about Andrew's company, Dalton only half listened. His focus was on Justine. He willed her to look at him again. When she did, he saw what he'd dreaded, unspeakable pain and the frightened look of a trapped animal. With her mother-in-law singing her praises, there was no way Justine could say she was filing for divorce.

Justine's mother followed the direction of her gaze. She was tight-lipped and angry. Then she smiled at him. His fists clenched. He understood the message.

He'd lost again.

"We need to talk in private," Justine's mother said as soon as the press conference was over. Without giving her a chance to reply, Helen grabbed her arm and drew her out of the waiting area to a quiet corner just outside the ICCU waiting area.

Justine didn't see any reason to resist. Thankfully the waiting area was clear of reporters and friends. She'd sent Brianna home. She'd heard over the radio and rushed over. At the moment, Beverly, Marcus, and Kent were visiting Andrew. The hospital couldn't do enough for them after they determined that Andrew was indeed waking up. Justine was still dealing with that, and wondering how long before she could file for a divorce. With all the praise she was receiving, it wouldn't be any time soon.

"What is going on between you and Dalton?" her mother asked sharply.

Justine didn't have to fake shock. "What?"

"I know you. Andrew's recovery might have been difficult to deal with, but you don't seem happy about it." Helen's gaze narrowed. "Neither does Dalton."

"Mother, I've been up since one this morning."

"Evade my questions if you want, but you listen to me. Don't throw away your happiness for a good-looking man who's just out for what he can get. Andrew is a wonderful, loving husband. Count your blessings instead of looking over the fence. Don't mess up."

There had been times in her life when she would have cowered, tried to appease her mother. Those days were thankfully over. "I'll give what you said all the consideration it deserves."

Her mother's lips tightened. "Have it your way, but don't come running to me when it turns sour and, believe me, it will."

Her mother huffed off. Justine was about to follow her back to the waiting area when her cell phone rang. She'd forgotten to turn it off. The frequency affected pacemakers. "Hello?"

"I'll wait at your house tonight after dark for as long as it takes," Dalton said. Then he was gone.

She wished she had the strength to tell him not to, but she couldn't. She needed to see him one last time. Her mother's words worried her. She didn't want to embroil Dalton in any negative gossip.

He deserved to hear it was over from her in person. Shutting off the phone, she slipped it back in her purse and prepared to continue acting a lie.

Patrick had heard the news on the radio and knew Brianna would be at the hospital with Justine. He debated whether he should go just to see her and try to gauge how she was doing. He decided to stay away. Hands deep in the pockets of his jeans, his head down, he followed the path of the walking course around the condominium.

He'd considered taking the *Proud Mary* out, but the ocean was no place to be when your head wasn't on straight. His certainly wasn't.

Leaving the paved path, he walked nearer the water and braced his arms on the railing that ran the length of the marina, then stared out to sea. Life sucker-punched you at times. He knew that as well as anyone.

What was Andrew's waking up going to mean to Justine and Dalton? He knew they were having an affair, but he'd learned long ago to stay out of other people's business. He liked both of them, and believed there was no reason for them not to be together, since it hadn't appeared as if Andrew would recover. Only now that had changed, and Andrew was very much in the picture.

Just like the unknown father of Brianna's baby was in the picture.

The squeak of a hungry sea gull caught Patrick's attention as it swooped down for food. Usually he enjoyed the sight. Not today. His mind was in too much turmoil. He'd never been torn by such strong emotions.

His hands came out of his pockets to wrap around the iron railing. He loved Brianna. He'd started falling in love with her the night she'd brushed him off at Justine's bookstore. He liked to think she cared for him as well, but that no longer mattered.

What was important now was what was best for her and the baby. He'd give her a few days to get used to the idea, let her talk with the baby's father. Brianna was too upfront not to contact the man. But if Patrick got even an inkling of an idea that the meeting had not gone well, he would do his best to get a ring on her finger.

He loved the woman; he'd love the baby as well. You didn't have to be the biological parent to love a child that came into the family. Brooke and the rest of his family had proven that with Amy and Mark.

Patrick pushed away from the rail and headed back inside the condo. The elevator door opened and Brianna stood there. Her face was wan, her eyes sad. He didn't think it was because of Justine. If he ever met the stupid guy who put that look on her face, the man was going to wish he hadn't.

He stepped on the elevator, effectively blocking her exit. "Did you eat this morning?" A safe question.

She shook her head. "I didn't want to chance being sick."

The door behind him closed. Patrick pushed four. "You need something in your stomach before you go to work. Decaf tea and toast, then I'll take you by your office to see what needs to be done. After that you're coming back and going to bed."

The elevator door opened on his floor. Gently he took her arm and went to his place. He knew how exhausted she must be when she didn't object. Opening the door, he sat her on the couch and went to the kitchen.

Patrick proved he was a man a woman could depend on. He'd cared for her as tenderly as her mother would have. It hadn't seemed to matter that she was carrying another man's baby.

It hadn't mattered to her either. Pitiful and needy that she was, something she had never been before, she still wished she could curl up in his lap, close her eyes, and rest. He'd let her, too. Just like he'd coaxed her into eating a half slice of dry toast and drinking a cup of tea.

"I've never known you to have tea and certainly not decaf," she said when they were getting in his truck. She hadn't resisted because she hadn't felt like driving. If she'd taken a taxi, Matilda would have told her parents and they would worry. She had caused them enough concern.

And deep down she wasn't ready to give up Patrick's friendship.

"I got it for you."

She hadn't known how to respond then. Twenty minutes later, when he was pulling into the parking spaces behind her office, she still didn't.

He had every right to think her immoral and loose, but he treated her with infinite kindness. Her eyes filled with tears.

"Are you all right?"

No, but I will be. "I'm fine."

His penetrating stare said he didn't believe her, but he helped her out. Silently they walked to the back door of her father's law firm. The smell of the chicory coffee caused her stomach to roll.

Patrick saw her expression and said, "As soon as we check in with Matilda, we're out of here."

She couldn't agree more.

Brianna woke up in her own bed shortly after three that afternoon. Lines of confusion darted across her forehead as she stared at the bright light streaming through her window, then she remembered.

She was pregnant.

She closed her eyes and sank deeper into the bedding. So much had changed in the past seventy-two hours. She was pregnant, unmarried, and the father was a Class-A jerk.

And she had lost Patrick.

Brianna almost whimpered as the pain of the loss hit her. How could she have been so stupid? It wasn't the baby's fault, she'd never think that. She was a grown woman and had made the choice to be intimate, and now the consequences had slapped her in the face.

Ready or not, she was going to be a mother.

The door opened quietly. Patrick peeked into the room. Her heart swelled with an emotion she couldn't define. It was extremely easy for her to imagine him doing that countless times to check on her. Why hadn't she met him first?

"Feeling better?"

Her body perhaps, but not her spirits. "Yes."

Coming farther into the room, he hunkered by the bedside. Briefly his palm cupped her cheek. She wanted so badly to prolong the contact. "You want to try a couple of spoons of broth? Eating smaller portions won't make your stomach rebel as much."

"All right." She didn't want any food, but knew she had to eat something or she'd never start feeling better.

"Be back in a jiff." Pushing to his feet, he started from the room.

"You must have other things to do. I'll get it later." She had no idea of when that might be. It was an effort to lift her head. She scrunched deeper into the bedding.

Patrick quickly retraced his steps and hunkered down once again. "There's nothing more important than making sure you and the baby are taken care of."

Tears crested in her eyes again. Pregnancy definitely took you on an emotional roller coaster.

Snatching a tissue from the box on the bedside table, he dried her tears. "A lot has been thrown at you, but things will get better."

She took the tissue and dabbed her eyes herself. "I know. I'm usually not this weepy."

"You're entitled. Just know that I'm here for as long as you need me," he said.

"But you shouldn't have to be," she said, not sure if she meant because she was pregnant or because he wasn't the father.

"I want to." He took her hand, his thumb gently stroking. "We were lovers, and now we're friends. I plan to stick around as long as you let me. I'll get that broth."

Her eyes stung as he left the room. She wished they were both.

Twenty-two

Justine finally reached home at half past ten. After the negative interview her mother-in-law gave, the hospital's switchboard had been flooded with calls from friends, family, and associates of Andrew. Many of those calling were well connected and politically powerful and had spoken directly with the administrator. He hadn't been pleased and wanted the hospital's sterling reputation restored. Thus, they were now bending over backward to give Beverly anything she wanted.

Extended visitation was at the top of her list. It had taken the social worker, Ms. Lancaster, to point out to her mother-in-law that Andrew needed his rest. Continuous stimuli couldn't be good for him. As for Justine, each time his eyelashes flickered, she felt as if she were falling deeper and deeper into a black hole.

Once inside, she practically ran to the back. She was barely off the portico before Dalton appeared. In seconds, she was in his arms.

"We'll get through this, honey."

Eyes closed, Justine tried to fill her mind with memories: the warmth of his muscled body, the spicy aftershave, the arousing softness of his beard, his deep voice that could arouse and soothe. "We need to talk."

As if sensing he wasn't going to like what she said, his arms clutched her closer. "Don't throw away what we have."

This is for him, for countless others, she thought. Slowly she pushed out of his arms. "We can't build a life on deceit."

"Jus—"

"We would be as guilty as Andrew," she said, talking over him. "Perhaps this is my punishment for breaking my marriage vows just as the accident was Andrew's. Good can't come out of wrong."

"That's bull," Dalton snapped, his hands clenched around her upper arm. "It's not your fault any more than it was mine when my wife left me for another woman."

Stunned, all Justine could do was stare at him.

Suddenly, she was free. "Yeah, the bad boy of Charleston's wife left him for a patient she met while in a psychiatric clinic for her violent outbursts. The woman, a psychologist, was there to kick her cocaine habit. Instead she got my wife hooked on the stuff, and on her."

"Dalton, I'm sorry," Justine said, reaching out briefly to touch his arm.

"I felt like crap when I found out about the affair." He shook his bowed head. "Here I was, a big macho man, and my wife wanted another woman. That she was bipolar and easily manipulated didn't matter. Her lover had given her something I couldn't. Finding out about it on the six o'clock news when they were arrested in a drug sting didn't help. I was scheduled to go to work the next day, but I called in sick. I didn't want to show my face." He stepped closer. One large hand tenderly cupped her cheek.

"At the time I was still fighting demons, until I came back and held you in my arms." His other hand cupped the other cheek. "Don't throw away what we have to do penance. Please."

"I can't," Justine said, her heart breaking. "Too many lives will be affected if I start divorce proceedings now." She swallowed. "He wouldn't even know what is going on. He may not remember."

Dalton's black eyes hardened. "And that excuses him?"

"No, of course not. But now I know how difficult it is to resist temptation."

Dalton muttered an expletive. "Don't you dare compare what we have to some sleazy affair. I love you."

She'd wanted to hear those words for so long and now they were coming too late. "We can't be happy building on someone else's misfortune."

"I'm not going to let you waltz right by what I said."

Tears sparkled in her eyes. "What difference does it make now?"

"A lot, admit it. I lost you seventeen years ago. I don't want to lose you again. At least give me that much."

No power on earth could have kept her from saying, "I love you so much it scares me."

"Justine." Despite her attempt to push him away, he pulled her close. "I've waited years to hear those words."

Unable to resist, she snuggled closer to his muscled warmth and strength. "I thought I was in love with Andrew, but it's sweet and gentle, with you it's different, it's powerful, fierce, and touches me on every level."

"I feel the same way."

"But that doesn't change things, since Andrew is just coming out of a coma. My life and that of his foundation will be under public scrutiny. Please help me. I can't be strong unless you do."

His chest heaved. "You can have tonight, but it's not over." His lips brushed gently across her, then she was free.

Shaken to the very core of her soul, Justine watched him walk away, tearing her world apart.

Shortly before noon the next day, Dalton entered It's a Mystery Bookstore. He'd given Justine last night, but he had no intention of getting out of her life. She had to learn to be a bit selfish like everyone else. He certainly was going to be. Andrew blew his chance and Dalton didn't plan on letting him have another one.

Now if he could convince Justine.

For a long uninterrupted moment he studied her helping a young mother and child select a book in the children's section. She'd kneeled down to show the little girl the book, flipping the pages, pointing out the pictures, and reading. The sight made his heart ache. One day he hoped and prayed that she'd do the same with their child. He was going to give it his best shot.

So far he hadn't seen her assistant or the manager. He'd picked lunchtime in the hope that he'd be able to talk her into going out for at least a little while.

She looked up and saw him. The love that shone on her

face, in her eyes, before it was quickly banked, did his heart good after a restless night of dreading that it might be all over between them.

"I'll be with you in a moment," she said, her voice a bit unsteady.

"Take your time. I'm in no hurry."

The young woman with the child looked around as well. She got that awed look on her pretty face that he was becoming very familiar with. "You're Edgar Gunn!"

"Guilty." Walking over, he extended his hand. "Pleased to meet you."

"My husband is a police officer, and he loves your books," she said, giddy with excitement. "He was on duty and missed your signing. I hate to ask, but could you please sign a book for him . . . if it's not too much trouble."

"It's not. I'll let you finish, and you can tell me which book later." He tipped his head. "Nice meeting you."

He walked off to the adult fiction section, but he had noticed the thrill in her voice when she talked of meeting him. He loved his fans, but there was only one woman he wanted to hear talk that way about him.

Justine was so nervous she could hardly help Michelle pick out a book for her young daughter, Cami. Dalton had come back just as he'd said. As she rang up the sale she had to admit she was flattered. What woman wouldn't want a man like Dalton to fight losing her, but in the end that was just what would happen. There wouldn't be a happy ending for them now, just as there hadn't been years ago.

"Here you go, Michelle." Justine handed the dark-haired woman the bag containing her purchases, which included a romance novel, *An Everlasting Love*, by Bette Ford, that she'd picked out for herself. "I hope all of you will enjoy your books."

"We will." Michelle turned to Dalton, who, after signing her book, had gone back to browsing the adult fiction section. "Nice meeting you, and thanks for signing my husband's book."

"You're welcome. Please tell your husband I appreciate his support."

"I will. Good-bye." Michelle took the small hand of her four-year-old and left the store.

The door had barely closed before Dalton crossed the room and stood in front of the counter. "You here by yourself?"

Justine didn't know why his question made her pulse race. Perhaps because of the barely banked desire she saw in Dalton's dark eyes. "Yes. Iris is at lunch, and the assistant is sick."

"What about your lunch?"

"I'm not hungry." The front door opened, and two laughing women came in. "Excuse me."

She met the women near the front of the store. "Good morning. Could I help you find anything?"

"We're just browsing," answered one of the women, her gaze following Dalton as he walked past them and out the front door. It closed quietly behind him.

"Now him you could have helped me with." They broke into naughty laughter.

Justine didn't think the comment was the least bit funny. "I'll be at the counter if you need anything." Going to the computer, she began checking stock, occasionally glancing up to see if the women needed anything.

Lunchtime was unpredictable. They could be busy, slow, or anything in between. Today was slow. She shouldn't, but she wished the women hadn't come in. She would have liked to have talked to Dalton. It was torture being so close and not being able to touch, but being away from him was twice as bad.

The door opened again. Dalton, a plastic sack from a popular restaurant in his hand, came directly to her and handed her the bag. "Eat."

She flicked a glance at the women, who had stopped browsing and now watched her like a hawk watched his next meal. "Thank you." As soon as she took the bag of food, he left.

Justine wanted to stare after him, but couldn't. Setting the food aside, she went back to checking stock, making mistakes, and having to repeat steps.

Her mind was on Dalton. The man she loved, but could never have.

"We're in bad shape," Brianna said, her head resting on the back of the tufted upholstery of the sofa in her great room.

"You won't get an argument from me," Justine said, her voice as miserable as Brianna's. They'd just finished dinner. "I haven't seen Dalton in three days. We finally find two good men, and we can't have them." She sat up on the sofa. "Correction, I can't. You're being too stubborn about Patrick. He's a great guy."

Brianna's sock-covered feet came off the coffee table and hit the carpeted floor. "You're talking to the choir here. He pampered me like a baby. He even drops by the office to see how I'm doing."

"Then don't let him get away. Tell him you want more than friendship," Justine said, aware that she wasn't in a position to give anyone advice on relationships.

Brianna's hand cupped her stomach. "I'm scared. He obviously doesn't think less of me, but what will happen when I start to show? When people think he's the daddy, or if he's repulsed by me when I get as big as his boat."

Justine rolled her eyes. "Stop being a lawyer. Stop trying to think of every contingency. Just go after the man you love."

"What!" Brianna's mouth gaped. "How did you know? I just realized myself."

"Because when you're in love it's easier to see it in other people." Justine sipped iced tea.

"You, too," Brianna said—it was more a statement than a question.

"Me, too."

"We certainly are a pair." Brianna sipped her decaffeinated Coke. "Both are ex-policemen and good men."

"I'm not sure if that doesn't make it worse." Justine came upright. "I better go and do penance."

Brianna stood with her. "How is it going?"

Justine looked down before answering. "The doctors are amazed at his progress. He moved his hand yesterday."

"The quicker he wakes up, the quicker you can file and end your misery."

Justine lifted her head to meet Brianna's eyes. She was sure the other woman wasn't going to like what she was about to say. "I've decided to put off filing until Andrew is out of the hospital and can care for himself."

"Are you crazy?" Brianna shouted. "That could be months from now!"

"It's not for Andrew," Justine said. "If I do it sooner, it might jeopardize the firm and the senior citizen complex. I can wait a little longer."

"Can you?"

Justine sighed. "It's the lie I'm trying to tell myself."

The doorbell rang. Brianna's eyes lit up. Her hand brushed across her hair, smoothed over the salmon-colored loose top and matching pants.

"The way you're primping, that's obviously Patrick, so I'm going." Justine dragged her bag from the end of the sofa. "I'll drop by tomorrow with dinner again and this time we'll drown our sorrows in ice cream."

"Deal." Expecting Patrick, Brianna opened the door. Dalton filled the doorway instead. His gaze snapped from Brianna to Justine.

"Dal—"

His mouth cut off the rest of what Justine had been about to say. She didn't, couldn't resist. It was like coming home after being away for a long time. Sweet. Welcoming.

"I missed you," he said when he lifted his head. He nipped her bottom lip. "Missed this."

Desire heated her blood. Her nipples puckered beneath the jacket of her suit. "Dalton."

"Should I leave the room?" Brianna teased with a smile.

"Not on your life," Patrick said.

Brianna whirled around and almost went into his arms. "Patrick!"

"I didn't mean to intrude, but I wanted you two to have these invitations." Coming in, he closed the door behind him. "Hello, Dalton, Justine."

Justine flushed and moved away from Dalton. "Hello, Patrick."

"Hey, man," Dalton said.

"Here." Patrick handed invitations in thick red and black envelopes with BLISS printed on the return address to Justine and Brianna. "They're having a pampering spa thing. I thought both of you would like to go. Before you say no, the shop will close at five to set up. Your invitation says six, an hour before the other guests will arrive."

"You did this?" Brianna said.

"I thought you both could do with some pampering," he said softly.

"Thank you." Brianna's voice wavered.

"If you'll drive out to my place afterward, I'll have barbecue with my special sauce waiting," Dalton said.

"Can you eat heavy foods now?" Patrick asked, his brow knitted in concern.

Dalton's eyes narrowed on Brianna. "You sick? I noticed at the news conference you were looking a bit off."

Complete silence filled the room and stretched out.

"She has the flu," Justine said.

"She has a virus," Patrick blurted.

Dalton's questioning gaze went from Patrick's chagrined expression to Justine's disturbed one before finally coming to rest on Brianna. "Which is it?"

"Neither," Brianna said. "I'm pregnant."

Dalton's hard gaze locked on Patrick for a long moment, then his shoulders relaxed and he hugged Brianna to him. "Can I find and kick his butt for you?"

"That pleasure is mine." Patrick said, his voice biting and cold.

She pushed out of Dalton's arms. "Thanks, but I fight my own battles. How about I skip the sauce?"

"Done. I expect all of you between eight and eight thirty."

"I don't think I should go," Justine said softly.

"I might not feel like driving from the store out to Dalton's place," Brianna said.

Justine looked at Patrick. He shrugged and shoved his hands into the pockets of his jeans. "Men tend to stay as far away as possible from Bliss when events are going on. Besides, I might have to show Dalton here how to grill."

"I'd appreciate it," Dalton said. "I wouldn't want to have Brianna and Justine drive out for nothing."

Justine could argue, but it was three against one. "All right. You don't have to gang up on me." She hugged Brianna. "I'll pick you up at five thirty. Take care."

"You do the same."

"I will." After one longing look at Dalton, she left.

Dalton started after her before the door closed. Brianna caught his shirt in the back. "Not a good idea."

He rubbed his hand over his face. "I guess not. I stopped by to ask you to talk some sense into her head."

"I already tried. Couldn't." Brianna looped her arms through both men's. "I'm tired of lying down, how about a card game?"

"You feel up to it?" Patrick asked, his brow furrowed in concern.

"Thanks to your excellent care I'm feeling better each day."

"If you get tired don't be stubborn. Tell me."

Brianna's brows arched. "I don't like taking orders."

"Then don't put me in a position to give them."

Laughter erupted. They both glared at Dalton. "Never

thought I'd see the man who could be her match. I don't think I'll stay after all. Night, you two, and play nice."

"He said play nice," Patrick said when the door closed after Dalton.

She didn't want to play nice. She wanted to drag him down to the floor and do naughty things to his body.

"What do you want to do?"

"It's best if you don't ask." She waved him to a seat. "I'll get the cards."

The doorbell rang again when she'd taken two steps. "I'll get it," Patrick said, going to open the door.

It was a toss-up as to who was the most surprised, Brianna's parents or Brianna. "Mama. Daddy. I didn't expect you."

"We wanted to check on you," her mother said, unable to keep her eyes off Patrick.

Her husband had the same identical problem. "Hello, Patrick."

"Hello, Mr. and Mrs. Ireland. I just came by to check on Brianna and make sure she takes care of herself." He smiled. "You know how stubborn she can be."

"You're asking for it," Brianna said, her eyes narrowed.

Patrick chuckled. "You wouldn't dare hit me in front of your father, the lawyer. I'd have an impeccable witness."

"He would recuse himself, of course," Brianna pointed out.

Patrick seemed deep in thought for a moment, then his smile came slow and bright. "Then it looks like I'd have to ask your mother."

"You would, too." Brianna playfully swatted him on the arm.

"In a heartbeat." He swiped his finger tenderly down her nose. "I better get out of here and let you visit with your parents." Opening the door, he said to her parents, "She's stubborn, but I'll watch out for her. Good night."

Brianna closed the door, unaware of the half-smile on her lips until she saw her parents staring at her. She wiped the smile from her face. "Can I get you something to drink?"

"He knows?" her father asked. He never was one to beat around the bush.

"Yes," Brianna said and left it at that. Telling them that he had known before she did didn't seem the thing.

"He still comes around?" This question was from her mother.

"Patrick is the kind of man who sticks, no matter what," she said, and could read their minds. *Why hadn't she picked a man like him to be the father of her baby?* Good question.

"I liked that young man from the first." Her father took a seat on the sofa. "Nice manners."

"He's grounded, thoughtful, and good-looking." Her mother sat beside her father. "Brianna, you should bring him over for dinner Sunday."

"Oh, no. Don't you dare." Hands on her hips, she stood in front of them. "No matchmaking. We're just friends."

"I don't believe either of us said differently. Did we, Susan?"

"Certainly not," her mother agreed. "Like Patrick said, you're too stubborn for that. Now come over here and sit down. We don't need anything to drink." She scooted over. "You need to rest when you can."

Brianna sat down between them. She wasn't fooled by

their feigned innocence. They liked Patrick and saw him as the solution to their daughter's problem. Arguing with them wouldn't do any good. She'd gotten her stubbornness from both of them and, although it wasn't well known, her mother was the worst of the three of them.

"Let me handle this by myself, please," she said.

"Whatever you say, Pumpkin."

"Whatever you say."

Brianna groaned. They were too agreeable. She was in for it now!

Twenty-three

Bliss was everything Brianna had heard it was—beautifully showcased with scrumptious, heavenly scented products and owned by three friendly, business-savvy women. Lorraine Averheart, the oldest and financial backer, was chic in an Armani pantsuit; Claire Bennett Livingston, the creator of the products, glowed in a Bill Blass dress in her final months of pregnancy; and Brooke Dunlap-Randle, the marketing genius, was stunning in a Ralph Lauren gown. All three women wore red and black, the signature colors of the popular and successful bath and body store in downtown Charleston.

Within moments after the introductions, Lorraine and Claire had taken Justine and begun showing her around. Brooke took Brianna.

"I'm so glad you were able to come," Brooke said. "We have seaweed hand treatment, eye massages and moisturizing masks, aromatherapy pedicures, Bliss mud masks, and massages."

Brianna glanced over her shoulder to where two muscular men prepared a massage table and chair. "There's going to be a long line for their services."

Warm laughter trickled from Brooke's red lips; the same color was on her toenails—her feet were in three-inch Chanel spike heels—and her fingernails. "Hope so. The first five minutes are free, but after that you need points."

"Which are obtained by buying products," Brianna explained.

"Exactly." Brooke tilted her head of classy short curls to one side, causing her chandelier earrings to brush against her cheek, and openly studied Brianna. "Patrick said you were sharp, but I wouldn't expect any different from a woman he cares about."

That was true as far as it went, but her foolish heart wished for so much more. "He's a great guy."

"That he is." Brooke wrapped her arms around her own slim waist. "When he was injured—" She swallowed before going on. "We were so scared. It took him a long time to recover."

The thought of what Patrick must have gone through still made Brianna's stomach roll. Her hand pressed against her abdomen to settle the churning motion.

Brooke's gaze dropped. "The baby making you feel queasy?"

Brianna started, tongue-tied. She felt betrayed. "He told you?"

"Don't be upset with Patrick," Brooke soothed. "He was concerned that the scents in here might make you ill or harm the baby. He'd read that some candles have lead in wicks and cause birth defects. I assured him on both counts. We're a close family."

Brianna picked up a bottle of lotion, then a jar of moisturizing cream, only to put them down again. She recognized the restless movements for what they were, nerves. Another by-product of her pregnancy. "He has a tendency to want to take care of everyone."

"That's what makes him so wonderful. He deserves the best." Brooke glanced around. "We better get started or you'll be late for your dinner engagement, and Patrick will have my head. What do you want to do first?"

Brianna knew she should probably let it go, but she couldn't. "You don't object to him still seeing me?"

"I'm thankful. Patrick hasn't dated since his accident. He's been happier lately than he has in months. Of course, Rafael talked of how beautiful you were, but it would take more than looks to keep Patrick interested." Folding her arms, Brooke leaned against the counter, which was filled with bath products. "The family is grateful."

Sadness washed over Brianna. Patrick would soon move on to other women who would know his special caring touch and loving. She'd lost him and it was her own fault.

"I'm going to have the eye massage and moisturizing mask first." Justine, the white terry cloth robe provided by Bliss draped over her arm, joined them. "Have you decided?"

What Brianna wanted, she couldn't have. "That sounds nice."

"I can't believe I've never been here," Justine said, staring around the store with excitement.

"After tonight, we hope that will change." Lorraine joined them and handed Brooke and Justine drinks in crystal flutes.

"Sparkling cider," Brooke said to Brianna. "We served

it at our preopening to save money, but have kept it as a tradition."

Brianna knew the clarification was for her. Justine was already sipping her drink. Patrick came from a wonderful, supportive family. "There's a lot to be said about tradition."

"I totally agree." Claire placed her hands on her bulging abdomen. "My husband and I live in my parents' home on Sullivan's Island. If I could get him to agree to it, I'd have our baby there."

Brooke laughed. "Fat chance. He breaks a sweat if you sigh hard. I'm surprised he hasn't been here to check on you. He only left two hours ago. Neglectful man."

As if on cue the door opened, causing the little silver bell to ring, and a handsome man in a gray tailored suit entered. His gaze centered on Claire. Entering behind him was a rugged, broad-shouldered man with two young children.

"That will teach you to tease me," Claire said. "Your family is here as well."

The little girl in a red and white polka-dot dress with a black sash broke away from the man holding her hand and, laughing all the way, ran straight to Brooke's open arms. Scooping her up, Brooke kissed her on the cheek. "Ready to help?"

The pretty little girl grinned. "I didn't get my new dress dirty. I won't run anymore. I was just running now so I won't do it later."

"Of course you were. Smart thinking," Brooke said just as the man with the boy reached them. He curved his arm around her waist and kissed her on the cheek. She introduced everyone to her husband, John, her children, Amy and Mark, and Claire's husband, Gray.

"Claire, you said you'd take it easy. Why aren't you sitting down?" Gray asked as soon as everyone had exchanged greetings.

Claire kissed her husband on the lips. "I'm fine. Better when I see you."

He put his forehead to hers. "Ditto."

"Mark, you ready to take orders and ring them up?" Brooke asked her son, who was dressed in a white shirt, red tie, and black slacks.

He held up his calculator and notepad. "Ready."

"Then let's get started." Brooke sat Amy on her feet. "I'll show Justine and Brianna to the back."

"I can do it," Lorraine said.

Brooke and Claire shared a grin before Claire spoke. "You might want to remain in the front. Hamilton is taking an early flight back."

Lorraine's eyes lit up at the mention of her husband. "He said he'd try."

"Looks like he did more than that," John said just before the front door opened.

Lorraine hurried to meet the distinguished man entering the shop. He drew her into his arms, kissing her.

"Ain't love grand?" Brooke said, leaning against her husband's rugged frame.

Brianna's throat clogged. Would she ever have that kind of utter devotion and love?

"This way," Claire said, leading them to the back of the store to change, her body gently swaying as she walked.

Brooke and Justine followed. Gray certainly adored his wife, Brianna thought. He didn't mind her bulging stomach or that she probably needed help putting her flat-soled shoes on. But he was the cause. What if the baby hadn't been his?

As Brianna went behind the curtained area to undress, she swept her hand over her still-flat abdomen. It would take a special man to love a woman whose body swelled with another man's child. If time had been on her side, she might have found him in Patrick. It wasn't.

They were friends, not lovers, and she wanted to cry.

Dalton stood on the front porch of his house and watched for Justine's van. He just hoped she showed. She didn't believe in deception, which was the reason she hadn't wanted to slip around to see him when they were in high school. She'd honor her marriage vows the same way.

The only reason she had allowed herself to be with him was because she thought Andrew wouldn't recover. Now that he had, he held her even stronger in his deceitful grip. She'd honor her vows even if it meant she and Dalton wouldn't have a future.

"They're on their way." Patrick closed the front door behind him and leaned against one of the four white posts anchoring the porch. "I finally got through to the store."

"Thanks." Both of them had become concerned when it was half past eight and the women hadn't shown. "Guess they had a good time."

Patrick chuckled. "According to my niece, they had a ball being pampered from head to toe."

Dalton's mouth tightened for just a moment. "They both deserve that and much more. Life isn't being kind to either of them at the moment."

"Nope, but they have us."

Dalton switched his attention to the other man. Patrick met his gaze head-on. He was just the kind of man that headstrong Brianna needed. "I guess I should thank you for not judging us. Justine and Brianna have been friends since kindergarten."

"So I heard. When you hurt one, you hurt the other," Patrick said. "Besides, I learned long ago to mind my own business."

"Appreciate it. Justine needs friends and a place to go where she can relax." Dalton switched his gaze to the driveway. "When I took her to dinner, she couldn't eat her food without people stopping by, asking questions." It wasn't lost on Dalton that he hadn't mentioned Andrew's name.

"So I noticed at your book signing."

Dalton wondered what else he'd noticed. Patrick was sharp. Dalton hadn't asked Patrick about his early retirement from the police force because that would give him leeway to ask Dalton questions. No way did he want to get into the worst days of his life.

He caught a glimpse of a vehicle turning into his driveway and straightened up. He was standing by the driver's door by the time the motor shut off and the door opened. "Hi. Food's on the table."

Justine bit her lip instead of getting out as Brianna did on the other side. "Dalton, I . . ." She threaded her fingers through her hair.

He easily read the apprehension in her eyes and knew the cause. "It was selfish of me to take advantage of the situation at Brianna's place. It won't happen again." He held out his hand.

She didn't move. "Try to understand, the only way I can possibly get through this is that we don't see each other as much." She swallowed. "Not being with you is going to be hard, but I know that if we're together too much, sooner or later, we're going to give in and make love."

She spoke the truth. Even now he wanted to send Brianna and Patrick away, lay Justine down on his bed, remove her clothes, and make love to her, then start all over again.

"Dalton, please help me," Justine whispered, her voice strained.

"Come on, you two." Brianna stood at the bottom of the steps. "For once I'm starving."

"Go on in and start. Patrick knows where everything is," Dalton said without looking away from Justine. He didn't speak again until he heard the front door close. "You know I love you."

"Yes," she whispered.

"Good. Then the only way I'll agree to not seeing you as much is that you promise not to forget that."

"Never. You're my heart, the other half of my soul. Loving you helps me get through the day."

Her words went straight to his heart. "All right. Give me tonight if not tomorrow. I want to hold you, touch you, but we won't make love."

She placed her unsteady hand in his. As soon as she was on the ground, he pulled her into his arms, nuzzled her neck. "You smell good."

"It's Bliss's Better Than Sex lotion."

"Say that again?" Dalton asked.

Justine's lashes lowered "Bliss has a line of products called Better Than Sex. I thought, considering how my life is going, I should try it out."

"And?" Dalton asked.

Her fingertips brushed across his lips. "You have nothing to worry about."

He had to kiss her. His tongue mated with hers, tasting the honeyed sweetness of her mouth. His body hardened, begging for release that wouldn't come. He went right on torturing himself, silently praying that this wouldn't be their last time.

"You smell good and look more like your usual fantastic self. You enjoy yourself?" Patrick asked as he sat a plate of food in front of Brianna.

"Yes." She picked up her fork, said her blessing, then cut into her sliced barbecued beef. "Delicious."

Patrick prepared his own plate and sat down at the table. "Are you that hungry or are you avoiding talking to me?"

She forked in potato salad. "Guess."

Reaching over, he took her plate, then moved his out of reach when she reached for his. They eyed each other before she got up from the table and got another paper plate. "Brianna, you try me."

She whirled. "You told Brooke. How many other people have you told? Did you take out an ad?"

His expression harshened. In seconds he was out of the chair and standing in front of her. His head lowered until their eyes were inches apart. "You can fight, yell, but you won't pick a fight with me so I'll run off. Get used to me. I promised your parents I'd take care of you, but even if I hadn't I'd still be here for you."

For how long? Her lashes blinked rapidly. "I can take care of myself."

"Then act like it. Getting upset can't be good for the baby or you." He put her plate on the table. "You want iced or hot tea?"

Her fist clenched. Her head bowed. "I don't know what I want," she admitted.

"Oh, honey." Lifting her into his arms, he sat and tucked her head between his chin and his shoulder. "Give yourself time. Your hormones are probably going crazy."

Up came her head. "What do you know about a woman's hormones?"

He wasn't going to back down. "I looked up pregnancy on the Internet."

The temper spike he'd expected didn't occur. "Why aren't you running as fast as you can in the other direction?" she asked.

His hand tenderly stroked her cheek. "It's not in me to walk away from those I care about."

He was one of a kind. She got out of his lap, picked up her fork, then put it down and looked at him. Misery shone in her eyes. "I may be the first."

"Whatever happens, I'm not going anyplace," he told her. Brianna tucked in her head. She didn't believe him. He'd just have to show her. Getting up, he opened the refrigerator and poured them each a glass of tea.

"Patrick?"

He placed their drinks on the table and sat down. "Yes."

She lifted her head. "I really had a good time at Bliss. Thank you."

"You get a massage from those guys?" He picked up his fork.

"No. We both passed." She sipped her tea, studying him.

"Like I told you, I give a great massage."

"I'll keep that in mind." Putting the glass down, she picked up her fork and began to eat.

"Do that." *And while you're at it, remember I'll always be there for you.*

"Why do I do it?" Brianna mumbled.

"Do what?" Justine asked, pulling onto the highway from Dalton's house. She glanced in the rearview mirror for one last glimpse, not knowing if she'd ever come back again. Dalton said he loved her, but she couldn't expect him to wait until she obtained her divorce. She swallowed the sadness that threatened to choke her.

Brianna glanced away before answering, "Push Patrick away when all I want is for him to hold me."

"You're scared, just like I'm scared." Justine's fingers flexed on the steering wheel. "I don't know when this mess with Andrew will be over so I can see Dalton without feeling guilty. You, on the other hand, are afraid to trust your great instincts because you were going through a rough time and trusted the wrong guy."

Brianna blew out a breath. "Not as rough as this."

"The difference is that you met and liked Patrick before you discovered you were pregnant." Justine stopped at a red light. "My advice is to grab him and hold on. He stands by his word. He's not going to run scared when you start showing."

"He hasn't said anything about us resuming our relationship," Brianna said, sadness creeping into her voice.

"Because he's aware of what a tough time this is for you," Justine said. "He has to have figured out that the father of your baby is no longer in the picture. All you have to do is look at Patrick and see how much he cares about you."

Brianna cupped her stomach and fought tears. "He could have his pick of women. Why should he settle for a woman carrying another man's baby?"

"Brianna Ireland, if I wasn't in the middle of a busy highway I'd pull over and shake some sense into your head. He'll be a lucky man to have you and he's smart enough to know it."

"I would be the lucky one." Brianna bit her lower lip. "Is he still following us?"

Justine pulled through the green light and glanced in the rearview mirror. She saw Patrick's black truck behind them when they passed beneath a streetlight. "So that's what he and Dalton were whispering about when we were leaving."

"You don't think Dalton would have let you drive home by yourself otherwise, do you?"

Justine shook her head. "He made life enjoyable again. I'm not sure I can get through this without him, yet I know if we see each other too much we might . . ." Her voice trailed off.

"Ain't that the truth." Brianna sat up and looked into the side mirror. "I might be crying buckets, my emotions all over the place, but I still have this urge to jump Patrick."

"We're a pair."

"And friends for life." Brianna lifted her left hand. Justine lifted her right. Briefly they clasped hands.

"We'll get through this and be stronger women," Justine said, flicking on the turn signal to pull up to the security gate at the underground parking garage of Brianna's condo.

The security guard recognized them and the iron gate slowly rolled open.

Brianna waved to Toni in the security booth as they passed. "We will, but in the meantime I think I'll follow your lead."

"What lead?" Justine pulled into a visitor's spot near the elevator.

"Not see so much of Patrick." Opening the door to the van, Brianna got out. "You're right. Again. I am afraid. I'm almost certain he'll be there, but until I'm one hundred percent sure I think it's best that we stop seeing each other."

Justine saw that Patrick had parked and was sprinting toward them. "They do make it more difficult, but I wonder if that's a good thing or bad thing. I'll tell him I'll wait near the exit."

Brianna waited for Patrick, although she wanted to run. Saying good-bye wouldn't be easy.

"You still feel all right?" Patrick asked, his beautiful eyes watching her closely. No man except her father had ever treated her with such exquisite care.

"I'm fine. I waited because I wanted to talk with you."

He frowned. "I'll come up to your place as soon as I see Justine home safely."

"That's what I wanted to talk to you about." She gathered her courage. "I appreciate everything you've done for me, but now I need some space to decide a few things. I'm asking for that time."

"How much time?"

She shrugged. "I don't know. A few days, a couple of weeks."

"All right." He jabbed the elevator call button.

"Thank you." She wished she could be happier that

she'd at last won an argument with him. The elevator opened, and she automatically stepped on. "Good night."

"Good night," he said as the elevator door began to close. "I'll give you that space just as soon as you aren't too tired to take care of yourself."

The door shut just as he got out the last word. She pushed the open button, but the elevator was already climbing to another floor. Score another one for him.

Brianna leaned against the wall and admitted she didn't want to argue with him. As she'd told Justine, even though she was unsure of their future, she just wanted to lie in his arms. Well, maybe at first, but then they'd get down to some serious lovemaking.

Luckily the elevator opened on three. She'd been so engrossed with thinking about Patrick that she had forgotten to punch her floor. He was a hard man to forget.

Speaking to the elderly couple who waited to get on, Brianna got off and went into her apartment. They were another reminder that love, for some, lasted. Her parents were another.

An image of Patrick popped into her mind. She firmly pushed it away and entered her place. No matter how much she wanted it, she couldn't be sure of a future for them.

Twenty-four

The next morning, instead of turning over, Brianna made herself get up when her alarm sounded. Showering, she dressed in a candy-apple red suit to make herself feel better, then left for her office fifteen minutes ahead of time. Traffic for once moved fairly swiftly downtown. She was congratulating herself on getting to the office twenty minutes early when she pulled into the parking lot and saw Patrick's truck.

The man doesn't know the meaning of the word quit, she thought. She parked beside him, entered the back door, and had another shock. "Daddy!"

"Hi, Brianna," her father greeted her from the small table in the kitchen. "I thought I'd drop by to see if I could help out a bit. Patrick is a pretty good cook. I'm having oatmeal, turkey bacon, and one of his whole wheat biscuits."

"Morning, Brianna." Patrick put her plate on a pretty poppy placemat. "Great timing, as usual."

Brianna tore her gaze away from him to see the soft scrambled eggs, turkey bacon, biscuits, and a bowl of cheese grits. He had to get up early to do all this.

"How did you get in?" she asked.

"I let him in. Your mother dropped me off on her way to her water aerobics class, and Patrick was waiting," her father explained, reaching for another slice of crisp bacon. "Good thing. The bowl of cereal I had wasn't enough."

"You need anything else?" Patrick set a cup of tea on the place mat.

Brianna's gaze went to his. He waited patiently for her answer. If she'd messed up with the father for her baby, at least she had picked out a good friend in Patrick. "Where's your plate?"

He smiled and her heart turned over. "Getting it now. Let me have that attaché. Sit down, and you and your daddy can talk shop."

Handing him the attaché, she took her seat in the cane-back chair that he held. "Thank you," she said, then turned to her father, who watched them with so much hope in his eyes it made her eyes misty. She couldn't fault him. He wanted the best for her. What parent didn't? Just as she wanted the best for the child she carried.

Yet sometimes, no matter how hard you wished or prayed, it just didn't happen.

Placing her napkin in her lap, she smiled at her father as Patrick took his seat. "You're here for exactly ninety minutes, then you're gone. Maybe you and Patrick can go chase a golf ball."

"I haven't played in years, but I'm game." Patrick buttered his biscuit. "I'll try not to embarrass myself."

"I can stay longer to help," her father said.

"You want me to take care of myself. I want you to do the same." She stirred her cheese grits. "What's fair for the duckling is fair for papa duck."

His father's mouth twitched. "I'd argue, but I don't think I'd win."

"No, sir, I don't think you would," Patrick stared at her across the table. "Not many have gotten the best of Brianna."

You have, she thought, and not once had he used it against her. For once it didn't bother her.

In the coming days, Justine's time was divided between the bookstore and the hospital. Andrew's mother was convinced that her daughter-in-law's presence was pivotal in continuing Andrew's progress. With Dr. Lane and Dr. Thomas's permission, Justine spent as much time as possible there. She wanted to expedite his recovery as much as anyone else.

Her freedom depended on it.

Each day saw some tiny improvement. Andrew went from moving his hand to opening his eyes. The blank stare progressed to his gaze actually following her or his mother around the room. He went from the barest movement of his fingertips to squeezing the doctor's hand to squeezing hers, attempting to speak, but unable to because he remained on the respirator. A week later they began to wean him from the ventilator. Next came the respirator.

Each day he made more progress. Each day she left the hospital hopeful that it would soon be over, and despondent that it wasn't.

Two weeks after Andrew began to wake up, Justine arrived home so tired she could hardly make her way to her bedroom. Although she was bone-weary, she knew she wouldn't be able to sleep. She thought of the perfect remedy. Dalton.

She continued through the great room and wished she wasn't so weak or he wasn't as tempting. They hadn't seen each other since that night at his house. It was for the best. She just didn't like it.

The cell phone in her purse rang with a familiar tone. "Hello, Brianna. How are you doing?"

"Better than you, if you're as tired as you sound."

"More so." Justine kept walking. If she sat down, she wasn't sure she'd get up.

"Then the surprise waiting for you on your portico should perk you up. Enjoy."

Justine whipped her head around and saw a small table draped with a yellow tablecloth and a white candle burning in a hurricane glass. All she could think of was that Dalton had better be there as well.

Her fingers fumbled with the locks, then she was outside. "Dalton, please be here."

"For as long as you want me." He stepped out of the shadows and drew her into his arms. "I missed you."

"Me too." She squeezed her eyes shut. "I was about at the end of my rope."

"When you are, just think of me, waiting."

She lifted her head. "That's the only thing that gets me through." Her voice trembled.

His hand tightened for a fraction of a second on her arm. "Sit down and eat. I'll fill you in on the progress of the house."

She sat and let his presence soothe her. She laughed as

expected when he told her of stepping in the pail of water he'd set aside to wash the paintbrushes, and drank a toast with him when he said he had finished the shelving in the second bedroom, which he planned to turn into a library/office. The third bedroom would be a weight room.

"I can't wait to see it," she said before she thought, then sadness hit her.

His hand touched hers. "Don't give up on us." He pulled her to her feet and pushed her toward the door to the house. "Go get some sleep."

It was in her heart and in her eyes that she didn't want to go. "Thank you." She kissed him on the cheek and slipped inside, but stayed near the glass door to watch him clean up.

Typically male, he'd brought disposable flatware and plates. He put everything in a wicker picnic hamper, folded the table under his arms after one long look at her, and left.

He gave without expecting anything in return. The palm of her hand touched the cool glass. One day she prayed she'd be able to give back.

That night, for the first time in weeks, Justine was able to sleep instead of tossing and turning. She actually overslept and was running late when she reached ICCU the next morning. She glanced at her watch and pushed open the heavy doors. Eight twenty-one. She tried to be there at eight every day and leave promptly at nine thirty to reach the store by ten. Then too, she wasn't up to seeing disapproval—or was it disappointment?—on Beverly's face.

Easing open the door, she entered the room. Beverly was standing by the head of the bed, holding Andrew's hand. Justine wondered again how she did it day after day. "Good morning, Beverly, Andrew." She included him because his head had slowly turned and his eyes met hers.

Each time they did, she felt uneasy. She knew it was because the vibrancy, the laughter in them, was gone. It was as if the Andrew they'd known was gone.

"Good morning, Justine." Beverly slowly turned. "We wondered when you'd come."

"I overslept," Justine said, coming to stand at the foot of the bed, her usual position unless Beverly asked her otherwise. She felt her uneasiness increase and wished he'd stop look—

"Jussss," came the hoarse rasp.

Justine went as stiff as a rod. Her eyes widened.

"He said your name! He said your name!" Beverly cried out with excitement, beckoning Justine to where she stood. "Hurry! Hurry!"

Justine rounded the bed without taking her eyes from Andrew. "Andrew?"

"Jusss-tieen," he whispered, his forehead pleated in a frown as if trying to understand what was going on, why his voice sounded rough instead of smooth and charming.

Beverly grabbed Justine's hand and clasped it between hers and Andrew's. "You're going to be fine, Andrew. You were in an accident, but you're going to be fine. Justine is here, and I'm here."

The lines in his forehead didn't clear. "Wh—aa?"

Beverly pushed the nurse's call button. A disembodied voice answered. "Yes?"

"Andrew just said Justine's name. Get Dr. Lane in here immediately!"

Justine didn't have time to think about Beverly ordering the doctors around; she was still trying to deal with Andrew saying her name first. Did that mean he still loved her?

A few minutes later, Dr. Lane came through the door in a rush. "He spoke?"

"Justine's name," Beverly answered.

Justine started to point out that it hadn't been clear, but Dr. Lane moved them aside. He pulled out a pen light. "Follow the light," he requested. When Andrew completed the task, the doctor took his hand and asked him to squeeze, then rubbed his finger and then the sharp and dull edge of a safety pin down Andrew's arms and legs. Next he checked his mouth. Each time Andrew responded. At times he seemed to search the room until his gaze settled on Justine.

"Juss—stie—nne."

"See!" Beverly cried in triumph.

"Mr. Crandall, do you remember the accident?" Dr. Lane asked.

Holding her breath, Justine kept her gaze on Andrew, watching for even a hint that he recalled what had happened and the reason. She thought she saw something in his eyes, but couldn't be sure. He continued to stare at her.

"He doesn't remember," Beverly said. "After what he's been through I think it's for the best."

"I agree. It isn't unusual for victims of traumatic accidents or experiences not to remember the occurrence or the events prior to it." Dr. Lane stuffed his hands into the pockets of his lab coat.

Justine recalled that Andrew said it was the first time

he'd cheated. What if he had been telling the truth? He didn't seem to want to take his eyes from hers. Perhaps he *did* love her.

The thought barely registered before she knew it didn't matter. Andrew had killed any love she had for him. Her heart belonged to Dalton, a man who wouldn't betray her, a man who thought of her first and always. She'd do all she could to help Andrew through this, but then she was leaving.

"He won't remember? Ever?" Justine asked, not sure how she felt about that.

Dr. Lane turned from studying Andrew. "Some never do."

"What difference does it make now?" Beverly took up a position on the other side of the bed. "Andrew is coming back to us, and he'll be as good as new."

Dr. Lane frowned. "I'd like a laryngologist to check him out. I expect the hoarseness, but not the stuttering."

"Do you think it's because of the cardiac arrests?" Justine asked.

The doctor shrugged his slim shoulders. "We might never know the cause. Depending on what the laryngologist finds, we can add a speech therapist to the physical therapist's schedule."

"I want the laryngologist here today," Beverly demanded. "Andrew's voice is as much a part of him as his smile. He can't lose that after what he's been through. He can't. I won't let it happen."

Justine didn't say anything. Beverly had pulled Andrew through so much, perhaps she could this time as well. However, one look at Dr. Lane's troubled expression, and

Justine felt that just maybe Beverly might have run out of miracles.

A foot massage shouldn't make a woman moan and get hot in all the wrong places. But perhaps that depended on the person giving the massage.

"I'll have to tell Brooke that this new product Claire developed is another winner."

Brianna's eyelids lifted just enough for her to see Patrick, sitting on the ottoman in front of her in her condo. She stared at him from her position in her leather library chair, her hands draped casually over the curved leather arms. Her foot was inches away from that part of him that her body hungered for. One little flex of her foot and—

Patrick put her left foot on the other side of his muscled thigh and picked up the right one. "Your parents enjoyed going out on the boat this morning."

Brianna's eyes closed. You knew you were in bad shape when even the mention of your parents didn't dampen your desire. "They had a wonderful time."

"We're going out again this weekend. Care to go with us?" Patrick asked, the ball of his thumb running down her foot, making her want to melt, preferably over him.

Her eyes opened again. She tried to determine if he was purposefully turning her on or was it just her body's intense reaction to him.

"Afterward we're going back to their place and cook what we catch." His sexy fingers slid up her ankle to her lower leg. He grinned when she cocked a brow. "Helps circulation."

Her blood was already hot and pulsing, thank you.

Time to try and get her mind on something else. "What if you don't catch anything?"

He laughed, and the sound soothed and excited her. She recalled so easily his playfulness in bed. "I made reservations at the Boathouse for four. Should I make it five?"

"Four?" The popular seafood and raw bar restaurant on East Bay near her parents' house was one of their favorites. She had little doubt that Patrick already knew this.

The smile slid from his face. "Dalton."

Brianna rose up. She'd kept Dalton up on Andrew's progress. When she told him Andrew was talking and had started speech therapy, there had been a long silence, then a "thank you" and he'd hung up. "He's having a rough time."

"Tougher because he can't be there for her." Patrick's fingers slid back down, his gaze still on her. "Nothing makes a man feel more helpless than not being able to take care of a woman he cares about."

All it would take for her to assuage the ache in her body and her heart was to lean closer and press her lips against Patrick's. A measly foot and he'd do the rest. She wanted to. She even inched forward, watched his nostrils flair, and felt his hand tighten on her foot.

Then what? Making love might satisfy the needs of their bodies. It wouldn't get her any closer to deciding if she was brave enough to risk Patrick walking away one day. She pulled first one, then the other foot from the ottoman and stood, immediately stepping away.

"Thanks for the foot massage. I'll let you know later about the boat trip and dinner." She went to the front door and opened it. "Good night, Patrick."

He swiveled around on the seat and looked at her for so

long that she started to squirm. He must have been a tough police interrogator. He was one witness that no one could have intimidated or flustered. Slowly, he came to his feet and stopped inches from her. "I'll be busy for the next few days. If you can make it, just leave a message on my machine."

There was no way she could keep the surprise and regret from her face. "All right."

"Good night."

"Good night." Brianna closed the door. She'd gotten what she thought she wanted. Space. And she couldn't be more miserable.

"Don't—want—that." Andrew slapped away the spoon of mashed potatoes his mother had been trying to feed him. The flatware clattered on the floor.

Justine watched the spoon skid beneath the bed. Beverly's hand clenched. Kent looked away. Marcus bent and picked it up. "We'll come back later."

"Stay," Andrew said, his stilted voice angry and defiant. "You—can-can't." His hands loosely fisted in frustration as he tried to find the words that had once flowed so eloquently from his mouth.

"You can't take over Andrew's firm or his speaking engagements," Beverly said.

From the venomous look Andrew sent her, he didn't appreciate her help.

Kent, who had stayed in the background after speaking, stepped forward. "Andrew, the foundation can't survive without incoming revenue. With each retreat Marcus has conducted, the attendance has grown."

"No-not me."

Marcus laid his big hand on Andrew's shoulder. "No one could take your place. I know that better than anyone. You're the man. I'm just standing in until you're able to do the retreats yourself."

Andrew lightly shrugged his shoulder. "Li-ar. Wan-want mine."

Justine couldn't imagine Marcus looking more hurt or shocked if Andrew had hit him. "Never. I love you, man, like a brother."

"You—want—mine," Andrew said, his eyes hard.

"I've never wanted what was yours. I was always content to stay in the background," Marcus defended. "You know that. You always said, take care of Justine and the foundation, and that's what I tried to do."

Andrew's eyes went to Justine. "M-mine."

Justine folded her arms. Day by day Andrew had grown more petulant and difficult to be with. His physical therapy was going well. He was even able to take a few steps by himself and feed himself, although Beverly liked to do it for him.

What he couldn't do that had been so much a part of him was speak clearly and eloquently. The words no longer rolled off his tongue with such unpretentious ease. His speech impediment flustered and angered him. He seemed to relish taking it out on everyone, as he was do-ing now.

Anger replaced the hurt on Marcus's face. "I hope you don't mean what I think you mean."

"Of course he didn't," Justine said. "He loves and values you and Kent. Perhaps you can come back later in the week."

"We'll leave then." Kent grabbed Marcus's arm when he didn't move. "Good-bye." The door closed behind them.

"How dare Marcus try to get huffy!" Beverly said, moving the bedside table from across Andrew's bed. "Without you, he'd be nothing. He'll return to nothing when you take over the foundation again."

"No—th-ing," Andrew said, his voice still echoing the raspy voice he'd had since awakening.

Beverly smiled benevolently, as if he'd just said something profound, then went into the bathroom and came out with a dampened washcloth she'd brought from home.

Justine studied them both. Had she really ever known either of them? She'd always thought Beverly sweet and caring. She understood her fierceness to protect her only child and son. This pettiness was a side of her mother-in-law that she'd not seen before.

As for Andrew, was this petulant and self-centered man who he really was? Had he hidden the real Andrew just as he'd hidden his affair? Thank goodness she had moved on, and didn't have to deal with them for much longer. "I'll be going."

"It's not eight," Beverly said, washing Andrew's hands.

"No, it isn't. Good night." Justine couldn't wait to call Dalton. They hadn't spoken in weeks. She wanted to tell him that she planned to start divorce proceedings the day Andrew was discharged.

No longer did she dread telling his mother and hers. Under Marcus and Kent's leadership the foundation would continue to prosper. If people blamed her and her business suffered, so be it. Being with and loving Dalton was worth any price she had to pay.

In the van she called Dalton's cell, but there was no answer. She then called Brianna, then Patrick. Neither had talked to Dalton for a couple of days. Patrick said Dalton had canceled their boating trip for that weekend. Worried, Justine drove out to his house. Her heart sank when she pulled up and didn't see his Jeep. The new brass lanterns glowed on either side of the carved door, but there was no answer to her repeated ringing of the doorbell.

She walked back to the van and drove home. The only thing that kept the fear and tears from falling was remembering Dalton's words—he loved her. She climbed into bed looking forward to the day he'd tell her again and they could be together.

Twenty-five

Brianna had never in her life wanted to harm another human—except Jackson, but she considered that justified—until now. She trembled with a rage she easily recognized as jealousy.

Not twenty feet away at the end of the marina two curvaceous women in skimpy bikini swimsuits were on either side of Patrick, their bodies pressed against his as if trying to make a human sandwich out of him. They were the same two bold women who'd worn disgracefully short sundresses last night at the monthly condominium meeting. They'd been hanging on Patrick then as well.

The only reason she'd gone was to see Patrick and accept his invitation for the boat outing and dinner afterward. She'd called, but his machine hadn't been on. She came home from work and saw him from her balcony and decided to tell him in person. Looked like she shouldn't have bothered.

Laughing, he looked up and saw her. Quickly she

turned away. The last thing she wanted was for him to know she was jealous. There was a park across the street. She'd just walk over there and act as if that were her intention all along. If he wanted those women, he could have them. She stepped off the curb without looking.

"Brianna, look out!"

Patrick's warning came an instant before the blast of a horn. She looked up and stumbled back as the late-model sedan swerved, barely missing her. Trembling, she stood on the sidewalk.

"Are you all right?" Patrick asked, his eyes running over her, his hands around her upper arms.

"Yes." Brianna thought his voice was as shaky as hers.

"What were you thinking!" Patrick yelled. "How could you be so careless? If I hadn't been looking, you might have been hit."

"All you were looking at were those two women hanging on you!" she yelled back.

His hands flexed on her arms. "You're the only woman I want hanging on me. The only woman I want."

Brianna started to cry and didn't seem able to stop.

"Oh, honey." Tenderly, he pulled her into his arms. "Please don't cry. I shouldn't have yelled. I was just so scared. I'd die if you were hurt."

The tears fell faster. Sobs were wrenched from her chest.

"Honey. Don't." Patrick picked her up in his arms and headed back to the condos. He didn't care about the curious stares, only the woman in his arms. Somehow he managed to open his door without releasing her. Inside his condo, he sat on the sofa with her still in his arms.

"I planned to wait, but the near accident reminded me

that tomorrow isn't promised." He kissed the tears from her cheeks. "I planned to stay away to see if you'd realize that you miss me, care about me. But, after what just happened, I can't. I love you, Brianna."

She gasped and stared up at him with tears shimmering in her eyes, watchful, waiting.

"The future isn't promised, honey. The child you're carrying might be the only one you'll ever have or there could be dozens."

He laughed at her incredulous expression, then kissed her lips. "Marry me, and let me be a husband to you and a father to your baby, *our* baby." He kissed her lips again. "I'd get on my knees, but I don't want to let you go yet."

She finally found her voice and her courage. "I'm scared, Patrick. Scared whatever you're feeling won't last when the baby starts to grow."

He stared into her eyes. "I love you, Brianna. My love will only grow stronger, deeper. The baby is an extra special blessing that I'll cherish as much as I cherish and love you."

She believed him. Tears of joy crested in her eyes. "Oh, Patrick. I don't want you to let me go either." Her hand gently palmed his face. "You're the special one. I got sidetracked because of the man I trusted and shouldn't have."

"I won't let you or the baby down, ever," he told her. "Trust your heart. Trust me."

She stared into his beautiful black eyes and felt tears crest in her eyes. She saw forever. "I love you so much."

"Brianna," her name trembled over his lips. "You did it."

"Because I know you'd pass the naked woman test."

A frown darted across his brow. "What?"

She laughed at the strange expression on his face. "I always said the man I loved, the man who loved me wouldn't care if a naked woman danced in front of him, he'd always come home to me."

"For me there is no other woman," he said softly.

The words went straight to her heart. "I know that now. Neither will you let what people say sway you or deter you. You listen to your conscience and your heart. From now on I'll listen to mine."

"Then you'll marry me?" he asked.

More happiness than she ever imagined swelled within her. "Yes. I'll marry you. I don't want to lose you."

"Never." His mouth took hers in a hungry kiss that set them both on fire. Picking her up, Patrick carried her to his bed and gently laid her down, then removed their clothes. He kissed her face, her breasts, laid his face against her quivering stomach. "You'll be loved and wanted," he told the baby.

Brianna felt tears sting her eyes again. She blinked them away. "We're blessed to have you."

His dark head lifted. "I'm the one who's blessed," he whispered, then proceeded to show her.

The next morning Justine received Brianna's call with news of her engagement just as she was leaving for the hospital. She couldn't have been happier for her best friend and Patrick. They made plans to meet for dinner the next day so Brianna could fill Justine in on all the details of the proposal, and discuss wedding plans with her maid-of-honor. Tonight she and Patrick were celebrating with her parents. They were both teary-eyed by the time they hung up.

Happiness was possible.

Justine kept her good mood despite the morning freeway traffic snarl she encountered a few miles from her house. She looked at the long line of cars and called Beverly. "Good morning, Beverly. I'm stuck in traffic. I'm going in to work. I'll come to the hospital around noon."

"All right, dear. Thanks for calling. Good-bye."

"Good-bye." Justine stared at the phone. Beverly sounded more like her old self. Shaking her head, she started to put the phone away, then dialed Dalton's number instead.

After a dozen or so rings she hung up. "Please come back soon," she whispered, then eased off the brake and onto the gas as the cars ahead began to move with increasing speed. Whatever the problem was, it must have been cleared up, she thought.

Five minutes later she neared the exit to the hospital and changed her mind about going on to work. She wanted to see Dr. Lane. He hadn't been able to give her a possible date for Andrew's discharge earlier in the week. She hoped that had changed now.

She sensed he was being more cautious after he'd been wrong about Andrew's chances of recovering. He'd apologized the day of the news conference. She'd accepted his heartfelt words. Mistakes happen. Andrew had wronged her, but she didn't want him to die. She just wanted the freedom to be with Dalton.

After parking, she rode the elevator to the ninth floor, where all the rooms were suites. Andrew had been moved there a week after he was transferred from ICCU. He might be angry with Kent and Marcus, but their management of his foundation, which included a comprehensive insurance plan, had allowed him to have the best the hospital had to offer.

Justine spoke to the nurse and continued down the hall. Mornings were always busy with the nursing staff getting their patients ready for the day. She stepped around a group of student nurses and a volunteer with a cart of periodicals for the patients, then stopped abruptly. A woman stood at Andrew's door. She pushed it open a few inches, then released it and turned. Their gaze met.

Teresa Moore, Andrew's ex-secretary, hesitated, then took a half step backward. The young woman looked at Andrew's door, then up and down the hall as if looking for an escape. There was none. His room was at the end of the hallway. Head tucked, she started toward Justine.

When she had almost reached her, Justine stepped into her path. Teresa's dark head came up. She bit her lower lip. "Hello, Teresa. Don't let me stop you from going in. I'm sure Andrew would like to see you. You haven't visited before. At least I haven't seen you."

The other woman's eyes darted around the hallway. "Hello, Justine. I've been kind of busy."

"I can just imagine," Justine said, unable to keep the sarcasm out of her voice. Andrew might not remember, but his little playmate would. "Sneaking around can be tiring."

Teresa's gaze snapped back to Justine. "What? You know?"

"Yes, I know."

She held up her hands, palm up. "No one likes to be the bearer of bad news. As it was, she still found a way to get rid of me to keep things hushed up," Teresa said, her voice filled with anger.

Justine frowned. Suddenly the pieces she thought were coming together no longer fit. "Keep talking."

Teresa glanced over her shoulder. "Why don't you ask her? I thought I'd ask Andrew for help, but she beat me to it."

Justine's gaze went to Andrew's door. Who was in there? If Teresa hadn't been "the other woman," then who had? Teresa stepped around her, and hurried away. Justine's chest felt tight. It was time to find out. Going to the door, she eased it open. Befitting the high-priced suite, the door opened without a sound.

In the sitting room decorated in muted shades of green, Andrew sat in the straight-backed chair his physical therapist had recommended. In front of him was a woman, bent at the waist, her hands on the arms of Andrew's chair.

"Stop calling the house and the office. Fun was fun, but you can't do anything for me now." She straightened, then said snidely, "You can't even do anything for yourself."

"Bit—"

Her scornful laughter drowned out his word. "Nothing you can say will hurt me. And, if you tell him, you can kiss your company and the money that pays for this and your therapy good-bye. No more calls, or I might tell him you made a pass at me, then there'll be hell to pay."

"There already is."

Nina whirled. Fear widened her eyes. "Justine!"

Justine stared at Marcus's wife. "Marcus deserved better. So did I," Justine said, feeling relief.

Nina rushed to her. "You can't tell Marcus! He'll go crazy!"

"Then I suggest you tell him first." Justine stepped around the other woman and faced Andrew. "Obviously you lied about remembering the accident. I see no reason for delaying divorce proceedings. I intend to file as soon as possible."

"I—lov—"

"Spare me the lies," Justine said. "Marcus is a better man than you ever hoped to be. He'll continue until the senior citizen's complex is complete, then he'll leave, taking Kent with him. Your personal finances will take a big hit. You better start preparing yourself for a less grandiose life-style."

"Justine, can't we talk?" Nina pleaded, her body trembling with fear.

"We have nothing to say." Her gaze drifted to the other woman's stomach. "Do you know whose baby you're carrying?"

Uncertainty flashed in Nina's eyes again. "This is Marcus's baby."

"You might not believe me, but I hope it is. You have twenty-four hours."

With a strangled cry, Nina rushed out of the room. As the door opened, Justine saw Beverly with a cup of coffee in her hand. Justine got the impression that her mother-in-law hadn't just arrived. There was no surprise on her face. *She knows.* That betrayal hurt almost as much as Andrew's.

"So she's the reason you didn't mind me being late," Justine said, facing her mother-in-law. "How could you do that to me? I loved you."

"Men stray sometimes. Nina means nothing to him," Beverly declared mildly. "Stay and together you and Andrew will be unstoppable."

"Not all men stray," Justine replied in anger. "And if he had, why didn't you tell him he was wrong and not condone and help him? I thought you loved me?"

"I do, but I love Andrew more," she said flatly.

"I see that," Justine said, her anger mounting. "You and Andrew have played me long enough. I'm leaving."

An anxious Beverly blocked Justine's exit. "You can't. Andrew needs you. He loves you. You saw how he responded to you."

"He should have thought of that when he began cheating." Justine looked at Andrew with disdain. "Was Nina the first or were there others?"

"I—lo—" Andrew began.

"Stop lying." Justine faced his mother. "How many others were there?"

For the first time Beverly looked uncomfortable. "Andrew loves you."

"I don't love him," Justine told her, then said to Andrew. "You killed any love I had for you." She spoke to his mother. "You both have. Thank you, because this makes it easier to walk away." Her chin lifted. "Andrew will have to find another gullible fool.

"The next time you see me it will be in court. Goodbye." Moving past the stunned Beverly, Justine walked away, feeling the shackles of her failed marriage fall away.

In her car, she called Brianna's office and left a message on her personal line to start divorce proceedings immediately and to cancel their dinner date. The second call was to the bookstore to tell Iris she was taking off for a couple of days.

At home, she packed a bag, and then got back in the van. Twenty minutes later, she arrived at her mother's house. Helen answered the door before the chimes ended.

"Justine, Beverly called. She was crying. She said you're divorcing Andrew because of some man," her mother accused. "Are you crazy?"

Justine fought to keep her anger under control. "Why do you always want to think the worst of me?"

Her mother frowned, seemingly caught off guard by the question. "I . . . I don't."

"We both know that you do." Justine jabbed her fingers through her hair in frustration. "I'm not even sure why I came to tell you."

"I just want the best for you," her mother said.

"Then why aren't you ever on my side? Why didn't you wait until you talked to me? Why aren't you more worried about how I feel than Beverly being upset?" Justine asked. Seconds ticked away without an answer. "I don't know why I even bothered. Good-bye." She started back to the van.

"What happened?"

Halfway up the walk, Justine paused. She did know why she came. She wanted her mother's love, her understanding. She wanted her mother to be on her side first and always. She retraced her steps. "Do you want to hear the truth or just Beverly's version?"

"I know it's him that has you all worked up. I saw the way he looked at you at the news conference. You've always been easily persuaded by Dalton," her mother said. "You were in high school, and you still are!"

Justine struggled to remain calm as they entered the house. "Yes, I am. And perhaps if you hadn't interfered I wouldn't have married Andrew and had to deal with catching him having an affair with Nina Hayes."

Her mother's eyes rounded in disbelief. "What?"

Justine told her everything. "Nina even got his secretary fired to hide their affair."

"I can't believe it," Helen murmured as they sat side by side on the sofa.

"It was hard at first for me as well, but I had no choice."

Her mother clasped her hands in her lap. "Do you really think I don't love you?"

"Yes," Justine said, the hurt making her voice tight and strained.

"You're wrong. I just didn't want you to make the mistakes I had by marrying a man with a reputation for going from woman to woman."

"Andrew didn't have the reputation, but he proved just as amoral." Justine hesitated, then placed her hand on her mother's. "Dalton isn't like that. He loves me, and I love him."

"Some people are going to think the worst of you, no matter what," her mother told her.

"It won't deter me. It would help if you understand and are with me," Justine said. "I'd like for us to try and find our way."

"I'd like that, too." She glanced down at her hands, then up at Justine. "Maybe it's time I told you something." She visibly swallowed. "Your grandfather made your father marry me. The marriage was doomed from the first. A month after your grandfather died, your father left." Her mother glanced away.

"For a while I blamed you. I kept thinking if I hadn't gotten pregnant, he would have stayed." Her hands clasped Justine's when she started to stand. "By the time I accepted that he wouldn't have stayed, I didn't know how to be a good mother to you."

It was a time for new beginnings. "Why don't we start over from this moment?" Justine asked.

"I'd like that," her mother said.

The hug was awkward, but it was a hug. Hopefully the next one and the next one after that would be easier and easier. "I'm going to Dalton. I may be gone for a couple of days. I'll call."

Anxiety flashed in her mother's eyes. "Jus—"

"I love him," Justine said.

Acceptance replaced apprehension. Her mother nodded. "Be careful and call me when you get there."

"Thank you." Justine hugged her mother again and then got back in her van, turned the radio to an oldies station. "Purple Rain" was playing.

Dalton's Buckhead home, at the end of a long paved driveway, was impressive. Single story, it stretched out in front of her with manicured lawns, green shrubbery, and lush flowers. No other homes could be seen through the dense oak trees surrounding it.

Getting out of the van, Justine went to the front door and rang the doorbell, which was almost hidden by English ivy. On either side of the double door was a bronzed lion and just below, on the second step, bronzed urns filled with flowering vines.

Justine stepped off the bricked porch and tried to decide

if she should go around to the back. He might be working in his office. She definitely wasn't leaving until she saw him. She was about to go around the side of the house when she heard the lock in the front door disengage.

Before he had the door opened completely, she was in his arms, his mouth on hers. "I love you. I love you," she repeated when he finally lifted his head.

His arms tightened. "I'm not sure I can let you go again. Leaving you was the hardest thing I've ever done. I left because it wasn't fair to you."

"You don't have to. Brianna is filing the papers tomorrow at the latest." She explained what had happened at the hospital. "We don't have to be apart anymore. Let people talk."

"Are you sure?" he asked.

"Yes," she answered without a moment's hesitation.

"Thank goodness." His forehead briefly touched hers. "I'm not sure how much longer I could have held out not seeing you, holding you. I love you so much."

"I love you, too," she said, adoration shining in her eyes. "We have another chance."

"Let's not waste another second." Holding both of her hands, Dalton got down on one knee. "Will you marry me?"

"Yes, a thousand times yes!" she said, laughing and crying at the same time.

Laughing, Dalton surged to his feet, kissing her. "You'll never be sorry."

"I know. Now, take me to bed, the only man's bed I'll ever want to be in."

Closing the door, hand in hand, they raced to Dalton's bed, their happy laughter floating behind them.

1. If Justine hadn't wanted to surprise her husband, she might never have learned he was having an affair. Do you think she was clueless because she had little experience with men or just that Andrew was good at covering up his infidelity? Can a woman "always tell" when her man is cheating?

2. Do you think men cheat more than women? Why? Can "cheaters" ever be reformed?

3. If you had been in Justine's position would you have signed the papers to disconnect life support? Why or why not?

4. Dalton and Justine were high school sweethearts. Why do you think we always remember our first love?

5. Brianna Ireland's unplanned pregnancy caught her by surprise and threw her into a tailspin. Her efforts to push Patrick away failed because her heart wasn't in it, and because of his unwavering love and support. Can a man love another man's child as much as he loves his own? Why or why not?

6. Dalton and Patrick both refused to give up on Justine and Brianna. Do you think the men were too persistent? When does a man cross the line between being assertive and being a nuisance?

7. Why do some marriages endure and others do not? What are ways to keep a marriage as committed and as passionate as the day the vows were made?

St. Martin's
Griffin

CPSIA information can be obtained
at www.ICGtesting.com
Printed in the USA
LVOW08s1943020217
523030LV00001B/122/P

9 780312 356132